MW01267955

G Banks

PEN CUSHION PUBLISHERS

PO BOX 85

New York, NY 10116

Typeset in Times Roman

ISBN#

Written by MIZ

Edited by: MIZ AKA Mark Adams

Typeset by: Deborah Cardona

Cover concept by: MIZ

Graphic Design by: Kevin Cosme

Cover Art by: Kevin Cosme

THIS BOOK IS DEDICATED IN THE MEMORY

OF

LORRAINE BROWN

WILLIE (WOLFE) HENRY BROWN

PINELLOUS DELORES NELSON

CAROL (T-MOMMA) BERNICE FELDER

RENEE ALBERTA ROGERS McADDLEY

TYRONE (TEE-ROCK) BAUM

DARRYL (HOMMO) BAUM

Miz Acknowledgements

First, I would like to send thanks, praise, love, respect, honor and everything within myself to the Most High God. You make all things possible. I love and thank you for blessing me with the gift to reach and entertain others through my writing. Most say the end is near, but I'm not worried because I believe in you. And though I have done some terrible things; even where some will never forgive me, I believe you still have me because you know my heart. Thanks to Jesus, your son, as well. After that, my love, heart, loyalty and honor go out to my parents, Alfred and Dorothy Adams. Thank you for giving me life and raising me to become the man I am today.

Much love to my siblings; Lorraine (R.I.P.) it's hard to think about you without hurting. I miss you so much. Words cannot explain it. My brother Freddy, a big brother I always looked up to. Michelle, some people wouldn't have businesses if it wasn't for you. You put them in positions to start their own. I know you can get it popping again. Nay, though you know how to talk a person's ear off (laughing), you have a lot of meaningful things to say. Put it in your book and get it out to the people. Cynthia, you give me inspiration to always keep my head up and believe in God. Thanks for all the help. You know the true meaning of family. Alfred Adams, Jr. (Shaborn), yo we did it again! (Laughing) Thanks for everything. When I'm at my lowest, you are always there to support me and get me back on track and on my feet. Neicey, Dot is our mother too. (Laughing) My success is yours.

Much love to my nephews and nieces. You are the next generation to take over: Aiesha, John, David, Steven, Darae (R.I.P.) love you and miss you. Kye, Baby, Sharrod, Shamira, Precious, Rick, Destiny, Shaniya, Omarion, John, Anthony (my boy! Laughing), Hakeem (Stay focus and come home). Steven, Jamel, Niasia, Lite Lite, Marquis, Day-Day (Glad you home. Let's get it!), Christina, Shaborn, Najae, Antwon, Anthony (Billy Muh'fu----- Bang! Laughing), Ashanique, Prince, Shianna (Smart girl), Shakira, Amaru, Brooklyn (Tootie), and can't forget Young Nik and their children. Too many to name.

Much love to my cousin Ocky (you my boy for life), my cousin Omar Vaughn (OV) It's about that time to share your hot music with the masses. Thanks for holding me down when I was in the pens), can't forget the cousins Malikah and Mya. Myra is definitely smiling down on her babies. So big of a family I'm stuck. Oh yeah, can't forget Tonya, her husband Bo, Zek, Taff. And the rest of the Browns, Reddings, Adams, Walkers. Pryor, McCants, Rivers and the rest of my family. We are truly huge!!!! My cousin Loretta Telford, Tonya Stewart (my sis), my other sis Stacey (love you girl), Laniel, Estelle what up? My girl Tyrel (love u), her daughter Shaquana, Wayne (fuck Snoop, I got ya name right. Laughing), Tasha Pilgrim-Stevens (N.A.Rock forever), my main man Daqual and Tasha, my niece Dakota water, Big Snoop and Aiesha, Boog, Nitty, Gremling Divine, Luv, Shameek, Oh and the few others from Lefrak I know. My whole LG massive!!!!! My whole Fort Greene massive!!! P.I., Na, K.I., KB, Darby, my boy Moedog, N.A. Rock! Lightskin Bar from the Fort, White Owl, my whole BK fam, Whitey from the Fort (Waiting for you to come home. Moedog said what up.), Big Lord, L, what up? Ready to come out of retirement?, Bo-Guard, my boy for life Rondu from the 'Ville(can't wait 'til you touch down bro), Gutter and the countless others behind those walls, bars and gates that I have tremendous love for, Frank Lewis(it was a pleasure to had met you. Hope you come out of that unjust situation), my sis Elenor (Young Nik's mom), my big sis Dimp and the rest of the Baum family, Berry, my boy Lashar, Rashien, Linda, rest in peace Mel-Sun, Sexy(author of Twofold), my boy for life Nut from Queens Bridge, my boy for life Tyhiem from Queens Bridge and the rest of the QB peeps. Sherm the worm (Good meeting you bro. hope you come home soon), lord, what up? The Jamaica Queens peeps, my boy for life Half, Sha boogie, Ta Ta, Troy, T.A., the good brother Kilo, Cor-ley(Duck, what up?), and the rest of the Jamaica crew, my Self Made fam. Too many to name. Hommo from Harlem, Born, Sha Bee, Ant, L.A., and the rest of the Harlem peeps, my boy Hook from the Brook, my boy for life Drama, Ant and countless others. If I forgot to shout you out blame my mind not my heart.

CHAPTER ONE

It was a very cold and windy night in New York City, and the streets of china town was quiet and desolate. The sharply dressed Chinese man walked nervously down the dark street. Just about every three seconds, his eyes would dart quickly in every direction. His knuckles turned a pale white from the pressure he applied to the briefcase he carried.

Mr. Chen was well familiar with the local Chinese gangs in the area and quietly cursed himself for not carrying any form of protection. He knew nowadays punks would shoot before committing a robbery. So many unnecessary murders.

Despite being small in stature, Mr. Chen was a very dangerous man. A former kick boxing champion and martial artist, he had the experience of killing a man with a single blow. However, his life was in serious danger and time was definitely not on his side. He had only twenty minutes left to get the important papers in the briefcase to its destination. His life depended on it. He was indeed a wanted man. The Chinese Mafia; the Triads of China's number one secret society and most feared organization, was out for his life. He had violated one of their most important rules; that is to never let anyone know of their dealings, or that they even existed. And now he had documents in his briefcase that could expose and ruin some very powerful and wealthy men. Once being a member of this dangerous group, he knew who was the top men and how millions of dollars entered the nations economy, and of course who profited from the illegal gains.

Mr. Chen was also wanted by the CIA (Central Intelligence Agency), and these were the people he was in such a hurry to meet to turn over the papers he possessed. This was his only option if he wanted to live. Because the CIA had information on him that could definitely send him to the electric chair or firing squad. With only a few minutes remaining, he looked at his watch and quickened his pace. He was only a few minutes away from being in the presence of CIA agents. They would then take he and the documents to headquarters to determine the papers authenticity before deciding Mr. Chen's fate.

As he walked down the very dark street, he could feel the presence of something or someone following behind him. He detected the sense of danger as the beast slowly tried to bear down on him. He was already on edge, and his jaw muscles tightened even tighter than he held the brief-case. The predator was within five feet away, and it seemed as though the hunter and hunted both were ready to strike and spring into action.

Just as the predator closed in, Mr. Chen spun around quickly delivering a deadly kick that stopped inches short of its intended target. The one hundred and seventy pound Pit bull dog froze in its tracks. It seemed as if the vicious dog could sense and smell the odor of death in the air, and knew it was not Mr. Chen's demise that was promised, but its own.

The dog quickly tucked his tail between his legs and ran away with a yelp. Mr. Chen turned back on his heels and continued to try and reach his destination quickly. He knew he had to hurry. Earlier, he thought about driving one of his cars, but quickly dismissed that thought. He was once a part of the Triads assassination team, and knew the possibility of one or more of his vehicles having had a bomb attached to it. He knew what they were capable of.

As Mr. Chen got closer to his destination, he could once again feel the presence of danger and a cold set of eyes following him. He figured this time when the vicious dog got within striking distance, he would have no mercy at all. He would kill the mutt once and for all.

However, the predator that stalked Mr. Chen this time was no dog but a man, and he was capable of killing and outsmarting any target he was paid to terminate. His name was Gregory Banks, but was called G-Banks by those who were closest to him, mainly from his past. Killing came natural to him. Something he did most of his life. He was a black man with a deep booming voice and infectious laugh. But laughing was something he rarely did, so only those he loved was afforded to hear it. All others received only a cordial conversation or a cold greeting.

G-Banks gave a terrible cough, and clutched his chest. He hoped he was not having another attack. He was diagnosed as having chronic bronchitis, a bad heart condition and respiratory problems. However, he was still a very dangerous man, but good health and age were no longer on his side.

He stopped momentarily and pulled a photo from his jacket pocket. After looking at the three beautiful young women in the picture, a warm smile slowly came to his face. But just as the smile came to his face, it disappeared even quicker. He cursed himself for taking out and looking at the photo. Now was not the time to get sentimental. The job at hand was far too dangerous to take things lightly and start making mistakes. He knew the last person hired to kill Mr. Chen ended up being the one to die, so one mistake could also be the cause of his demise. No, he would definitely have to take this job more seriously.

G-Banks spotted Mr. Chen approaching the two CIA agents, and knew that now was the moment of truth. He was more than ready to make his move, but waited patiently. However, Mr. Chen could sense that something was not right as he greeted the two agents, and he too was ready to make a move if need be.

"Mr. Chen," greeted an agent with his hand outstretched, "we've been waiting on you."

His partner took the briefcase from Mr. Chen's hand and held it close to his side. He then smiled and opened the back door of the unmarked police vehicle so Mr. Chen could enter. Everything happened so fast before the Chinese man could enter the car.

The assassin G-Banks stood thirty feet away and with calm precision, he pulled out a shiny black nine millimeter with silencer attach and took perfect aim. The first shot hit an agent square in the forehead and the briefcase fell from the dead man's limp hand. His partner screamed out and took cover. But he was way too slow. Before he could reach the car's door, a bullet pierced his skull. He fell dead to the concrete only inches away from his partner.

Mr. Chen crouched down low and desperately looked around for an escape route. But he could not leave the briefcase behind. As he quickly crawled on the ground and got a hold of it, he felt the presence of someone behind him and approaching. When he was sure his stalker was in striking distance, he leapt from the ground and turned with a deadly kick connecting with his target. The sounds of bones breaking excited him.

However, his moment of triumphant was indeed short lived. He looked down and the dead pit bull dog from earlier lay dead near his feet with a look of fear in his lifeless eyes. He was highly disappointed because he knew the assassin was still lurking in the shadows. He knew he had to move quick. But as soon as he took a step, a bullet ripped through his eye socket. A piercing scream filled the air as G-Banks stepped out of the darkness.

"What happened to death before dishonor?" he asked as he pulled the trigger again.

The second bullet was well placed into Mr. Chen's forehead, and the china man was dead before falling to the cold pavement. G-Banks walked closer and picked up the briefcase. He looked around at the massacre and knew cops would be in the area in a matter of minutes. He did his homework, and knew when they would be making their rounds in the vincinity. However, before disappearing, he once again pulled the picture of the three beautiful young women from his pocket and stared at it long and hard. He then placed the photo back into his pocket. Yes, the three beautiful young women, he thought with a smile. His mind had then went back to 1995 when it all began. He remembered it all like it was yesterday as he faded back into the darkness of the streets.

THE BEGINNING-1995

Chapter Two

"Tracy, get your black ass in here!" yelled her crack addicted mother, who sat on a brown couch with the springs sticking out of the side of it.

The living room was a mess. Empty crack vials and beer cans littered the nasty looking green carpet that hadn't seen a broom or vacuum in months. The walls looked as if it was sweating dirt, and the big beautiful picture of Tracy on the wall when she was younger looked completely out of place in such a filthy environment.

Most of the time, people from off of the streets would occupy the space in the small apartment in exchange of getting Tracy's mother Darita high. Because she was always broke. The only times she had some kind of income, was when she received her welfare benefits each month. But as fast as she received the money, it disappeared even quicker on drugs. At times, it would already be spent before she physically had it in her hands. She would get so much drugs on credit from the neighborhood dealers before the money even got on her card. Most of the time, it was hardly anything left for she and her daughter to survive. The drugs had become to mean everything to her, and when she could no longer get anything on credit, she would simply allow other addicts to share the little space in her apartment for a free get high. So, the small apartment was always crowded and smelled of crack cocaine and unwashed bodies. A terrible mixture!

"Tracy, didn't I call your black ass?!" yelled Darita. "You better get your ass in here now! Don't make me have to call you three motherfucking times!"

Tracy entered the living room with a justifiable angry look on her face. She wore the blue gym shorts she'd gotten from school, a dingy white tee-shirt and a pair of old Reebok Classics that were leaning to the side.

Tracy was only 13 years old. But her young body was maturing very quickly; maybe due to the fact of her having sex at such a young age. Her young breast was small and round, and her youthful behind sat up high. She was very pretty. Her jet black skin tone and chinky eyes gave off the appearance of an African/China doll. Her long black hair was pulled back into a ponytail with a straight part down the middle. However, she did not feel pretty at all, because her mother always refer to her as an ugly black this, or a terrible black that. The young girl's self-esteem was basically torn to pieces. It had gotten to the point where she began to hate the word 'black' in itself, and oftentimes wished that she was white or perhaps light complexioned like her two best friends the twins; Monique and Monica. Tracy had even once put white shoe polish all over her skin to add cream to her chocolate complexion, but all it did was cake up and give her a terrible itch.

As soon as Tracy entered the living room, she had to take a step back, because the first thing to hit her was the potent crack smoke as her mother deeply inhaled the poison. Darita's two crack buddies also inhaled from their stems taking the drug's smoke into their lungs. Tracy hated living here. She often wondered what it would feel like to live like the people on television. In fact, she could not even remember the last time she watched television, because that too, her mother had sold for about eight crack vials. Once in a while, she would be able to catch a movie or rap video whenever she ventured over to Monique and Monica's apartment. That is until their step father Derrick, would say she had to go home because he wanted to spend some 'quality time' with the twins. She knew what that meant, and hated him for it.

Tracy turned her attention back to the scene in front of her and felt angry as well as hurt. She looked at the two crack head ladies sitting across from her mother, and then her eyes fell on the 45 year old, dirty looking Puerto Rican man that was staring at her young body lustfully. From the look in his eyes, she already knew why she was called from her bedroom.

"Girl," said her mother after nearly choking to death on the poison she inhaled, "take Joey in the back room and show his ass a good time."

Tracy looked at the disgusting looking man and instantly the tears fell from her eyes burning her cheeks.

"No!" she said angrily, tired of being her mother's whore. "I'm not doing it! I'm tired of this shit!!!!"

"Bitch!" yelled Darita as the stem dropped from her hand and broke into two pieces, "who the fuck you think you talking to?! I'll fucking kill your black ugly ass in here! You hear me? I know you out there in the streets fucking and sucking dick anyway you little heifer, so you just do what the fuck I tell you to do!" Then looking at her two crack head friends, she replied, "This little black ass bitch made me break my stem."

The Puerto Rican man stood up from the beat up couch nervously playing with his zipper while waiting for the mother and daughter to finish their dispute.

"Little black ass bitch!" continued Darita, talking about her child as if she were an animal. "She lucky I didn't kick her ass out of here yet."

Tracy sucked her teeth as the tears fell from her eyes.

"Come on!" she said angrily to the dirty man looking at her young body lustfully.

Darita smiled triumphantly while turning her attention to the man. "Wait a minute motherfucker," she said sarcastically. "You didn't give me my shit yet!"

The man fumbled inside of his pocket and produced three crack vials, handing them to her with a rotten mouth smile.

"And try not to get that ugly black ass bitch there pregnant, 'cause I'm not raising no more of them motherfuckers in here!" said Darita as her young daughter led the way to her bedroom with the dirty perverted man following closely behind.

Tracy wished she knew who her father was, or least found out his name. Because she would not hesitate to try to reach out and contact him. She really needed his help to save her from this terrible ordeal and bad hand that life had dealt her. But Darita had told her nothing concerning him, except that he was a black ass bum who could not live up to his responsibilities. She thought about how pretty her mother used to be. She was light complexioned with very long straight hair. But now her face had a dull sunken in look, and her hair had fallen out in patches causing her to everyday wear the same dirty beige scarf on her head. No one could believe how much her appearance had changed for the worse in such a short period of time. She now looked downright disgusting! Once caring, loving and showing her baby girl unconditional love, she now treated her like shit! It all began when her mother was forced to move into the tough and notorious Cabrini-Green housing projects located in one of the roughest parts of Chicago. Darita was abandoned by Tracy's father, causing her to be financially strapped for cash with no direction. She had no one to help her, and struggled to make ends meet for she and her daughter. However, before long, Darita began drinking and gossiping with the other single mothers in the projects that didn't have anything to do with their lives. That was the beginning of the end for her, and things only gotten worse when she allowed herself to get involved with a man younger than herself who turned her on to smoking crack. Darita had really hit rock bottom and it was her daughter Tracy, who she once loved with all her heart that ended up being the one to suffer.

Tracy and the dirty man entered her small bedroom. This was the only clean room in the filthy apartment. But the room did not have many things in it. All of the stuffed animals she once had all over the room and the small television set, were now gone. The room now only boasted a small bed and a dresser. On top of the dresser sat some of Tracy's favorite books. They were the only things Darita did not get her hands on yet to sell to feed her crack habit.

The crack head man unzipped his pants, revealing a dirty stink penis that looked as if it had not been washed with soap and water in months! The smell of him alone made Tracy fight the urge of throwing up.

12

"Listen," snapped Tracy as she pulled her shorts down and bent over the bed, "don't touch me with your dirty ass hands either!" She hoped the man would be quick. She blocked out everything and began day dreaming, that perhaps she was someone else.

The dirty man stroked himself to a full erection and positioned himself behind her. He guided himself into her and moaned at her tightness. But unknown to him, mentally Tracy wasn't even there. She had become somewhat immune to the pain and humiliation, and thought about better things as the man stroked into her young body. Tracy thought about the future when she would be of age to be out in this cold world on her own. She would finally no longer have to put up with her crack addicted mother and the sexual abuse. She was only 10 years old when she first had sex, if you can call it that. It was a hot summer day when her mother had a 16 year old crack dealer sitting in the living room. Darita was practically begging the youngster for a few cracks on credit, promising to pay at a later date. Tracy could hear them talking as she sat in her room and played with her white Barbie doll.

"Yo bitch, I don't do no muh'fucking credit!" snapped the young boy Damien. "Shit, I thought you called me to buy something."

"Please Damien," pleaded Darita licking her chapped and crusty lips. "I get a check next week and you know I'ma spend it all with you. Don't I always come to you? Come on baby, don't do me like this."

"I told you I don't do credit," Damien said with a sinister smile. Normally, he would had walked out of her apartment not wanting to hear anymore. But he truly enjoyed watching the woman who was old enough to be his own mother, beg for crack. Four years ago, before she started smoking crack she acted as if she was going to beat his ass one day for smoking marijuana in the hallway in front of her door. Now look at her, he thought with a smile.

"Come on baby," pleaded Darita looking desperate. "I'll even suck your dick. Baby please, just give me a rock."

13

Damien laughed as if she had just said the funniest joke he'd ever heard.

"You fucking crazy?" he said incredulously. "I'm not sticking my dick anywhere near your corroded ass. If I knew you were calling me up here to fuck for crack, I would've bought my Pit bull Danger up here to fuck you. He loves human pussy."

Darita looked at the young boy and licked her lips as if what he'd just suggested was not beyond what she would do for some crack.

Damien's face had then lit up when he remembered that she had a very beautiful young daughter who he knew was a virgin. Now that, was a piece of ass he would pay for, he thought with a smile.

"I'll tell you what," said Damien. "I'll give you ten rocks if you let me fuck your daughter."

Darita dismissed his offer with the wave of the hand. However, when he pulled the crack vials from his pocket and began shaking them in his hand like dice, she seemed as if she was reconsidering the offer. She thirstily licked her dry lips and decided to do it. She came to the sick conclusion that Damien was only 6 years older than Tracy, and she would probably be fucking in a year or two anyway. So what the hell, she thought.

"Give it here," she said while looking at his closed hand. "But she's young Damien, so please take it easy on her. She's in the back room, but she may not give it up to you. Let me talk to her first."

"Nah, don't worry about that," smiled the young crack dealer, handing Darita the crack vials and walking to the room. "I'll take good care of her."

He entered the room and closed the door as Darita pulled her stem from between her breast and opened up one of the capsules. Sitting down on the couch, she took a hit from the stem and blocked out everything, as her baby girl Tracy cried, screamed and fought as she got raped.

$$$$$$$

"And don't cum in me either motherfucker!" said Tracy to the old Puerto Rican crack head man. He pulled out of her and released his semen all over her tee shirt.

Tracy quickly got up and walked to the bathroom, leaving the dirty man in the room alone to straighten himself up.

After washing up and peeing, Tracy laid across her bed and wished she was living with her friends Monique and Monica. But after giving that some thought, she dismissed that wish because she knew the twins' situation was not all that much better than her own.

Chapter Three

"I wish that motherfucker die!" sobbed Monique. "I hate his ass."

"Me too," cried her twin Monica as they cuddled together in bed. "Forget mommy, we should just call the police. I'm tired of this."

"They wouldn't believe us."

The two were talking about their stepfather Derrick. He had been raping and molesting the twins since they were nine years old. They were now 13 and still going through the same sexual abuse. Their mother Clurisa knew what was happening but had always turned a blind eye to things as if nothing was going on. She would simply pretend that she had a perfect, caring and loving family. When she saw signs of the abuse, she totally ignored it. Most of the time, she was so drunk it didn't even matter. Even when she was sober, which wasn't often, she would never try to hear what her two young daughters were trying to tell her. The twins often wondered what Derrick had done to her for her to not see the obvious that he was destroying their family. They often wondered why their mother had picked this bad man over them. Wasn't a mother's love for her children suppose to be stronger than all else? Unknowingly to the twins, their mother Clurisa, when she was a child, had also gone through being sexually abused and raped. So, she should have known better and addressed the situation but her own situation was never addressed. She carried the pain of it throughout her life, not revealing it to a soul. She thought letting others know what happened would only make matters worse. But what really made things worse was keeping her pain bottled up inside of herself instead of dealing with it head on. Maybe had she told someone and reached out for help, her two young girls would not be going through what they were going through now. Growing up, Clurisa was repeatedly raped and sexually abused by her older brother Jesse. The first time it happened, she was only 14 years old. She had just come home from summer camp when her brother, high on heroin stumbled into her bedroom and forced himself onto her. She was a virgin up until that day. What made things worse was that the rape was not a quick ordeal. The heroin in Jesse's system made his penis harder than it had ever been and it literally tore her apart and took hours for him to cum. Clurisa felt as though she was being split in half as she screamed at the top of her lungs. She cried for help as blood from her private area stained the white sheet on her bed. She knew Jesse was crazy, and after threatening her if she told someone, Clurisa kept the incident to herself. Being scared to expose her brother, the sexual abuse became a routine of torture in her life. Her fear was his power. The rapes only stopped because Jesse was one day found dead in his bedroom from a drug overdose. But it really did not stop there, because now once again she acted as if nothing was happening. Also, it was as if she had blamed herself for what her brother had done, and held that same blame for the twins for what Derrick was doing to them. Like the day when Monique walked into the kitchen while Clurisa was cooking breakfast. With tears falling from her eyes she asked, "Momma, why do you let him do this to us? You know what Derrick is doing to me and Monica. You act like you don't even care. He's not even hiding what he's doing to us. I know, you know he's raping us."

"Girl," yelled Clurisa, "get your ass out of this kitchen! My husband is not thinking about you and your sister's nasty lil' asses, like I'm not enough for him or something. Shit, y'all ain't nothing but two little hot asses anyway. Somebody needs to put something in you!"

"Momma," cried Monique. "We tired of it. I'm not letting him rape us anymore. The next time he touch us momma, I'm going to call the police."

Her mother spun around and with all her might, she threw the spatula she had in her hand, just barely missing Monique's head. She then squinted her eyes, pointed her finger in the young girl's face and said, "You little bitch, so help me God, if you ever call those white folks up in here I will kill you. And I mean it!"

Monique quickly stormed off to her room. She would always remember the look in her mother's eyes. It was a look of pure hatred and she would never, as long as she lived forget that look.

"We can't call the police," said Monica to her twin as they lay in bed together. "It would only make things worse. Plus, nobody ain't gonna believe us anyway, 'cause you know momma is gonna take his side like she always do."

"I know," pouted Monique. "Man, I just wish he die. I'm tired of this. But don't worry; I'll come up with something."

The twins were very pretty. They were light-skinned, shoulder length hair, green eyes and nice slim bodies with youthful protruding butts and breast. They looked just like their mother when she was younger, before the drinking changed her complexion giving her a dull look as well as bloodshot eyes.

Clurisa began drinking when she found out her husband Derrick was having sex with many of the women in the Cabrini-Green housing projects. Once again, instead of placing the blame on him, she constantly blamed herself for his infidelities and actions. If only she had not gained weight he would not be cheating, she thought. Never mind it was only ten pounds she gained throughout their marriage. He looked at her in disgust. In the process of trying to lose the weight, Clurisa had also lost her self-esteem. She began drinking alcohol so heavily that even when she was sober, she still looked drunk and reeked of liquor.

"I wish daddy didn't die," sobbed Monica as she and her twin watched the Oprah Winfrey show on television with the volume turned down low.

"I know, right?" responded Monique not taking her eyes from the television.

Their father Robert Chance was a good man who loved his wife and daughters with all his heart. The twins, was his everything and he would spoil them rotten, giving them anything they wanted. But it all came to a tragic end one day, while coming home from work his life was cut short by a stray bullet. There was a war going on at the time between two notorious gangs: The Gangster Disciples and the Vice Lords. However, some stated that the two gangs had nothing to do with the shooting death of Robert

Chance, but that he was hit by a stray bullet from a group of young boys playing with a gun. Whatever the circumstances, their father was dead with no one to protect them in this cold world.

After being a young widow for two long lonely years, Clurisa felt that it was time for her to live again and felt so alive when she began dating the factory worker she saw everyday coming home from work. Derrick was the perfect gentleman. He treated her like a queen; sweeping her off of her feet. But after marrying, their relationship quickly soured and began to fizzle out. Derrick had changed and she did not know where this change had come from. It was definitely a change for the worse, and Clurisa and her two young girls had become the recipients of his foul actions.

The bedroom door had suddenly flew open and Derrick stepped into the twins' bedroom wearing only his boxer shorts and no shirt. He was brown-skinned, 200 pounds, 6 foot 2, and wore his hair in cornrow braids. He had an evil smirk on his face. He slowly walked over to the small television and turned it off as he openly massaged his private area with his left hand.

"Your momma went out with her friends drinking," he said with a smile looking as if he had a few drinks already of his own. "So tell me," he continued looking at the twins with lust filled eyes, "who gets fucked first?"

"Won't you get out of our damn room?!" yelled Monique as Monica looked on in fear.

They were very afraid of Derrick and had never spoken back to him in such a disrespectful tone of voice, so Monica could not believe her twin had just yelled at him with such authority in her voice. It even caused derrick to flinch for a moment. The tone of her voice had caught him completely off guard as he took a startled step backwards. Monique was the outspoken twin, but had never made an attempt to yell at Derrick in such a manner.

After the initial shock wore off, he became even more angrier as he balled up his huge fist and screwed up his face. "Little bitch," he said through clenched teeth, "I'll break your fucking jaw if you

19

ever fix your mouth to yell at me again. I'm the fucking man in this house! You hear?! And until you start paying bills and putting food on that table in that kitchen, you better watch your mouth. You remember what happened to you last time, don't you?"

He didn't have to remind Monique. She would never forget it as long as she lived. It was last summer. Clurisa was in one of her usual drunken stupors. Derrick entered the children's bedroom with a noticeable hard on. "Monique," he said to her, "make a nigga happy."

"No," she pouted. "I'm not doing that anymore for you."

Without warning, Derrick punched her in the chest so hard, that even he panicked thinking he had stopped her breathing. The young girl fell to the bed holding her small chest before rolling onto the floor in pain. The pain was so unbearable that no sound would escape through her lips.

"What did you do to her?" cried Monica rushing to her twin's aid to make sure she was okay. "What did you do?!"

Derrick had become so terrified, he ran from the room and out of the apartment.

Once outside, he stood in front of the white high rise building and smoked a cigarette, scared that Monica had perhaps called an ambulance or even worse…the police!

Upstairs, Monique had caught her breath as tears fell from her eyes. She and Monica hoped Derrick was gone for good. But they were sadly disappointed when they heard him enter back into the apartment. He headed back towards the twins' bedroom. He always had a thing for young girls even before marrying Clurisa, and now it was her daughters who had to suffer for his sick and perverted preference. He peeked into their bedroom and after seeing that Monique was okay, he began to feel cocky again as he entered the room with his face drawn tight. "Next time," he said threateningly, "any of you little brats refuse me, that's going to happen again."

$$$$$$

Monique stared at Derrick and knew she would never forget that day. But she was tired of being raped, and would not have given in to his demands again had it not been for her sister Monica being present. She didn't want to get her twin physically hurt by her not cooperating. If her twin wasn't there, Monique was ready to die before given in to this sick man. She figured death could be no worse than what she and her twin were presently going through. She looked at Monica crying silently next to her and knew she would have to do it. She bit down hard on her bottom lip and pulled off her nightgown as the tears fell from her pretty eyes. Why did their mother allow this man to come into her life and do this to her two young daughters? Why did her love disappear from them after meeting Derrick? Why was she hiding behind a bottle? Why didn't other people in the projects recognize what was going on? And why did those that did know acted as if they didn't know, or just didn't care? All of these questions were going through Monique's mind as she lay back on the bed with her legs apart. She silently hoped her mother would come to her senses and get rid of this sick man. But of course, Clurisa had come to love this man more than the two beautiful twins who came from her own womb.

"Monica," said Derrick sitting on the girl's small bed, "pass me that jar of Vaseline off of that dresser. And don't even think about sneaking out of this room, because your ass is next."

She went and got the Vaseline as Derrick positioned himself between Monique's young legs. Sometimes the twins wondered who situation was worse; theirs or their best friend Tracy's.

Chapter Four

"Yeah," said Tracy with a comb in her hand as she sat on the couch and parted Monica's hair, "my mother is still tripping."

Monica sat on the floor between her legs. Monique was reclining back on the dusty looking recliner chair. They were in Tracy mother's apartment and was glad Darita was not presently home. They didn't want to hear her mouth or be forced to inhale any second hand crack smoke. The girls figured she was out trying to get a free high or out begging as usual. Whatever the case, they were happy she was not home. Tracy didn't care about the people her mother left in the small apartment. As soon as Darita would leave, she would kick them out, open the windows to get rid of the smell no matter how cold it was outdoors, and clean up as best she could. She hated living in filth. The apartment was not fit to raise a dog, let alone a child.

"My mother had the nerve to try and sell me to some pimp ass nigga," continued Tracy as she combed Monica's long hair. "But when his ass saw how Big June and them crazy niggas from the dark side that be on the side of the church was looking at his ass, he damn near broke his neck trying to get away from my mom's crack head ass," she laughed as the twins joined in.

"Shit," said Monique, "you probably would've been better off with him. At least you would've been making money and looking good while he had you hooking. Me and Monnie," she said using her twin's nickname, "probably would be rich by now if old ass Derrick paid us every time he came into our room for sex. No for real, all jokes aside. I know you tired of having sex just like we are."

Monica said nothing. She was the quiet twin. She just sat on the floor between Tracy's legs as she quietly rapped the words to Da Brat's song "Funkdafied." She wished she could hear it on the radio but knew Tracy's mother had sold the stereo. However, she knew all the words to the song by heart being Brat was her favorite female rapper and was also from Chicago.

"I'm tired of getting raped," continued Monique. "All last night I could not sleep. I kept thinking about leaving and I'm ready."

Tracy and Monica looked over at her waiting to see what she was getting at.

"I think we should run away," she continued.

"Where?" asked Tracy, very interested in what her friend was saying. She herself had many times thought about running away only to back out at the last minute, because she had no idea where she would go especially with no money.

"Anywhere is better than here," answered Monique.

"You sound like one of them slaves we saw in school, in that movie 'Roots'," joked Monica.

"Anyway," continued Monique not paying her twin no mind as Tracy laughed. "If y'all down to run away, we can go to Detroit or California."

"No," said Monica being more outspoken than usual. "I think if we go anywhere, we should go to New York. Who knows, we may even meet Big Poppa."

"Yeah," smiled Tracy. The Notorious B.I.G. was her favorite rapper and she had always fantasized about meeting him.

"'Black and ugly as ever/however I stay Coogie down to the socks,'" she rapped one of his songs. Pausing after putting two long braids on each side of Monica's head she asked, "Where are we going to get the money to get there?

"I already thought of that," answered Monique always being the one with a plan. "If it works, then we're good. I planned the whole thing out last night. Tonight, just pack your shit and meet us in front of the building in the morning. Tray, be there exactly at 3:00."

23

"In the morning?!" asked a wide eyed Tracy.

"Yeah," answered a calm Monique, "in the morning."

All last night she thought about it over and over, and now was the time to put her plan into action. She just hoped that everything went according to plan. Because if it didn't, Derrick would kill them, and that she was sure of.

$$$$$$

Later that night at the Jackson's residence, the twins sat at the kitchen table and ate the dinner Derrick had prepared for them. They knew this was indeed the last supper. They were unbelievably quiet and Derrick was glad they were, because surprisingly Clurisa was not drunk tonight. During dinner she continuously smiled at her family, acting as if they were the perfect functional family. Just looking at Derrick and her mother, Monica felt sick to her stomach. She felt like throwing up. It was definitely a rare night because not only was Clurisa sober, but also Derrick had showered her with kisses and attention throughout the evening as if they had just gotten married. He was known to do this once in awhile, and it was perfect timing for Monique's plan.

Inwardly, Monique smiled because she knew her plan would be carried out even better than she had anticipated.

"The two of you," said Derrick to the twins as he pushed himself up from the table, "clear the table and wash the dishes."

He winked at his wife with a smile and she stood up from the table as well. She giggled like a school girl when he pinched her behind and led the way to the bedroom. The plan was going better than they thought it would. Because usually after dinner Derrick would watch television for hours but when he and his wife had they ten minutes of sex, they knew he would immediately go to sleep.

I guess he wanted some older pussy tonight, Monique bitterly thought to herself.

24

"I'll take care of the dishes," she said to her twin when their parents were out of earshot. "You can make sure all of our clothes and stuff we need is packed."

"Alright," Monica nervously smiled as she walked away to their bedroom.

Monique could not believe that her plan was finally coming to fruition. She hoped everything turned out fine being that she, her twin, and Tracy would now be out in the streets on their own. But just thinking about the sexual abuse they were going through was enough to give her the strength and courage to do what she felt she had to do. So she put the fear of the unknown behind her and finished the dishes.

Monica walked to her closet, reached down and grabbed the two blue duffel bags filled with clothes that sat on the closet's floor. All the things they thought they would need had been neatly packed. Remembering to get their toothbrushes and toothpaste, she quickly dashed into the bathroom.

"Can't leave without this," she smiled to herself as she entered back into the bedroom and placing the items into her bag. She sat on the bed and took one last long look around the small bedroom she and her twin shared since they were born. The last four years in this bedroom had been pure torture for the young girls with Derrick around. She could not believe it was all finally coming to an end.

Monique entered the bedroom wiping her wet hands on her sweatpants. It was a school night but she knew their school days in Chicago were over. She sat on the bed next to Monica and they talked about all of the possibilities that awaited them in New York. It was finally 2:30 in the morning, and Monique knew she should've gotten some sleep early yesterday like her twin had done. She was now tired and was fighting to stay awake.

"Come on," she said to Monica as she looked at the clock on the dresser. "It's that time, and I'm tired as hell."

"Well," said Monica, "then let me go in the room. The last thing we need is for you to go in there stumbling around waking them up and getting caught."

She quietly walked towards the room with her socks on. Putting on her sneakers would have made too much noise.

"Okay but be careful," whispered Monique. "I don't want my plan to backfire now."

Monica gently pushed her mother's bedroom door open and peered inside. The sounds Clurisa and Derrick made brought a smile to her face. They both were dead asleep to the world as the two snored loudly. Every time Derrick inhaled, Clurisa exhaled.

Monica got on her hands and knees and crawled into the dark bedroom. She knew where everything was located and headed in the direction of what she'd come for. In the big black leather recliner chair located in the corner of the room, sat the pants Derrick wore yesterday. The big belt buckle felt as if it weighed a hundred pounds in Monica's small hands. She slowly and quietly pulled the pants off of the chair. It landed with a soft thud that seemed very loud to the small frightened girl.

As Monica crawled back out of the bedroom dragging the pants behind her, she hoped and prayed Derrick did not wake up turning on the lights and catching her. Because if he did, she knew she would be in very serious trouble. Just the thought made her bump her head against the door trying to quicken her pace. She stopped, silently cursing herself when she heard her mother or Derrick moving around on the bed.

When the movement stopped and the snoring continued in sync, she crawled out of the bedroom and felt excited the moment her eyes fell on her twin standing in the hallway waiting on her.

Monica stood up and the two quickly headed back into their room. Monique took the pants and began rifling through the pockets. She knew Derrick had got paid two days ago, and hoped he didn't deposit any of it into the bank. The two front pockets were empty except for his keys and two condoms. She then pulled the thick brown wallet from the back pocket. After pushing his identification and two phone numbers aside, she found four hundred and fifty three dollars. It was not a lot of money but she knew it was enough for the three of them to leave Chicago.

"Hurry up Monnie," whispered Monique as she dropped the pants to the floor. "Put your sneakers on. We gotta get outta here before he gets up to use the bathroom or something."

Monica slipped on her sneakers and grabbed her coat off of the bed. They then slung the duffel bags of clothing over their shoulders and quickly and quietly exited the small apartment without even looking back.

$$$$$$

Tracy stuffed her clothes and underwear in a big black plastic garbage bag. All morning and yesterday, her mind had been on the plan of running away. She hoped the twins had been successful getting Derrick's money and getting out of the apartment. What if he awoke realizing that something was wrong and capturing the twins before they could get out of the building? What if they never showed up? These two questions were going through her mind for the last three hours.

Tracy peered into the living room and saw her mother Darita and another crack head lady getting high. She had to come up with a plan to get pass her mother with the big bag of clothes. She looked around and an idea hit her. She quickly put on her coat and walked into the living room holding the bag as far away from her body as possible.

"What is that?" asked Darita looking at the bag before taking a hit off of her stem.

"This is garbage," answered Tracy with her face scrunched up. "And it stinks!"

Knowing how clean Tracy liked things to be, she looked at her daughter and said, "You don't have to take that shit outside. Just put it in the hallway."

"Doesn't she have school tomorrow?" asked the crack head lady as if she cared.

"Bitch, I don't know," answered Darita nonchalantly as she took another hit from the pipe inhaling the poisonous drug.

Tracy opened the front door and stepped out into the quiet and semi-dark hallway. She quietly closed the door behind her and made her getaway. She knew her mother was too occupied with her drugs and company to come see about her, so she slowly walked away not caring if she ever saw her mother again.

When she got in front of the building, she began to worry. She didn't see Monique and Monica and it was already five minutes past three 'o clock. She then looked behind her and saw the twins hurrying towards her.

"Come on!" Monique said quickly. "We have to hurry up and get out of here!"

"New York City it is," smiled Tracy as the three walked away from their building hoping to never see it again.

Chapter Five

New York City was nothing like what the young girls expected it to be. It was indeed a far cry of what the music videos had depicted. There were no pool parties, happy faces, hot weather or people having the look of love on their faces. Instead, everything moved fast, the people rudely bumped into one another as they rushed about their business, and the weather was cold.

Tracy, Monique and Monica stood on the corner of 34th street in midtown Manhattan in front of a jewelry store. They watch the people go about their business not paying others any mind. This was their second day in New York and they were already broke. Between their bus fare, the cheap hotel room they stayed in and food to eat, they were now left penniless. Now with no food to eat and stuck in the cold with nowhere to go, the girls didn't know what to do.

"I told you we should've gone to California," shivered Monique. "At least we would've been warm."

"I'm ready to try and get back home," announced Tracy holding her plastic bag of clothing close to her body.

"We can't go back!" cried Monica. "Even if we were able to get back, Derrick would kill us!"

"Excuse me, can you spare a dollar?" Monique asked an old white woman walking by. "We just need some—"

The old lady clutched her purse tightly and kept walking. The girls had been standing out in the cold almost all morning and all they were fortunate enough to get from begging was two dollars and seventy five cents.

"Let's sneak on the subway," suggested Tracy. "At least it's warm down there."

This was the best idea they've come up with since standing out in the cold. Now they just hoped they would be able to sneak on the subway without paying their fares.

As they walked in the direction of the subway, a young sharply dressed pimp with a mouth full of gold teeth gently grabbed Tracy by the elbow as she tried to walk by him. He smiled brightly as he pulled her aside.

"Hey sweet thing," he smiled. "Let me get a moment of your time and I guarantee you won't regret it."

When Tracy stopped to hear what he had to say, it was then he noticed the two equally beautiful twins also walking with her. The twins stopped walking as well. However, being from Chi-town, the young girls were no strangers to pimps and players. So they knew what he was before he even began talking.

"Damn!" exclaimed Goldie. "Just my luck, I ask for one and I get three. Shit, who said pimping ain't easy? May I ask you three young ladies your names?"

Monique sucked her teeth, turned away and asked a Puerto Rican man walking by, "Excuse me, can you spare a dollar?"

The man dug in his pocket and came out with a dollar giving it to her as he kept walking.

"Thank you!" yelled out Monique not wanting anything to do with the young pimp talking to Tracy.

"My name is Tracy, and these are my friends Monique and Monica."

"Tracy, my name is Goldie. And I can see you and your friends here done fell on some bad luck. But y'all ain't gotta worry about anything from this point on, because Goldie is here. You see that pimp mobile parked across the street?" he asked pointing out a blue Maxima to her and Monica. He didn't wait for an answer as he continued talking. "I say we all get into that warm machine

there, and talk a little business. All y'all need is some manage-
ment. So what's up? Y'all gonna barbeque or mildew?"

"Barbeque or mildew?" asked Monique with her cute little face
screwed up, causing Monica and Tracy to laugh. "You can't be serious," she continued with her hands on her hips. "You're a poor
excuse for a pimp or whatever you call yourself. But pimps in the
Windy stopped using that line long ago."

"Bitch!" yelled Goldie blowing his cool. "You don't know who
the fuck you—" he stopped mid-sentence when a brand new White
limo with tinted windows pulled up to the curb. He already knew
who was in the car. He just hoped it wouldn't be an altercation. He
knew he would never be ready for that. He watched the car come
to a slow stop and it seemed as if his heart had done the same.

The girls, as well as the people walking by had no idea who
sat in the expensive looking car. Most of those walking by stopped
to see who would emerge from it. They figured it had to be a celebrity, and their curiosity got the better of them as they waited patiently to see who it could be.

When the sexy black woman chauffer emerged from the car
and opened the door for the expensively dressed black man, the
people standing around looked in awe. But not knowing who the
man was, most shrugged their shoulders and walked on to get out
of the cold.

The man stepped all the way out of the car. He was in his late
forties, and wore the biggest diamond ring on his pinky finger that
the three young girls had ever saw in their life; whether in person
or on television. He had on a grey double breasted three piece suit
and a black derby on his head to match the chinchilla coat and al-
ligator shoes. He walked as if he owned the world, and his presence suggested that he was a very powerful and important man.

Tracy, Monique and Monica wondered who this man could be
as they stared with their mouths open. He quickly walked pass the
three girls and Goldie as if he didn't even notice them standing
there. He entered the tall building behind them. Monique turned

around and saw the building was a legal firm. She figured him to be a rich lawyer like Johnny Cochran or someone.

"So, what's up baby?" asked Goldie trying to get their attention again. Moments ago he looked like a million dollars, until the tall black man pulled up in the white limo. Now the young pimp looked like a cheap imitation of someone trying to succeed with a weak game plan.

Goldie knew exactly who the man was, and wanted to hurry and cop his three beautiful young prospects before the man exited the law firm. He did not want any problems.

"What's up?" he asked again.

"What's up with what?!" asked Monique with an attitude.

"With the business plan I was telling y'all about," explained Goldie trying to make his cop. "I got a phat crib y'all can stay at and everything."

Tracy and Monica were with it. Any place was better than freezing in the cold, but Monique had figured if she wanted to continue getting sexually abused, she would've stayed in Chicago with Derrick.

"Look," said Monique pushing Tracy away from the pimp, "we don't want to be your hoes. The most you can do for us, is give us a few dollars if you can spare it."

"I can spare more than a few dollars," smiled Goldie while pulling a stack of bills from his pocket. "Let's get out of the cold and talk about it."

"Do you have any other hoes?" asked Monique as if she was interested.

Hearing such a question, Goldie looked at her as if she had just slapped him upside his head with a frying pan.

"Of course," he answered with a smirk. "I can't even picture the thought of me being whoreless baby. I was born a pimp, not made."

"Well," she said being too fast for her own good, "then you should count your blessings and be happy with the ones you have. Never fuck over your for sho' pussy, trying to get mo' pussy, because you might just end up with no pussy."

Tracy and Monica burst out laughing at Goldie as he looked coldly at Monique and thought about his next move. If he was fortunate enough to cop the three young girls, he would definitely make the one in front of him life a living hell. He would fuck over her like she had never been fucked over before.

"Excuse me," Monique asked a black man walking by, "can you spare a dollar?"

The man stopped, dug in his pocket and gave her two dollars and continued on his way.

"Thanks you!" she called out. A few more dollars and they would have enough money to buy something to eat, and pay to get on the subway to stay warm.

"I like you," said Goldie with a fake smile. "I like your style. You're a born hustler, just like me. Shit, we can make some very beautiful things-", he stopped mid-sentence once again when the tall well dressed black man exited the law firm.

Goldie was at a loss of words. The man's chauffeur opened the car's door for him before he reached the car.

"Excuse me mister," said Monique to the rich looking man, hoping to get the few dollars that she, Monica and Tracy needed. "Me and my sisters are cold and hungry, can you spare a dollar or something?"

The man turned around slowly with a frown on his face and peeped the whole scene in front of him as if noticing the small group for the first time. He pulled a big stack of money from his pocket as he looked over the three young girls and their bags of clothing. His mean slit eyes had then settled on the young and skinny wanna-be pimp with the mouthful of gold teeth. Goldie looked as though he were going to shit himself.

The man pocketed his money and quickly looked at the girls with that same look.

"Get in the car!" he ordered in his booming voice.

"What?!" said Monique with attitude. "Listen, all I asked you was, can you-"

"Get in the car!" he barked again causing her to flinch.

The look in the man's eyes warned that this was not the man to play games with. He was nothing like the pimp she was speaking to a few minutes ago. He was completely different from Goldie, and for some reason, something inside of her told her she had better obey this man.

Monique quickly climbed into the big spacious car. The man then looked at Monica and Tracy with the same cold eyes and glare, and they too climbed inside of the warm car.

Before the man got in behind them, he spun around and looked at Goldie.

"I should've killed you last time," he said coldly. "Now, get your little punk ass out of here before you come up missing. And for the last time, I don't want you back in this area."

Goldie quickly walked away glad to be out of the presence of the man who put fear in his heart like no other.

Gregory Banks slowly slid into the expensive car and closed the door, as the chauffeur pulled away into the busy Manhattan traffic.

Chapter Six

The big white and green house in Bethpage, Long Island was very well furnished. This was definitely a house of the rich. The expensive paintings on the walls were of African art and every room entered made a person's mouth drop open leaving one completely astonished.

Monique, Monica and Tracy sat in the big kitchen that boasted so much space, that it could have easily been a business meeting room. The long table seated eight, but only the three girls and the man who brought them here sat at the big and long table.

The maid prepared a very big meal and the girls stuffed themselves full, not knowing when they were going to get another meal like the one they'd just got finish eating. They could not recall ever eating so much. The food was delicious. Tracy really enjoyed it, being her mother hadn't cooked in years. Well, not food anyway. All she cooked nowadays was the crack in her stem. The only time Darita stove saw fire, was when a dealer gave her a few pieces to cook his product. He would also bag up his cracks in the apartment, which meant that every plate they owned was full of scratch marks from the gem-star razors the dealers would use to chop the big rocks into small pieces.

To survive, Tracy was forced at a young age to learn how to steal from the local grocery stores and supermarkets. And whenever she had money, the Chinese restaurants and other fast food spots became her food provider. Though the twins had dinner regularly in their home, they had never enjoyed a dinner like the one they had just eaten.

The girls wondered who this man was and what he had planned for them. His actions were friendly but his cold demeanor and silence frightened them something terribly. When they'd first entered the car in Manhattan and drove off into the traffic, the first one to speak was Monique, as usual. She looked hard at the man and asked, "Where are you taking us?"

The cold eyes didn't even look in her direction as he answered.

"Be quiet! When I want you all to talk, I'll let you know. Until then, be quiet."

There was no more conversation. The girls quietly sat in their seats and nervously looked at one another. When they reached their destination, they marveled at the big house with the three car garage. They could see the big swimming pool behind the house from a distance, and when they entered the house they thought they had died and gone to heaven. The house was gorgeous and when the man gave the order to have food prepared, the maid put the delicious food together so quickly, it appeared as if she put it together before the order was given. After eating, the girls rubbed their full stomachs, and when G-Banks gave a nod of the head, the maid quickly cleared the table and disappeared for the night.

"My name is Gregory Banks," he said suddenly to the three girls as he looked closely at them. "All I want you to do is answer my questions. Is that clear?"

All three nodded their heads.

"Good," he said before looking over at Monica. "Did you all run away from home?"

"Yes," she answered.

"Where are you all from?"

"Chicago," smiled Tracy.

"Where in Chicago?"

"Cabrini-Green Projects," she beamed with pride.

"Why did you all run away?" he asked Monique.

The outspoken twin did not answer, and neither did Monica and Tracy. They all looked away as if in shame. They never told anyone about the rapes and sexual abuse, and now this man who they did

36

not know had asked them a question none of them were ready to answer.

Mr. Banks could see something was wrong but decided to let the question go unanswered, for now. He looked up in deep thought as he reminisced about his own early days in Chicago. Originally, he was from Durham North Carolina, and was rumored to had run with Frank "Pee Wee" Matthews gang, the "Chicken Thieves" named in honor of Pee Wee's childhood prowess for illicit poultry procuring. The Chicken Thieves was loyal to Frank Matthews, who was dubbed "America's biggest dope peddler." But in the early 70's when Frank posted a $350,000 bond and vanished, it was said that Gregory Banks had found himself moving alone in Chicago, locking down the 144 Unit Randolph Towers and surrounding areas. By the time the younger and hungrier thugs in the area began to form little drug gangs, G-Banks was already in the process of making his next move up the success ladder. Unlike any of the Black gangsters before him and after, he was able to buy off judges and politicians, just like the White mobsters has done for so many years. And that was because he had done and continued to do very important favors for some very important people.

"I have to take the three of you back home," said G-Banks looking at the three young faces. "We can leave in the morning."

"We can't go back," cried Monique as the tears fell from her eyes. "I'm tired of him!"

"I can't go back either," said Tracy shaking her head from side to side.

He was no dummy. He knew something had happened to these girls and could see that someone or some people had frightened them to death. He would get to the bottom of it for sure, but decided for now not to press the issue. He knew they were not ready to talk about the horrible things that was happening in their young lives. But it would all come out in due time.

"Okay," G-Banks said making up his mind. "You all could stay here for a few days until I can figure out a few things. What building do you all live in?"

"We're all from the same building," answered Monica. "That's my twin Monique," she pointed. "And that's our best friend Tracy, but she's more like a sister than anything. I'm Monica, and we're from building 624 W. Division Street."

"Write your apartment numbers down," he ordered. "Also, write your last names and all the rest of that stuff. Have it for me in the morning. Now follow me," he said standing up from the table. "I'll show you all to your rooms."

They were walking out of the kitchen area when he suddenly turned around facing the girls.

"Why were you all talking to that pimp on the sidewalk in Manhattan?" he asked.

The girls laughed and then Tracy answered.

"He was trying to get us to work for him but Monique," she laughed and pointed at her friend, "put that nigga in his place."

G-Banks face twisted into an angry mask as his eyes slit into two thin lines causing the girls to immediately stop laughing.

"Let's get something straight," he said looking into their faces. "Don't ever think playing with pimps is a game. Just be grateful that little wet behind the ears boy didn't know what to do. This is New York, and there are pimps out here who will chew you up and spit you out before you could even recognize what color shoes they had on! And another thing and I mean this. Don't any of you ever use that filthy language you just now used, around me ever again. Do I make myself clear?"

All three nodded, and as his eyes pierced through to their souls, they realized he waited for a spoken answer. "Yeah," they answered in unison.

"It's yes not yeah," he corrected as he turned and led the way to the guest bedrooms.

The house was huge! When he pushed open the first bedroom door, Tracy stepped inside of it. When she saw the big Queen sized bed, she turned around waiting for the twins to come into the room and join her with their bags.

"You all can sleep in separate rooms if you'd like," he said. "There's four bedrooms on this floor. I'll be upstairs in my room, and the maid is downstairs if any of you should need anything. But if you all want to sleep together, then feel free. The bathroom is at the end of the hall, so make sure you all brush your teeth and wash your behinds before getting into them beds." With that said, he walked away heading to his own master bedroom.

"This is crazy," said Monique stepping into the big bedroom with Monica following closely behind.

"Usually I can figure people out quick but that man is strange," she continued as she closed the bedroom door and sat on the big bed.

"Look how big the TV is in this room!" Tracy exclaimed as she walked over and turned on the 57 inch color television. The show "Real Sex" came on the screen and two white couples were having sex. Tracy's heart began to race as she tripped over herself to change the channel. "What the fuck was that?" she asked no one in particular.

The twins laughed.

"That's cable," explained Monique, "And you better stop cursing 'cause if Mr. Banks catches you, we may be outta here faster than we came."

"I ain't going anywhere," laughed Tracy. "You won't hear anymore curses from me. You bets' believe that!"

Monique joined her laughter before she began unpacking her clothes from her bag.

"What are you doing?" asked Tracy with a playful attitude. "This is my room. Y'all rooms is somewhere down the hall."

Monique sucked her teeth and said, "I'm sleeping in here tonight. I'll find my room in the morning. Plus, I'm not used to sleeping by myself so tonight we're together."

"Me too," chimed in Monica causing them to laugh.

"What 'chu think Derrick and your mother is doing right now?" asked Tracy. "You think they called the police?"

"No," answered Monique. "Us running away will just be another excuse for my mother to have a drink. And all Derrick wants is his money back and some more young coochie. But one thing is for sure, the last thing he would do is call the police. They might start asking his ass some questions if he did call 'em. What about your mother?"

"She probably celebrated me leaving her house," laughed Tracy. "She might even had a crack party with no music." She demonstrated a real fast dance with her eyes comically wide open, causing the twins to go into a fit of laughter.

"You stupid," giggled Monica. Then getting serious, she asked, "What do y'all think Mr. Banks does for a living? This house is a mansion! You only see houses like this on television."

"This one room is bigger than our whole apartment in the projects," said Tracy. "And I don't know what he does for a living. But he don't look like a singer though."

"And he sure ain't no rapper," laughed Monique.

"Well it's that time," announced Monica taking her toothbrush and night clothes from her bag. "I'm taking my bath first. Y'all can go after me." She then left in search of the bathroom.

"See what's on TV," requested Monique.

After getting comfortable on the bed, Tracy turned the TV with the remote to the Cosby show and the two of them watched the sitcom and laughed. Tracy didn't know how long this good living was going to last, so she decided to just enjoy the moment and make the best of her time away from her mother. She smiled as she stared at the television screen.

$$\$\$\$\$\$\$$$

Upstairs in his bedroom, G-Banks sat at a small desk as he looked over the latest stock reports. He had a lot of money invested and had already made huge profits. He was already a multi-millionaire, and at times wondered why he worked so hard for more money when it would take a lifetime to spend what he already had. Plus he had no one to share his wealth with or anyone to leave it to if he passed away. He never knew his real parents and when he was old enough to locate them, it disappointed him terribly to discover that they were two dope fiends who wanted nothing to do with him. It was his adopted parents that showed him love and provided a decent living; that is until they were both killed in an automobile accident leaving young Gregory to go back to the adoption agency. And when things did not work out for him there, he found himself on the mean streets of North Carolina. Surviving for young Gregory had proved to be more difficult than he thought. Because of his young age, there were no jobs for him, and he had no place to stay. But hanging around pool-halls and becoming acquainted with North Carolina's biggest gangsters, he had quickly become one of the most feared and ambitious money getters in Durham, North Carolina. And when Frank took him under his wing, things could get no better for the gangster. He was set.

G-Banks looked around the big bedroom he slept in. He then sat the papers he was reading down on the desk before standing. This was definitely a nice house, but it was in no comparison to the Los Feliz home he paid 2.4 million dollars for that boasted a 4,800 square foot Spanish style property with four bedrooms, four and a half bathrooms, a grand living room that opens up to a loggia and a mosaic-tiled outdoor pool. Or his 18 million dollar cliff-perched San Francisco mansion he owned with guest quarters, a private path to the beach, and views of the Golden Gate Bridge. He was a travelling man but always found it very relaxing to be in New York when he could. He appreciated the quietness of Bethpage, Long Island and spent most of his time here.

G- Banks walked over to the big walk-in closet and after using a key to open the big lock on the door, he stared at the assortment of weapons neatly hung on racks and hooks.

After being satisfied, he closed the closet door, locked it and walked to his bed and laying down. He placed the closet door key on the nightstand, cut off his night lamp and as soon as he closed his eyes, he thought about the three pretty young girls sleeping down-stairs.

Before drifting off to sleep, he made up his mind to fly out to Chicago early in the morning to straighten out the situations with the girls and their parents. He had no intentions of even thinking about raising any children. His life was already too complicated.

Chapter Seven

"Has my flight reservations been taking care of?" G- Banks asked the beautiful brown-skinned woman sitting across the table from him.

"Yes darling," answered Amy Devoe before taking a sip of her steaming hot coffee. "It was taken care of last night."

Amy was one of G-Banks' many female companions, who was competing to be the number one lady in his life. She was the daughter of a very wealthy prominent business. Anything Amy wanted she got, except the role of being G-Banks' only lady. She was very beautiful, but he did not have the time or the patience to be in a committed relationship. He had always made it clear in the beginning of his many conquests that a committed relationship was not something he was looking for. He didn't want to answer to anyone or compromise himself. No, it was much easier to stay single. If he ever needed company, a woman was only a phone call away. He had never been in love. He was a very serious man and his work came before anything and anyone.

"Okay," said G-Banks looking into Amy's eyes. "While I'm gone, you can take the girls shopping. I want you to get rid of all that disgusting stuff they call clothes. Just because they ran away doesn't mean they have to look like it. But they're only staying here for a week, and then I'm taking them back home where they belong. Because I'm not watching no brats, and raising children is completely out of the question," he frowned while shaking his head from side to side.

"Darling," smiled Amy putting her cup of coffee down on the table. "We can raise them together. I've always wanted children. Wouldn't that be marvelous? I mean, just think about it, you and I and our three little girls. I'm even willing to have one of our own. I would make a perfect mother and you my dear, would make an excellent father and husband," she smiled.

G-Banks dismissed her with a look that questioned her sanity. He was ready to get rid of her, let alone the three little girls.

"Oh my God!" squealed Amy when Tracy, Monique and Monica entered the kitchen wearing their pajamas. "They are such cute little angels. Please come and sit down."

The three girls stopped in their tracks staring and wondering who the pretty expensively dressed black woman was, as their eyes then travelled in the direction of G-Banks.

"Get your little butts upstairs and put on some clothes before coming into this kitchen," he ordered.

"Okay," said Monique turning on her heels and marching back upstairs with the two following closely behind her.

"Ooh," squealed Amy as they exited from the kitchen. "They are so beautiful!"

G-Banks picked up his newspaper and began reading with more important things on his mind. As Amy talked he paid no attention to her as if she weren't even there. She flew in from California late last night and joined him in his big king sized bed. If he didn't need her to watch the girls while going to Chicago, he would've sent her home by now.

"Good morning," chorused the girls entering back into the kitchen.

"Good morning," replied G-Banks before putting down his paper and standing up. "Have a seat."

Amy looked on with the biggest smile on her face. The scene before her made her feel as though she were witnessing something very, very special.

The girls sat at the table as G-Banks walked over to the big brown oven and removed a big tray of hot pancakes, sausages and eggs. He fixed three plates of food and poured three cups of cold orange juice for the girls.

"You are so beautiful," smiled Amy looking at Tracy. "You should become a model. I have contacts, you know."

Tracy dropped her eyes and could not look into Amy's face. She was not use to compliments and could see nothing beautiful in being black. She didn't know what this lady was up to, but it had to be something. She could not see what the lady was saying to be true in regards to her. Of course this woman had to have interior motives she thought, she just didn't know what.

"And you two are beautiful as well," said Amy looking at the twins. "I love the color of your eyes."

G-Banks placed the breakfast in front of the girls, before sitting back down in his chair across from them.

"Thank you," chorused the girls before bowing their heads and giving thanks to God for the food they were served. It was something the twins had always done before eating, Tracy watched the two and followed suit.

G-Banks stood up, looked at his expensive watch, took one of his credit cards from his wallet and tossed it on the table in front of Amy.

"While I'm gone," he said, "take the girls shopping, and get them whatever it is they want. Just make sure it isn't any of that garbage young girls are wearing these days with their bodies exposed. That kind of dress code is not permitted in my home. Also, get rid of that other stuff they wore here. Buy a whole new wardrobe and give the clothes and bags they brought here, to the Salvation Army or something."

"Good," smiled Amy. "I know just the places to take these little darlings. I'll show them how to dress and how to shop. I say we ladies, first stop at all of the top designers; many who are my personal friends and associates. How about that?" she smiled at the girls.

Tracy, Monique and Monica had the biggest smiles on their faces. They could not believe this man was buying them a whole expensive wardrobe and anything else they wanted. They looked at Amy and was beginning to like her already, as they looked at her with smiles and nodding their heads in agreement to what she just said.

G-Banks leaned forward and gave Amy a kiss on the cheek and walked out of the kitchen.

"So ladies," smiled Amy. "Are you all ready to go out and spend Gregory's money?"

The girls laughed and all three screamed out, "Yes, yes, yes!!!!"

"Good," said Amy. "I remember I saw Janet Jackson wearing this beautiful—"

$$\$\$\$\$\$\$$$

G-Banks thought about the three young girls, as he was being driven to the airport. He wondered for the twentieth time had he done the right thing by taking the young girls off of the streets and bring them home, as opposed to just giving them some money in Manhattan. After turning it over and over in his mind, he knew he'd made the right decision. He knew the girls would not had been able to survive on their own in the mean New York City streets had he not come to their rescue. Something told him had he not gotten involved, the young inexperienced pimp Goldie might had done something very terrible to those girls; worse than what they had already been through in their young lives. He remembered the first time he encountered the young pimp. It was a cold night when G-Banks was coming out of his lawyer's office. He saw the young pimp beating up a young white hooker. Goldie was accompanied by a much older pimp who looked on with an unreadable expression on his experienced face. G-Banks never interfered with people's street business. Especially that of pimps and hoes, but what he did not appreciate was the crowd of people forming to watch the spectacle in front of his attorney, Mr. Shapiro's office. There were about ten hookers milling around watching the lopsided fight. G-Banks could picture his attorney scared to death and maybe hiding under his desk for fear that the rowdy street people in front of his firm would perhaps smash in his door and rob him, being that he was known to make large sums of money. He was considered to be the best lawyer in New York among his peers and important clients, and G-Banks knew he was alone and assumed that he may had already called the police to remove the undesirable group from in front of his firm.

Goldie grabbed the hooker by the neck with one hand, and with the other he held a wine bottle. He was just about to smash her in her already bleeding face with the bottle, when suddenly his hand holding the bottle stopped in mid-air by a hand that gripped Goldie's wrist so tightly the bottle fell from his limp hand.

"What the fuck are you are you doing?!" yelled Goldie as the old pimp and the hookers looked on wondering who was the sharply dressed black man that just handled Goldie like a child.

"Look here," said G-Banks sternly. "Take your business down the street. We don't want this type of nonsense going on in front of the firm."

"I don't give a fuck!" yelled Goldie in a high pitched voice as he snatched his hand away from G-Banks' loosened grip. "Nigga, my name is motherfucking Goldie! And if you ain't no cop, you better never interrupt me when I'm checking a hoe!"

G-Banks wore a long black Cashmere coat and he slowly slipped his hand into the coat's pocket and fingered the cold black nine milli-meter. His chauffeur slowly pulled to the curb, and he was ready to make his move. He didn't believe in letting anyone strike first.

The old pimp accompanying Goldie stared at G-Banks. It was something about him that was so familiar. Then it hit the old pimp like a ton of bricks! His mind raced back into time. He could not believe it. His eyes got big as saucers and his lips quivered as he grabbed Gol-die by the arm to save the young fool from sure enough death that loomed ahead.

"Come on little nigga," pleaded the old pimp. "You don't know who you're fucking with. I'll pull your coat to who he is later. I taught you the game, now I'm teaching you how to stay alive. Young blood, this is way over our heads. Come on."

He then looked at the hookers as he pulled Goldie away to safety and barked out, "All you coochie infested bitches, you heard the man, get your stink asses off this block. Now!!!"

All of the hookers quickly dispersed, as G-Banks released his hand off of the gun inside of his coat pocket. He was sure the old pimp recognized his face from the old days when he used to be a bit reckless with his killings. He was grateful the old timer saved the young fool from getting killed. Because he didn't want to commit such an act in front of the firm. He wasn't really concerned with the witnesses, because he was so well connected, the case wouldn't even had made it to trial.

No longer thinking back on the incident, G-Banks leaned back in his seat and picked up the car's telephone. It was a call placed to Chicago.

"Hello," he said into the phone. "Yes, let me speak to the senator…Tell him it's Gregory Banks, and I'm sure he will adjourn the meeting that he's in. He's been waiting on my call…yes, I'll wait."

After a minute of waiting, the senator came on the line.

"Gregory," said Senator Pardon loosening his tie. "I've been trying to get in contact with you for quite some time now. I have a very serious and embarrassing problem. Whatever you want, I'll give. What I need you to do is—"

"We'll talk later," interrupted G-Banks. "I'm on my way to Chicago now. I'll give you a call when I get there," he said hanging up the phone. He never took care of business over the telephone, and never understood the recklessness of some men's mouths; especially that of powerful men.

The chauffeur pulled up to the airport. After getting his luggage checked and being seated in first class, G-Banks leaned back into his seat and closed his eyes as he waited for the plane to take off.

Chapter Eight

The tall handsome white man laughed out loud as the blue-eyed, blond haired woman with silicone breast held on tightly to his arm, giggled and hung onto his every word. Moments ago in the hotel's lobby surrounded by reporters and photographers, the two acted as if they hardly knew one another. But walking towards the hotel room they shared, it was evident that the two were secret lovers.

The woman name was Clara Sue Pardon, the wife of Senator Bobby H. Pardon. Clara was having a love affair with Congressman George Giddens. Because of the way the two carried on in Senator Pardon's presence, with the smiles, flirting eye contact and constant touching, he knew their relationship was more than casual friends. One day the senator approached the congressman about it, only to discover that not only was his wife cheating on him but also the smart congressman knew a secret about the marriage that no one else knew and threatened to go public if the senator decided to make trouble. What the congressman had hanging over the senator's head was that, he knew Clara was actually poor white trash. She did not come from money or a stable family. She was a beautiful white girl from the trailer parks, and was the product of an incestuous relationship. Her father was also her mother's brother. One day the father/brother got into a terrible accident that had left him partially paralyzed from the waist down. He was awarded a very handsome lawsuit and it was with some of that money that he paid to have his pretty daughter/niece attend one of the best expensive colleges and receive the best education she can get. Added to the money, the color of her skin and beauty worked nicely for her. She was in. It was there, that she had met and fell in love with her future husband and now senator, Bobby H. Pardon. Of course his family had objected very strongly to the relationship due to Clara's background, but the loved the two shared proved to be stronger than their objections. However, his family, including Bobby and Clara, knew the importance of her keeping her background a secret because of their status in society agreed, so the secret lasted for many years. Now somehow the congressman attained the information and was using it to his benefit.

It all started at the mayor's celebration party for once again being re-elected for the second term. All night long, Clara had noticed the

eyes of the congressman following and undressing her, as her husband walked around and talked politics and shook hands most of the
evening.

Everyone was elegantly dressed, and only three black people
was present in the mayor's home: Judge Harold Washington, his wife
Lucille, and the mayor's butler who walked around with drinks and
caviar on two separate trays. The white people took drinks off of the
tray and placed half empty ones back, as they talked non-stop. Clara
hated these functions, and hoped this one would end soon. The music lowly playing, reminded her of elevator music, the women were
stuck up snobs and most of the men were stuffed shirts and boring.
What Clara just really wanted to do was spend time with her husband.
They had a very exciting marriage; that is until Bobby's politics had
seemed to become more important than their sex life. Maybe, that
was the reason why for the life of her, Clara could not peel her eyes
away from the handsome congressman that kept his eyes fixed on
her breast as he smiled and licked his thin lips.

Clara's vagina began to get moist and she could take the stare
no longer. She stood up from her seat and quickly headed towards
the bathroom to freshen up a bit.

As she turned the corner and walked down the long quiet corridor, she was surprised to hear someone behind her clearing their
throat. She quickly spun around and saw the handsome congressman walking towards her with a smile. She could not move. She felt
as though she was paralyzed with fear. Her hands had become swea-
ty and her heartbeat increased something fierce in her chest. She
didn't know what to do or say. Where is my husband? She thought to
herself. She really wished that he was here to save her from this
awkward situation with this handsome man, but of course, he was
down the hall and around the corner talking politics as usual.

"You're looking very beautiful this evening Mrs. Pardon," smiled
Congressman Giddens standing in front of her and looking into her
blue eyes.

Clara shyly turned her head away.

"It's okay," he said while gently touching her chin with his finger to force her to look into his face. When she did, he leaned forward to bring his lips to hers. The kiss was passionate as he explored the sweet insides of her mouth. As they kissed, he gently rubbed her buttocks and with his free hand opened the bathroom door leading her inside. This man was smoother than Bill Clinton, she thought jokingly.

After locking the bathroom door, he made love to Clara like she had never had love made to her before. She was open! Needless to say, since that day in the mayor's bathroom, the two of them had been sneaking around behind the senator's back and to Clara for some reason, she felt that it made the affair with the congressman that much more exciting. She had no idea that he and her husband had spoken about it.

"I had to examine the effects of redistricting," smiled Congressman Giddens with the boring political talk as he dug into his pocket for the hotel room key. "The logic behind our argument in favor of a benefit is that majority-minority districts are drawn in a way that packs black voters, who are overwhelmingly Democratic, into minority districts and creates new or heavily realigned districts with mainly white voters, which should help Republicans. Do you know what I mean?"

"Yes, but who really gives a fuck?" laughed Clara as she grabbed him by the tie and led him into the room. After closing the door, she pushed him towards the big king sized bed and began kissing him as she helped remove his tie and shirt. But before she was successful in getting either of them off, they were interrupted by a loud knocking at the door.

"Oh what the hell!" the congressman said angrily while straightening his shirt and tie while walking towards the door.

"Room service sir!" yelled the deep voiced waiter outside of the door.

Congressman Giddens sighed, opened the door and angrily looked at the black waiter in uniform with a dinner tray on a small table and a bottle of wine. "I did not order anything!" he said to the waiter.

"I know sir, and I'm sorry. But this is complimentary of the hotel," smiled the waiter while pouring a glass of wine and handing it to the congressman.

He quickly downed the bitter sweet liquid and before slamming the door in his face said, "Don't bother me anymore that will be all!"

"You're such an animal," smiled Clara as she dropped her dress to the floor and held her arms open wide for her lover to enter them and take her.

Congressman Giddens laughed while walking slowly towards her. Suddenly, he had a strange look on his face as he stood in front of her. It was then that he realized that the wine he drunk was poisonous. Without warning, he reached his hands slowly to his throat and then fell into her arms. The weight of his body landing on top of her caused Clara to fall backwards onto the beds as he fell to the floor with a look of horror on his face.

In a panic, Clara knelt down and looked into his motionless wide open eyes. She then grabbed his wrist and realized that he had no pulse, before letting out a blood curling scream that was sure to awaken everyone in their rooms inside of the luxurious hotel.

$$\$\$\$\$\$$$

G-Banks removed the fake beard and waiter's uniform he wore. He placed them in the back seat of the car he was driving while leaving the hotel's garage. He calmly put back on the expensive clothes that lay neatly folded across the passenger's seat of the rented car. He then slowly pulled out of the hotel's garage.

He had one more stop to make before leaving Chicago. He made a few turns as he headed towards the notorious Cabrini-Green housing projects. He was determined to take care of the situations concerning the girls and their parents, because he had no desire to be stuck with three young girls.

He expertly drove through the Chicago streets and it wasn't long before he began to see more black faces and run down ghettos. He noticed things had not changed much since his last visit.

Finally making it to the Cabrini-Green projects, G-Banks cut off the car, fingered the nine millimeter in his overcoat pocket and then stepped out of the car.

Guys were standing around selling drugs as they smoked their reefer and talked in the cold windy weather as if it was a hot summer day. G-Banks did not recognize any of the young thugs standing around in the cold. But he was sure that most of them had heard of his legend, whether it was from the streets, their fathers, uncles or other relatives that spoke his name in the same light as past legendary gangsters. He walked pass the young brothers and headed towards building 624 on west Division Street.

After walking into the building, he decided to first go to Tracy's mother's apartment being that it was on the third floor and the twins' apartment was on a higher floor.

As he approached Tracy's mother's apartment door, he noticed a terrible stench coming from the apartment. It smelled like…shit! He knocked on the door two hard times before it was opened by a very skinny woman wearing a dirty beige housecoat and scarf on her head. G-Banks had to take a step back to escape the potent crack smoke that exited from the apartment.

"What do you want?" asked Darita with her face screwed up as she peered out of her door.

"I'm Gregory Banks and I would like to talk to you about your daughter, Tracy."

She looked him up and down taking note of how expensively dressed he was and then her eyes fell on the Rolex watch he wore. Even without diamonds flooding it, you can tell it was a very expensive watch. She licked her crusty dry lips as her mind went to work.

"Come on in," said Darita opening the door wider so he could enter. She smiled exposing a mouthful of yellow teeth that hadn't seen a toothbrush in months.

G-Banks hesitated before entering the small filthy apartment. The first thing his eyes came in contact with was four crack head women sitting on a dusty looking couch smoking crack from their stems.

"Y'all bitches go in the back with that shit!" said Darita. "You see I have company."

The four crack addicted women looked at G-Banks before scurrying off to the back room. They didn't know what the handsome rich looking man wanted with Darita, but they hoped she would be able to score a nice amount of drugs. But of course, Darita had it already in her mind that if she was successful in getting some money from this man in front of her, all four of her smoking buddies was getting the hell out of her apartment. Never mind they made sure she got high off of their drugs all morning.

"Have a seat," smiled Darita.

G-Banks looked at the filthy couch before declining the offer. "No thank you, I rather stand. I didn't plan to be here long anyway. I just wanted you to know that your daughter Tracy is okay. She's in New York City with two of her friends, at one of my places. I have plans to make sure they find their way back home and that you shouldn't worry."

"Sheeit," laughed Darita. "I ain't hardly worried about that little black ass bitch. If she does come back, I hope she's ready to do what the fuck I tell her to do, to make sure I'm okay. Sheeit, as much as I did for that little heifer. If she ain't willing to act right, then she can stay where the fuck she at!"

He could not believe his ears. How could a mother have so little love for a child she gave birth to? For some reason, he knew he was not going to get anywhere with this lady. The conversation was going nowhere and he definitely was not in the mood to argue with a crack head with no sense.

"Well," said G-Banks. "I really don't care. I'm just here to let you know that she'll be back home in a few days."

"I don't want that little black bitch here!" snapped Darita angrily as she wiped her snotty nose with the back of her hand. "She's not welcomed back in here!"

He looked around the dirty and smelly apartment and thought that no one should be welcomed in such a filthy environment.

"Give me two hundred dollars and you can have her little ass," she continued while licking her crusty lips.

He looked at her for what seemed like an eternity before pulling a huge stack of money from his pocket and a business card with his name and number on it. He peeled three hundred dollars from the huge stack and placed the money and card in Darita's excited hand.

"I'm not buying your daughter," G-Banks said in disgust, as she smiled down at the money in her hand. "I'm giving you this money in hopes that you will put it to good use and get you some help! You have my number, and when you come to your senses give me a call. Don't waste your time calling me for more money. I have nothing for you, besides your daughter."

With that said, he opened the door and slammed it behind him as he left the nasty small apartment. He then pressed for the elevator to make his final trip to Monique and Monica mother's apartment. He hoped it would be no worse than what he had just encountered.

He exited the elevator on the fifth floor and knocked hard on the second apartment door he came to. The door swung open and he stood face to face with a woman who was in a drunken stupor.

"What do you want nigga?" slurred Clurisa holding onto the door for support.

"I need to talk to you about your daughters, Monique and Monica," said G-Banks.

Before Clurisa could reply, the door swung open wider and Derrick stood there in a pair of jeans with no shirt on. "What's the problem" he asked pushing Clurisa out of the way.

"I'm here to inform you and your wife, that Monique and Monica had run away to New York City," answered G-Banks. "But they are safe and in good hands. I'll bring them back to Chicago in a few days."

"What did they tell you?" asked Derrick with his eyes squinted.

"What do you mean, what did they tell me?"

"About me," answered Derrick with his eyes never leaving the gangsters'.

G-Banks had already figured the girls were being molested, and now it was evident to him as who was doing the molesting.

"Mrs. Jackson," he said ignoring Derrick and trying to talk to Clurisa, "I have your daughters in New York and I would really appreciate if you and I can talk."

"Talk to my husband," she slurred. "I don't have a damn thing to say. Shit, I don't even care anymore. Those girls are way too fast for their own good anyway; with their titties in everybody's faces. So, if you have anything to say, then say it to my husband."

"Listen here," said Derrick. "I'm the man of this here house. If you want to bring their little asses back, then you do that. I got a beating coming to their little asses anyway, for stealing my motherfucking money. I don't know who the hell they think they are, and I don't know who you think you are either, but I'll tell you this—"

G-Banks walked away before Derrick could finish his statement. He had not the patience or time to argue with a child molester. As he walked away, he had no idea how he was going to look after three little girls, but one thing was for sure, he knew he could not send them back to the horrible parents and nasty environments that he just left from.

"Why would anyone have children they are not ready to have and look after?" he mumbled to himself as he exited the building quickly walking back to his car.

Within twenty-four hours, his life had become even more complicated. He had a lot to think about. God had definitely dealt him a hand that he was not sure if he knew how to play.

He reached his rented car and pulled away from the projects, at the same time pulling his cellular phone from his pocket. He then dialed a number as he drove through the Chicago streets.

"Hello," said G-Banks into the receiver. ""May I speak to Senator Pardon please?"

"I'm sorry," said a woman on the other end, "but the senator is not taking any calls at the moment."

"Tell him it's Mr. Banks."

"Oh yes Mr. Banks," she said in a different tone. "He's been waiting on your call. One moment please."

After waiting two minutes, Senator Pardon was on the line sounding as if he had been crying. "Hello Mr. Banks," he sniffed, putting on an academy award performance. "I've been waiting on your call. But there's a lot going on at the moment, so it's a bit impossible to talk to you right now. But everything is in order."

"Good," said G-Banks. "I've heard the terrible news concerning our friend Mr. Giddens, and I would like to send my deepest condolences to you, your wife and of course to the family of Mr. Giddens. It's a terrible shame."

"Yes it is, Mr. Banks. And we appreciate your condolences."

"Oh yes, and uh, senator?"

"Yes Mr. Banks."

"I know this is not a good time, but I was hoping that you can assist me with a little personal problem that I have. It is a small matter, dealing with Family Court."

"No problem. I'll call my good friend Judge Clark, and have him give you a call before you leave Chicago. And uh,....thank you for everything," said the senator before hanging up the phone.

G-Banks looked at his watch and decided to call Amy and the girls to see what they were up to, and to let them know that he'd be back in New York after taking care of some legal issues.

As he drove through the streets of Chicago, he decided to end his relationship with Amy. He had enough headaches already.

Chapter Nine

2010

Things Done Changed!

"A yo Bar, you going out to the yard?" asked the slim guy with curly hair.

"Why nigga?" asked Barkim ignoring Slim's question. "Boy, I don't know why you asking. It's not like you coming outside to workout with me. I'll put that 480 pounds on that weight rack and crack your whole chest plate," laughed Barkim causing a few inmates to laugh as well.

Everyone in the recreation room knew Barkim was serious when he made the statement, despite his laughter. He was one of the strongest guys in the medium facility prison located upstate in New York. Actually, there were only two other inmates in the jail stronger than him; Big Uno and Scott, and both were his workout partners. Barkim stood at six foot two, and weighed over two hundred and thirty pounds. His chest stood out more than any other body part, and he always kept his hair and beard well groomed, as if he was waiting for a visit from the outside any minute. His brown complexion was the color of a piece of chocolate, and he had a very easy going personality.

"When I come back from working out," he said, more to himself than anybody else, "I'm going to take my shower, heat up my food and watch the re-run episodes of the 'Wire'. I never saw that one when Stringer got killed," he said referring to a character on the show.

"Yo, that shit was crazy!" said a short dark skin guy everyone called B-More, being he was from Baltimore, Maryland. He claimed to know everything and everyone from the state. "I know the whole story without even watching it," he boasted. "That shit is true, and it's based on niggas I know from my town. It was a dude named Little Melvin—"

"Man, shut up!" laughed Barkim cutting him off. "Nobody asked you for a history lesson on the shit. Just because you're from B-More, don't mean them niggas was fucking with you. Plus, I should fuck you up just on the strength that you're from out there," he joked. "We show y'all niggas mad love when y'all get locked up in New York. But when New York niggas get locked up down there, y'all be try'na front on us and shit. I should choke your ass out."

Barkim was laughing, but another inmate standing near, looked on with his face screwed up as he stared at the Baltimore native while nodding his head in agreement.

Noticing what was going on, Barkim laughed even harder. He then looked at the clock above the CO's desk and grabbed his net bag containing his jug of water and workout gloves off of the floor.

B-More also noticed the guy face fighting him and quickly said to Barkim, "Nah yo, you got it all wrong. New York and Baltimore is cool in the jails down there. We be warring with them DC niggas just like y'all. Sometimes we even move together."

The CO's radio cackled out loud with a static voice and the red-neck CO stood up out of his chair and yelled, "On the rec!!!"

Barkim and the other inmates rushed through the door to go to the yard and gym in the Otisville Facility. When he stepped onto the compound, he heard someone calling his name from behind. Without even turning around, he knew who the voice belonged to.

"Come on Uno!" Barkim shouted over his shoulder as he climbed the small hill in front of the mess hall.

"What's up Bar?" asked a chubby guy named Poke who was carrying a keyboard instrument in a big black case.

"What's up?" responded Barkim as Poke walked beside him. "Where you going, up to the music room?"

"Yeah," answered Poke. "I wanna hear how 'dis beat I just made sound, coming through the speakers real loud. I just put it together like two hours ago."

"Jesus, je, je, jesus," chanted Big Uno catching up to Barkim and Poke.

"Oh boy," laughed Barkim glancing sideways at Big Uno.

"Nah, nah, nah," stuttered Big Uno. "I got, I got, I got three songs I did, I did last night."

Big Uno was a brown skin, 5 foot 10, very muscular brother from Guyana. At times when he talked, he stuttered and he was very hyperactive. He was known to change his personality quite often. Meaning, he would be a devout Christian one month, thugged out three months later, a positive poet weeks later and so on. Presently, he was in full Christian mode.

"When we finish working out," he said to Barkim, "I want 'chu and Scott to hear these songs I wrote. Matter fact, we can go up to the music room when we finish our sets. They'll let me, they'll let me sing it up there."

"Yeah come on up," invited Poke. "You can hear it over this crazy beat I just made."

"Man I ain't going up there," laughed Barkim. "I'll hear it tomorrow. I'm jetting back to watch the 'Wire'."

"Come on up Uno," repeated Poke. "Bring Scott with you. I got something mean for you to spit over."

"Aiight, aiight bet," replied Big Uno.

They walked down the long hill and before they knew it, they were at the gym door where they had to drop their ID card into a brown wooden box as a funny looking CO stood posted to make sure no one slipped by him without depositing their ID in the housing unit slots. After dropping their IDs', Poke entered a black door and disappeared up to the music room, as Barkim and Big Uno headed to the equipment room to get two weight belts.

"What's up Uno? What's up Bar?" greeted a nerdy looking light skinned guy wearing thick glasses. He sat in the equipment room by himself taking program cards in exchange for equipment being used. This was his program and what he got paid a dollar and change a day to do.

"What's up stupid?" laughed Barkim as others called his name out and greeted Big Uno.

"Alright, alright, alright," greeted them back. Then looking at a guy tying his sneakers, he asked, "Yo, you seen my boy Big Scott?"

"Yeah," the guy answered. "He's already in the weight pile waiting for y'all."

"Come on Bar!" yelled Big Uno.

"Hold up I'm coming," said Barkim handing him the weight belts and pins. "Take these over to the weight shack. I'll be there in a second."

"Aiight," replied Big Uno rushing out of the gym door to the weight shack as if they had just yelled out 'last call for chow.' He couldn't wait to lift all the weight in the yard.

"So what's up?" Barkim asked the light skin nerd guy. "You got a girl for me or what? I heard your sister came up yesterday. Dudes said she's dimed out. What's up nigga? You gone plug me in or what?" laughed Barkim.

"Nigga put in an ad," laughed the nerd.

"What?!" joked Barkim balling up his huge fist and standing over him.

"Alright, alright," laughed the nerd with his hands up pleadingly playfully. "I can't plug you in with my sister. But there's a lot of girls out my way that I can probably hook you up with. Matter of fact, I got this girl's address that you can write to. Yo, she's bad! I used to try to talk to one of her sisters who went to school with me."

"You mulatto ass nigga," laughed Barkim. "I don't want none of those suburban Long Island white girls."

"It ain't nothing wrong with the pink toes," joked the nerd. "No for real, the girl I'm telling you about is black. I'm talking real black! But real pretty black. Yo, she's one of the prettiest chicks around my way."

"That's what I'm talking about. An African Queen," smiled Barkim. "Give me her name and address, you yellow ass nigga."

"I'm telling you, she's bad," replied the nerd while pulling a note pad from his net bag and writing the information down.

"Her name is Tracy," he said handing Barkim the piece of paper with the information written on it. "Her pops is suppose to have a lot of money or some shit like that. I believe it, because Tracy and her sisters is also the best dressing bitches out there and they all push the latest whips."

"Alright," said Barkim stuffing the paper in his pocket. "I'll see you after I'm finish working out."

He then rushed to the weight shack knowing Big Uno and Scott was cursing him out for taking so damn long.

As he got near the weight shack, he noticed four guys he knew standing around and being entertained by a real smooth old timer claiming to be the baddest pimp in his day.

"Man, I'm telling y'all," said old timer Tea-bag moving his hands dramatically with every word spoken. "I've been down for twenty five years now, and never missed a visit," lied the old player.

It had been many visit days he sat alone in his cell, like so many other inmates. It was three years ago that he met his wife through a friend, and began getting visits every weekend. The other twenty two years in prison had been pure hell with no outside contact, but miraculously, he maintained a real smooth persona as if nothing bothered him.

"Man, that bitch gone tell me," continued Tea-bag, "when I get out, I bet' not fuck with no other bitches. She said if I fuck with other bitches, she gone fuck with other niggas. Look here, dig this. I told the bitch, you can't do what I do. A shovel can dig many holes, but one hole being dug by many shovels? Shit, you'll only ruin yourself."

Everyone laughed.

"Yo Bar!" shouted Scott from inside of the weight shack. "Come on man, we waiting on you!"

"I'm coming!" he yelled back. "Let me say something to this fake ass Ice Berg Slim."

Looking at Tea-bag he asked, "Yo man, how official are you with writing letters?"

"Sheeit," said Tea-bag. "I'll make a bitch rest her head on the question mark and put her feet up on the period."

Everyone standing around laughed.

"I bullshit you not," continued Tea-bag. "I been doing this shit for dudes my whole bid. I bagged niggas bitches, and I bagged niggas bitches back for them, so you can say that I definitely lead in assist. Now what kind of letter do you want the player to hook up for you? Because that's what I am, a player, not a pimp. P-i-m-p means a punk imitating my position."

"I want you to hook up an introduction letter for me," said Barkim.

"Okay, what's the young lady's name?"

Barkim dug in his pocket to remember the name. After looking at the piece of paper he said, "Her name is Tracy. I think she's one of those middle class chicks from Long Island."

"I got you young blood," smiled Tea-bag. "I'll see you after you're done working out."

"Alright," said Barkim putting the paper back into his pocket. He then entered the weight shack and began playfully arguing and explaining to Scott and Big Uno as to why it took him so long to join them.

Chapter Ten

Everyone sitting around the kitchen table laughed so hard, tears fell from their eyes.

"And listen to this," said Tracy through her laughter reading the letter in her hands to G-Banks, Monique, and Monica. "'Tracy, I believe you're the most powerful stimulus a man can have. Believe me when I say, it would be a pleasure for you and I to touch hands before the ground turns white.'"

"What does that mean?" asked a confused Monica.

"Before it snows," explained G-Banks while looking at Tracy for her to continue reading the letter.

"Okay, here's my favorite part," smiled Tracy. "'Baby, my loving you would have to be as natural as breathing.'"

"Ummm," smiled Monique. "That boy is romantic."

"That boy is crazy as hell," said G-Banks causing the girls to laugh. "That sounds like some old back in the day down south pimp talk. How old did that boy say he was?"

"Thirty years old," answered Tracy.

"You know what?" said G-Banks, and then continued before the girls could say anything. "That boy there probably didn't even write that letter. I'll bet my last dollar that he paid some old fool to write that thing."

"But look how cute he is," squealed Monica picking up the picture lying on top of the envelope.

"And look at his chest," smiled Monique peering over her twins' shoulder to get a better look at the picture.

G-Banks smiled to himself as he looked at the three beautiful young women he raised from very young teenagers. He couldn't even picture his life without his three angels. He had to admit, he done a hell of a job raising the three. They were college educated, business minded, intelligent, goal oriented young women that had a lot of good qualities. He raised them well. He wanted them all to go to Harvard or some other expensive and well learned schools, but they wouldn't have any of that. They wanted to be in the mix of things in New York City and attend school. Also, they wanted to be close by to their father at all times, especially Tracy.

Monica had graduated and was an accountant, and presently dating a doctor five years her senior. She still was very quiet and reserved, especially around people she didn't know.

Monique; her twin, was still the very outspoken one. Never biting her tongue for anyone, she never minced her words. She attended CUNY, and her major was psychology. She loved to manipulate and play with people's minds. She could not wait to become a professional psychologist. Like her twin, she possessed a very sexy gaze, and when it was something she wanted, she would simply look at a man with those sexy eyes and he would normally trip over himself to make sure she got whatever it was she wanted. But she was not a sleep outside of her relationship type of woman. If she ever did it, she knew it would only be for one thing she always craved; power! She was presently involved with a police officer who was completely in love, and would do just about anything for her. Because in his words, she was his 'exotic sexual siren.'

Tracy attended John Jay's College and had pursued dream of becoming a lawyer. She was still gorgeous, and had so much verve and sheer animal magnetism that her presence was felt even before she entered a room. Under G-Banks' parenting and guidance, she truly learned to love herself and appreciate being black. Because of her father, her self-esteem was at an all time high. She KNEW she was pretty. G-Banks called her, his little 'African princess', and growing up, got her involved in learning about African kings and queens, doctors, leaders, top models, and other great people of our race who was just as dark as her. She loved the ground her adoptive father stood on. At times she would act so over protected, he would have to remind her that she was not his wife or mother.

G-Banks had always stressed to his three girls the importance of first loving yourself before loving others. He said that's the only way, one would you be capable of loving another human being. He taught those girls a lot about life, style, character and being successful. He would even make dates with his three adopted daughters on many occasions to show them how a man is suppose to treat a woman. He would take them out to very nice restaurants, give them flowers, and compliment their beauty and intellect. He would always ask how their day was, and listen intently to their responses. Just the little things he did showed them the meaning of commitment. He taught them the meaning of having money, but that it was not to be worshipped. He also encouraged them to participate in community activities and to always learn from their mistakes. However, as a single father, there were times when he didn't know what to do or what advice to give when he was confronted with situations that only a woman could handle or understand. Like whenever the girls went through their menstruation cycles. Man, they would get so cranky, and their attitudes would be all over the place. G-Banks had a solution for that; whenever they were going through their 5 day forecast, they were to stay very far away from him and vice versa. The girls would laugh, at him and simply say how much they loved him.

G-Banks smiled brightly as he looked at his three beautiful girls; now women, sitting around the table laughing and talking.

"How did that boy in jail get your information anyway, Tracy?" he asked before having a minor coughing fit. G-Banks had been diagnosed as having heart problems and a strong case of bronchitis. At times it became difficult for him to breathe. Even in the winter months, he slept in an air conditioned room. He had no idea where this bad health had come from being that he was always healthy. It just snuck up on him one day, like a quiet assassin.

"He got my information from a boy that went to school with me, according to this letter," answered Tracy. "A guy named Alvin who used to always try and talk to Monique."

"Alvin?!" asked a surprised Monica. "What is he doing in jail? His family had always given him money."

"But he wanted to be a thug soooo bad," said Tracy. "Copying slang from rap videos, with his pants hanging off his butt."

"But Alvin?!" laughed Monique. "That boy doesn't have a thug bone in his body. I hope he's not getting raped in there."

Everyone laughed, including G-Banks through his fit of coughing. Tracy went to the refrigerator to get him a cold glass of water. She and the twins loved him more than life itself, and continuously hoped and prayed that he would always be okay. Growing up, they learned everything there was to know about their father, except what he did whenever he disappeared from home days at a time. He made it clear that it was never to be discussed. When he had to do a hit, he would leave the girls in good hands until his return. Before he knew it, the girls had reached an age that they began taking care of themselves when he wasn't present. He was still doing hits for the powerful people he knew, but was seriously considering retiring. His health just wasn't up to par with the occupation.

"So, are you going to write him back?" asked Monique.

"No, I don't think so," answered Tracy picking up the photo and looking at it again for the tenth time.

"Why not?" smiled Monique. "I thought you liked those big football player/thug looking type of guys."

"I do, but I don't know anything about this Barkim guy. And who wants to talk to a friend of Alvin, A.k.a. Gansta A?" asked Tracy causing everyone to laugh.

"Don't tell me that's what he calls himself these days," laughed Monica. "Oh my goodness."

"In Barkim's letter, he said that's what they call Alvin now," laughed Tracy. "I can't even picture it."

The twins didn't want to encourage their sister to get involved with a man in prison, but they did feel that if she chose to get involved with Barkim, they would support her. They knew she had always pushed guys away whenever she felt the relationship was getting serious. She told the twins that she just didn't find a man yet, that she considered her type. Of course, Barkim had fit the ideal description of the men she liked, but for some reason his letter sounded more like game than who he actually was.

"So, are you going to write this Barkim guy back?" Monique asked again. "And what is his real name?"

"I don't know," answered Tracy. "I mean, he's in jail for crying out loud! Oh, and his real name is Noris Houston."

"You can't judge a man just because he's in prison," said G-Banks sitting his glass of water on the table. "A lot of great minds and great men, and women, are behind those walls and gates. As you know, even Malcolm X was once in prison," he said knowing that Malcolm was his daughter's favorite leader and hero, after himself of course.

"I'll tell you what," he said standing from the table with a small smirk on his face. "I'll go with you upstate this weekend coming, and we'll see if he's the real deal or someone who would only waste your time. How about that?"

Tracy looked at the picture of Barkim again, and then at the man she loved as her father, and said with a smile, "Daddy, he better be the real deal."

"Even if he's not," said G-Banks walking out of the kitchen, "you'll always be my little African princess."

"I know daddy, I know," said Tracy looking at the picture again.

Chapter Eleven

"Something told me don't fuck with your ass," said Barkim. "Shorty wasn't feeling that 1968 pimp shit. That's why she didn't write back."

"Nah young blood," said Tea-bag while running his hand across the long braids that came down to his shoulders. "My shit probably just flew over the young girl's head. Bar, I don't spit nothing twice and eat nothing cold, everyday my game elevates, so how can I say something old?" the old player rhymed as he chewed a piece of gum he'd gotten from his female correction's counselor.

It was rumored that she and Tea-bag had something secretly going on, and she regularly put money on his books to make sure he always had something to spend on store day. No one knew if the rumor was true or not, but the old player made it a point to spend the maximum every time his buy date came around. Those who knew him knew that his wife never sent money through the mail, so most did not doubt the rumor.

Barkim, Tea-bag, Big Uno, Scott and Troy stood in front of Barkim's housing unit. They all were laughing because Barkim was dissing Tea-bag about the letter written for him. It was said that prison preserved individuals; whether true or not, all five inmates looked younger than their age had portrayed.

"Look," said Troy with his hand held out in front of him as he spoke to Barkim. "You done let this fake ass pimp write that letter to that girl for you, and he fucked that whole package up."

Everyone laughed except Tea-bag. He shook his head, said something under his breath and checked under his fingernails hoping he had no dirt under them.

"Look here man," said Tea-bag looking at his watch. "I ain't put two banana peels on my heels and slip into this game. I was born into this shit. Y'all can stay here and flap your traps all you want, but I gotta go pull my gators out and prepare 'em to take that long ass swim upstream to that visiting room. They should be calling me in a hot minute," he said looking at his watch again as he walked away to his housing unit.

"Fa-fa-fake ass pimp!" stuttered Big Uno causing everyone to laugh. Tea-bag looked over his shoulder with a half smile. He did not want to get Big Uno started. Especially with not being sure what mode Big Uno was presently in. He was way too big for you not to be sure. He stood 5'11 tall, but with a physique that could only be described as...damn!!!! He was without doubt, muscle book material, and tea-bag was too wise to feed into what he had to say, so he even laughed at the statement and continued his pimp strut to his housing unit.

"What happened to La?" Troy asked no one in particular.

"Just because this jail is wack," answered Scott, "he thought it couldn't happen here. He let little ass GT bust him in the head with a lock in a sock while he was watching wrestling on television."

"Damn, he let the goat herder do that to him?" laughed Troy causing everyone to laugh.

Just then, two big white co's walked across the grass, and headed down the compound as they talked.

"That muh'fucker's an asshole, said Scott in reference to one of the C.O's.

"Yeah," agreed Barkim. "Two weeks ago, he had the nerve to say something to me when I dropped the letter in the mailbox that Tea-bag wrote for me to shorty. I spilled a little water on my pants from my jug of water in my net bag, and that clown wanted to be funny and say, 'Houston, what's that wet spot on your pants? Had a wet dream?' I looked at his ass and said, 'it's pimp juice. I accidently spilled it on the letter going to your wife.' "

They all laughed and could picture how red the co's face must have gotten at Barkim's statement. They also knew that Barkim was now on his 'give somebody a ticket list.'

"You know he wanted to slug you," said Scott. "But he's probably too stupid to know how to write a ticket."

They laughed at the true statement.

"Houston," interrupted a short fat white co that came out of Barkim's housing unit, "you have a visit." He then disappeared back into the housing unit.

"Who came to see you?" asked Big Uno.

"I don't know," answered Barkim truthfully. "I have no idea. It might be my little cousin Boo. He didn't say he was coming up though. I don't know who it could be, but it's only one way to find out," he said as he walked into his housing unit to shower and get dressed.

"If-if-if you get a food package make sure I get some of that," Big Uno said loudly hoping Barkim heard him.

Scott and Troy just shook their heads as they looked at Big Uno. Everyone knew Big Uno had an appetite that was serious. It was always said, that a person would rather clothe him, than feed him.

$$$$$$

Barkim wondered why his cousin drove up to see him so early, as he finished showering and dressing. He had to walk up the long one mile hill to get to the visiting room. His cousin Boo usually came after the 11:30 am count and here it was only 9:00 in the morning. He hoped nothing had happened to his family, He didn't want or need a bad news visit. Throughout his bid, he witnessed many inmates get those visits, and he prayed that he himself would never get one of those.

"Maybe it's my ex-girl," he laughed to himself as he walked up the long hill to the visiting area. "I mean, my time is getting shorter. Isn't that what they say? Bitches start popping up when they know you're coming home?"

He briefly thought of his ex-girl from the past and had to smile.

"I can't front though," he laughed to himself as he entered the big brick building, "shorty pussy extorted me." After climbing the stairs, he was face to face with a prison guard in a small area.

"ID," said the short white male C.O. sitting at a desk. "And what do you have?"

"Chain, cross and belt," answered Barkim.

The C.O. wrote it on the pass, logged in the visit and stood up to pat Barkim down, making sure he had no contraband. After searching and giving Barkim back his ID card, the C.O. opened the visit door and said, "Have a good visit."

Barkim stepped into the visiting room and looked around at the many inmates and visitors, as he scanned the huge room for his cousin or a familiar face. He could have swore he saw a very beautiful dark skinned young lady smiling and waving in his direction. But he never saw her before in his life, so he knew the girl wasn't waving at him. To get some sense of direction, he headed towards a fat ugly white female C.O. and asked, "Who came to see Houston, Ms.Allen?"

She smiled and pointed at the pretty dark skinned girl who waved at him moments earlier. "I believe that's your visitors right there," said the C.O.

As Barkim headed towards the table, he noticed for the first time the very serious looking man sitting next to her. He didn't mind talking to the girl, but the man for some reason, unnerved him.

"Hello Barkim," said Tracy in her very sweet voice. "Have a seat."

When he was seated, she said, "Hi, I'm Tracy. The one you wrote the letter to."

Barkim smiled and relaxed. He instantly knew, he was plugged in with a winner!!!

"Okay," he said. "I didn't know who was coming to see me."

"I hope I didn't disappoint you," smiled Tracy.

"Not at all," said Barkim quickly almost stumbling over his words. "So, so what's up? How you're doing?"

"I'm fine. I got the letter you wrote and figured instead of writing back, I'd just come up and see you personally. You know, see what you are about. I hope that's not a problem."

"Nah, that's cool," said Barkim stealing glances at G-Banks wondering what was his purpose for being here and not even introducing himself. Not one time did the old timer smile as he looked coldly into Barkim's eyes causing him to glance away quickly.

"This is my father Gregory," smiled Tracy. "He offered to come with me, being I've never visited a prison before."

"I prefer you call me Mr. Banks," said the veteran gangster finally speaking for the first time since Barkim joined their table. He stuck his hand out and when Barkim shook it, he noticed the strong firm grip and strength the old timer possessed.

G-Banks let go of his hand and seriously asked, "Did you write that letter to my daughter? Be real with me. I hate liars."

Barkim was locked up amongst gangsters 24 hours a day, so he couldn't understand why the old timer made him so nervous. The man's aura commanded respect, so Barkim decided to be real with his words. His only defense was to be himself.

"No, I didn't write the letter," said Barkim. "A fake wanna be pimp in here wrote it for me. I sent the letter for rec, but if I knew your daughter Tracy was this gorgeous, I would've wrote her with my own words from the heart. I'm not a bad dude, I just got caught up in a bad situation. I'm trying to get my life back together. I have plans on starting my own construction company, being I did construction my whole life."

G-Banks looked at Barkim for the longest twenty seconds. He then looked at his daughter and a smile slowly came to his face.

"I like this guy," said G-Banks to Tracy. "He may not be a bad guy after all. Take your time to get to know him, and see for yourself whether or not you see yourself with him. Remember, follow your head and heart."

He then turned his attention back to Barkim and asked, "Who is the tall guy sitting two tables from us?"

Barkim looked, and his eyes fell on a big bald head guy that used to work out with him but proved to be too weak to continue on.

"Yeah I see him," answered Barkim. "Why? What's going on?"

"Is he screw facing me?"

Not understanding, Barkim looked at the guy not paying anyone, not even his visitor, any attention. He knew the old timer was mistaken.

"No," said Barkim. "He's not screw facing anyone. He's just looking in this direction."

"Norris, either that boy is screw facing me, or he's a very ugly man."

Barkim and Tracy fell out laughing.

"You two go on and get acquainted," said G-Banks standing up. "I'm going to this vendor machine and see what they have. Do you want anything, Norris?"

"You can call me Barkim."

"I said do you want anything, Norris?" repeated G-Banks with his eyes squinted.

Barkim chuckled and said, "I'll just take a soda."

"I want some hot wings daddy," smiled Tracy while still looking at Barkim.

G-Banks nodded and headed off to the vendor machine.

"Why your pops try'na gangsta me?" laughed Barkim when her father was out of ear shot.

"Don't mind daddy," said Tracy. "He's always been very protective. Anyway Mr. Barkim, what do you do in here, and why are you in prison?"

"Well Ms. Tracy Banks," smiled Barkim. "To answer your first question, I don't do much in here besides workout and read books to keep the mind sharp. It's not much a person can do in here. The last governor took away the college programs. And to answer your second question, if you haven't looked on the computer and checked," he smiled knowing she had, "I'm in here for arm-robbery. But I'm done with that life. I don't have any big money schemes when I get out of here. I just want to get a job and work so I can stay out there. I mean, look what I'm missing being in here," he winked while looking over her body causing her to blush.

"Tell the truth," continued Barkim. "I know when you first were coming in here, you thought I'll be on one side of the glass and you on the other and we had to talk over a phone, right?"

"No," answered Tracy. "Actually, I figured it would be a contact visit. But I did think it would be like that show that used to come on HBO called 'OZ'," she laughed.

"It is," laughed Barkim. "You see that big bald head guy right there?" he asked pointing at a stocky brother talking to a girl. "That's Anal-becee right there."

Tracy laughed so hard she damn near fell out of her chair.

"Nah," he smiled. "I'm just playing. That stuff doesn't happen in here like that. Television always portray people in jail fucked up; excuse my language. I can't speak for other states, because I never been in prison anywhere else, but New York ain't really on it like that."

"Do you follow politics?" asked Tracy changing the subject trying to see where Barkim's head was at.

"Do I?" smiled Barkim. "I have to follow politics in here, because I'm a product of it. That's why I'm still in prison after my second parole board even after I did everything that was required to get paroled. Politics kept me in here."

"So what do you think about us having a black president now?" she asked.

"It's cool in a sense," said Barkim. "I mean, he's taking orders like all the other presidents, but it's very important to have someone black in there. It gives children hope that they can be whatever it is that they want to be. But I have to see what this dude does to say whether he's a good president or bad one. Who knows? This thing might be deeper than what any one of us knows."

She respected his opinion.

"Are you one of those five percenter things I heard about?" she asked.

"Yes," smiled Barkim. "I'm one of the five percent. I am the maker, the owner, the cream of the planet earth and father of civilization and god of the universe," he quoted parts of his lessons. "I represent the nation of gods and earths. As a black man, I'm god. And as a black woman, you're my earth, a goddess."

"How romantic," she smiled. She knew in the very near future, she would have to build with him, because she knew her history quite well also. G-Banks had taught her well. But of course, it would be a time for that.

78

As the two sat and got to know one another better, G-Banks came back to the table carrying two packs of hot wings and three sodas. They ate and talked, and people began to get up and take pictures with their loved ones in the back of the visiting room. When Tracy saw the inmate taking pictures, she went in her pants pocket and pulled out her picture receipt she purchased before coming inside.

"Let's take some pictures," she announced standing from the table. Barkim also stood up, but G-Banks didn't. He remained seated.

"Come on," she said leading the way towards the picture guy. "It's just you and I. Daddy doesn't like taking pictures."

Barkim walked behind her and had to smile to himself. He looked at her ass not believing how round and perfect it was. Even the inmate taking the pictures stole a glance and gave Barkim a complimentary nod of the head letting it be known that he had the best looking woman in the visiting room. Barkim would definitely be the talk of the jail later when he got back to the dorm.

He smiled, grabbed Tracy from behind playfully and waited for their turn to take pictures. Tracy gave the picture guy the receipt and she and Barkim took six photos together.

As they walked back to the table admiring the pictures, they noticed G-Banks having one of his coughing fits. Barkim had a look of surprise on his face as he looked at the old timer. Because it seemed G-Banks now looked ten years older than he did a few minutes ago, before he and Tracy went to take the pictures.

"Daddy, I told you to watch what you eat," said a concerned Tracy. She then looked at Barkim and said, "I'm sorry, but I have to get him out of here. I'll be back by myself next week, and I'll write to send you my telephone number. You can call collect, okay? But I have to run now."

"I understand," said a sympathetic Barkim while helping G-Banks to his feet.

They made it to the front desk and Tracy got a piece of paper from the C.O. as Barkim got his ID card back as well. G-Banks tried to shake his hand but his coughing fit had him damn near doubled over. Barkim pat his shoulder gently and then gave Tracy a hug and kiss. She leaned closer and kissed him softly on the lips.

"I'll be back next weekend," she said pulling away. "My father and I brought you a food package as well. I hope it is things you like. And write me. This time, you write the letter."

"I promise," laughed Barkim. "I will. And thanks for the package."

He then watched G-Banks and Tracy exit the visiting room before going to the back to get searched. He had a half smile on his face. He was very happy to hook up with the beautiful Tracy, but he did feel bad about her father's health issues. He sincerely hoped the old timer would be okay. He then smiled as he looked at three of the pictures he and Tracy had taken together. He was so caught up looking at the pictures and into his thoughts, he didn't even realize the searching C.O. was waiting on him to come in and get searched.

Chapter Twelve

The bum wearing thick glasses and filthy clothes was sprawled out on the sidewalk with his legs outstretched and a cup in his hand begging for change. Occasionally, he would glance at the Federal court building across the street. He jingled the loose change in his paper cup and continued begging the patrons walking by.

"Can you spare a quarter or a dime?" he begged in his raspy voice with his cup out.

A pretty white woman looked into his red bloodshot eyes and dirty face and clothes with disgust before dropping a dollar bill into his cup.

"Thank you ma'am," smiled the old bum revealing a mouthful of yellow teeth. He then quickly glanced back towards the court building and smiled inwardly when he saw the rich looking group of men coming out of the court house.

The boss Big Al, walked down the court house steps flanked by his six body guards. Wearing dark shades, a blue three piece suit, with a Cuban cigar dangling from his lips, he fit the perfect description of what a rich black gangster should look like.

Everyone walking by looked in awe at Big Al and his henchmen all wearing dark blue and mean faces. Most of them knew who the gangster was being that he was a regular in the newspapers and television with the coverage of his criminal trial.

The dirty bum begging for money, sat his cup down on the ground, got up and followed the group of gangsters at a short distance. He then increased his speed, because he knew Big Al and his henchmen were about to get into the black stretch Mercedes Benz the chauffeur had waiting for them at the corner.

On two different occasions, Big Al repeated the same routine of not having his driver pick him up in front of the court building. Instead, he walked the one block radius seeking the media attention he so desperately craved. He truly enjoyed it, and loved the fact that he was labeled by the press as the new black godfather, and compared to Nicky Barnes. However, his shine was presently being dimmed by the new elected first black president; Barack Obama. The president picture and image was everywhere! So, Big Al did not get his usual media attention and the look of annoyance showed on his face as he walked to his car being escorted by his body guards.

"Excuse me, excuse me!" yelled out the bum wanting to get close to the celebrity gangster. "Black godfather, black godfather!"

The group of gangsters spun around and the smile on Big Al's face turned into a look of fear as he peered at the big gun with silencer attached being pointed at his face. His henchmen quickly went into action, but they were too slow being that the bum already had the drop on them from the beginning.

"Putt, putt, putt, putt, putt, putt," spit the .40 caliber handgun as the henchmen caught bullets to their faces, heads and chest. They were dead before they even hit the pavement.

"Please no!" pleaded Big Al as he backed up against the stretch Mercedes Benz waiting for him. "Please don't kill me."

"Putt, putt, putt," spit the handgun tearing away pieces of his face, neck and head.

The bum quickly stepped over his body and he himself got into the waiting Mercedes Benz and closed the door behind him. "Take me to Jim," instructed G-Banks to the small black driver behind the wheel.

"I was already given the order Mr. Banks," replied the chauffeur as the car leapt into traffic.

Everything had transpired so quickly. Those walking the busy Manhattan streets did not hear the gunshots. All they saw when the Mercedes Benz pulled away from the scene were seven dead black men sprawled out on the ground in a small circle with body parts missing.

G-Banks slightly lowered the car's window and from a distance in traffic, he could hear various men and women voices screaming in horror at the scene that he left behind.

The chauffeur expertly drove through traffic, got on the highway, and within an hour, they were pulling up in front of the big white mansion out in Teaneck, New Jersey. They drove through the big black gate surrounding the property, and down a long road like path leading to the house.

As soon as the car stopped in front of the house, four very big and tall black men all sporting baldheads waited for G-Banks to emerge from the car. They all knew how the gangster looked, but was completely caught off guard by his bum disguise when he stepped from the car. It took them a second to recognize him and relax.

"Lead me to a shower and bring me some fresh clothes," instructed G-Banks to the open mouth gunmen. After recovering from their slight shock, they led him to a bathroom big enough to be a project apartment.

"Leave the clothes in front of the door," again instructed G-Banks, "and tell Jim I'll be with him shortly."

The men nodded and walked away, as G-Banks closed the bathroom door and began taking off the dirty, smelly bum clothes he wore. He paid a real bum for the clothes so the smell was definitely authentic. He grinned when he looked down at his big toe hanging out of one of the beat up boots he wore.

After disrobing completely, he brushed his teeth removing the yellow American cheese he had smeared over them. He then used the Visine eye drops to get the red out of his eyes from rubbing them vigorously before doing the hit.

After showering and dressing, he tucked his gun into the waistband of his pants and stepped out of the bathroom in search of the big man everyone called Jim. He knocked on a huge brown door before entering.

"Come on in!" bellowed Jim sitting behind a big desk. He then nodded to the three gunmen sitting inside of the office with him and they all stood up and exited out of the room as G-Banks stepped all the way in, closed the door and took a seat directly across from him.

"I see you took care of my problem," smiled Jim as he stood and wobbled over to the bar. He was a heavyset man and resembled what the late rapper B.I.G. would've looked like in later years had he still been alive.

"You want a drink?" asked Jim while making himself a glass of gin and juice.

"No thanks," declined G-Banks.

"It pains the family very deeply of what we had to do to Big Al," said Jim nursing his drink. "This was a man that I grew up and played stick ball with in the streets when we were kids. His mother calls me son," he said sadly. "And now I have to break the news to her. I loved Big Al like a brother, but you can't mess things up for everyone else. You know, with all the media coverage, unnecessary cases and the like. I thought that flamboyant type of shit went out of the window with Nicky when he, you know, turned sour."

G-Banks sat there looking at Jim realizing that the man talked too much. He was only paid to do a job, and now the man standing in front of him was on the verge of revealing everything about this so-called 'family'. He wondered how long would it be before someone else from this 'family' would contact him to silence Jim.

"I don't mean to be impolite," said G-Banks cutting the man off. "But I have other important matters to tend to. So if you don't mind—"

"Yes, yes," smiled Jim walking back to his desk, reaching under it and pulling out a briefcase. He sat it on top of his desk and opened it revealing stacks of hundred dollar bills, and then pushed it towards G-Banks.

"Count it," smiled Jim while sitting back in his chair.

G-Banks stood up, closed the briefcase and said, "I trust that it's all there. However, if that is not the case, I do know how to contact you."

Jim's throat had suddenly become dry as cotton. He shook off the indirect threat and said with a smile, "Mr. Banks, it was a pleasure doing business with you."

"Same here," replied G-Banks walking towards the door.

"Oh uh, Mr. Banks?" said Jim causing him to turn back around. "I received word that you were once a part of the legendary Frank Matthews's crew. Is it true that Frank is still alive?" smiled Jim.

"I have no idea," answered G-Banks with a poker face. He would never reveal any information concerning his childhood friend 'Pee-Wee' to anyone.

Jim was unsatisfied with the answer and tried a different approach to befriend G-Banks.

"Well," smiled Jim, "would you like to attend this weekend's heavy weight title fight with me? My good friend Mr. King is sure to have some extra seats for the two of us at ring side."

"No thank you," replied G-Banks as he spun on his heels and exited Jim's office. He was approached by the three gunmen to be escorted out of the huge mansion. Upon stepping out into the nice cool weather, G-Banks' chauffeur sat outside with the door opened to his Maybach car.

"Good evening Mr. Banks," said the chauffeur.

"Good evening Valerie," said G-Banks stepping into the spacious car.

The chauffeur closed the door, and ran around to the driver's side of the car. He got inside and drove off down the path leading away from the mansion.

G Banks   Miz

"Put on some music," he instructed as he stretched out in his seat and opened the briefcase in his lap to count the money he'd gotten from Jim to make sure it was all there. He did not want to have to pay Jim another visit.

The chauffeur did as she were told, and the sounds of Al Green's song 'Let's Stay Together' came through the expensive sound system in the car, as they headed back to G-Banks' Long Island home.

He closed the briefcase and decided to count the money when he got home. He leaned back and closed his eyes enjoying the sounds of one of his favorite singers.

Thirty minutes later, a police siren could be heard behind the Maybach. G-Banks looked behind him and could see the police cruiser was signaling for him to pull over.

"Valerie, are you speeding?" asked G-Banks.

"No sir," she answered. "I'm doing a little under the speed limit, sir."

"Pull over," he ordered.

The chauffeur did as she were told, and turned the music down as well.

The white male officer approached the vehicle and G-Banks rolled down his window.

"What is the problem officer?" he asked.

The officer looked in the car and was surprised to see the distinguished looking gentleman, and his whole countenance changed. He expected and hoped the car contained a young black drug dealer or perhaps one of those damn rappers selling millions of records.

"Uh, you were speeding and I had to pull you over," lied the officer.

"Go and see my chauffeur and give her the ticket," said G-Banks. "However, I doubt that is the reason we were stopped. Perhaps, you may have thought that a young black man trying to escape the ghetto life was in this car, and you just decided to do a little harassing to keep him trapped in his place. But as you see, that is not the case here. However, if you should feel that a black is a black, then feel free to harass me and we'll later take it up with my lawyer Mr. Shapiro and my good friend police commissioner Joe Edwards. The decision is yours."

Realizing that he had stopped the wrong black man, the racist officer quickly apologized.

"No, no sir. I'm sorry. All of this is very unnecessary. In fact, let's just say we forget this whole incident had even occurred and you have a good day, sir."

The officer quickly spun on his heels and headed back to his patrol car where his black female partner waited.

G-Banks let his window roll back up and his chauffeur pulled back into traffic. But before she could turn the music back up, he went into one of his coughing fits. He was doubled over as he let the window roll back down to fight for air. He wasn't breathing right.

"Are you okay, Mr. Banks?" asked the concerned chauffeur. "I can get you to the nearest hospital in about three minutes."

"No, no, no," said G-Banks through his coughing fit. "Just get me home to my daughters. They'll know what to do."

He was feeling terrible, and knew in his heart that the occupation he lived to do and learned to love was soon coming to an end.

Chapter Thirteen

"Daddy, Barkim is coming home!" Tracy excitedly announced. For the last ten months, she had been going upstate every weekend, writing letters and sending money orders to help his stay in prison a bit more comfortable. She couldn't believe it when he told her that he only made eight dollars every two weeks for the hard labor he did in prison. This was what they called a job in prison. He explained to her that there were outside businesses that had big money contracts with the department of corrections. It now made perfect sense to her as to why the parole boards weren't letting people go. It was all about business, but they led the people to believe that it was about rehabilitation and to make the streets safer. Tracy knew that was a lie, because every time she picked up a newspaper crime was still at an all time high and most of the things happening didn't even make the papers.

She came home one day after visiting Barkim, and told her family in disbelief of how he told her the prisoners were being treated in there. G-Banks being as knowledgeable as he was, took it a step further, sat his daughter down and schooled her about the prison's slave labor. He said prisons had become designed to lock up Black and Spanish men and women and to keep them there throughout their most productive years. He said they had long ago abandoned the thought of rehabilitation and only cared about punishing minorities and keeping the business of prisons flourishing. Tracy had no idea major companies owned stocks in prisons. Even the inmates that worked and made things in the various industries: clothing, optics, license plates, furniture, and so on at the most, only received 96 cents an hour for their hard labor and time. So, these outside companies and the department of corrections were the only ones profiting from the inmates labor. Not the communities from whence they've come from, where most of them would one day return. The prisons even had contracts with the telephone companies charging the inmates families outrages rates for them to get through. They charged not only for the call, but would also charge the same for the connection. Tracy was just glad that Barkim would soon be home and would no longer have to deal with the crazy conditions that inmates had to deal with.

"So, your man is coming home, huh?" smiled G-Banks. He enjoyed seeing his daughters happy. They had come to mean the world to him.

"Yes daddy!" laughed Tracy very excitedly. "He said he should be home in two more months."

"That's good," he smiled. "Tell him I want him here at the house the very first week he gets out of there. I know he has to get back on his feet, so maybe we can take him shopping or something when he comes home."

"Okay daddy, I'll tell him."

"Where are Monique and Monica?"

"They're in the living room with Bryan and Joe."

G-Banks walked out of his home office followed closely by Tracy. They entered the living room to the chatter and laughter of Monique, Monica and their men.

"Good afternoon Mr. Banks," both men said in unison as they stood with outstretched hands.

G-Banks first shook the hand of Monica's boyfriend, Doctor Bryan McCall, and then shook the hand of Monique's boyfriend, Officer Joe Green.

"Don't let me disturb you all," said G-Banks. "You all finish talking. I just wanted to say hello."

"Well, I would love to," said Bryan looking at his watch. "But I was just about to leave anyway. Unfortunately, I have to get back to the hospital."

"Joe has to leave also," said Monique. "He has to go and buy me that Louis Vuitton Trolley Bosphore rolling bag and the Sac Bosphore bag that I wanted. Right, baby?"

Joe nodded like a puppet as G-Banks shook his head and laughed.

"There goes my retirement fund," sighed Joe.

"Okay gentlemen," said G-Banks before exiting the living room. "It was a pleasure seeing you two as always. We'll talk another time."

He then headed towards the stairs to his spacious bedroom.

"Okay baby," said Monique rushing Joe out of the house. "I'll see you when you come back with my bags."

"I'll get your bags baby, I'll get your bags," replied Joe causing them all to laugh.

Monique could have gotten her own bags, but she liked to send Joe on errands. She and her twin kissed their men goodbye as Tracy stood near. She wouldn't be alone without her man too much longer.

"Don't worry," smiled Monica. "Barkim will be home faster than you can imagine."

"I know," smiled Tracy not being able to wait for her man to come home. She and Barkim had become very close through the visits, letters and phone calls.

"Are you sure you wanna get involved with an ex-con?" asked Joe spoiling everyone's mood.

"I'm just saying," he continued. "You can do much better than this guy. I work in Brooklyn, so I know everything there is to know about this Barkim character. You want to date someone nice? There's a great guy that I work with—"

"Joe!" said Monique cutting him off. "Stay out of my sister's business."

He knew not to say another word. Because Monique would definitely have him in the dog house indefinitely, and that he could not bear.

Tracy gave her sister a look as if to thank her, and Monique gave her a smile in return that said she had her man in check. Bryan and Joe left out of the house, and the girls ran up the stairs to Tracy's room full of laughter because they knew Tracy wanted to talk their ears off about her Barkim.

$$\$\$\$\$\$\$$$

G-Banks was about to lie down because his chest was giving him pains that he never felt before, but before his body could touch the bed, his private telephone had began ringing. No one was allowed to touch this phone but him. He snatched it up on the third ring and said, "Hello. Who's calling?"

"Hello, Mr. Banks. This is Tony Castellano. Remember I had uh, talked to you out in Brooklyn?"

"Yes," answered G-Banks remembering the Italian mobster quite well.

"Good, good," smiled Mr. Castellano. "I'm ready to make that move about what we've discussed. But we have to keep it very quiet, because if my people found out that I used a black guy, I could end up—"

"Mr. Castellano, I'll contact you when the time is right and we'll discuss it then," said G-Banks hanging up the telephone before the mobster could get another word in. He did not like talking business over the telephone. Especially with mobsters, because he knew they were prone to be watched by the feds.

He walked over to his closet, took the big lock off of the door and opened it up, revealing an assortment of weapons: hand grenades, guns, knives, cross bows and bottles of poisonous liquids. He took out two nine millimeters with silencers attached, and just when he was about to close the closet door, he went into the most terrible coughing fit he'd ever had. He grabbed his chest, as both guns fell from his limp hands to the thick money green carpet. It felt as though his chest was closing in on him, and he could barely breathe as he fought for breath.

Hearing the terrible coughing, Monique, Monica and Tracy rushed into his bedroom. Seeing him lying on the floor, they quickly dropped to the carpet to aid him. They paused in shock when they saw the two guns lying beside him. But what surprised them even more was when their eyes fell on the half opened closet door revealing the arsenal of weapons. Their mouths dropped open and they could not believe their eyes.

Tracy was the first to recover. She looked at Monique and ordered, "Go and get daddy's medication and a cold glass of ice water! Monica, pass me the pillows from off of the bed."

Both sisters quickly did as they were instructed.

"Don't worry daddy, you're going to be okay," whispered Tracy with tears falling from her eyes as she rubbed her father's face and planted soft kisses on his forehead.

"Here," said Monica passing Tracy the fluffy pillows to put underneath his head.

Monique ran back into the bedroom with the tall glass of water and medication, handing them to Tracy. She put the medication into his mouth, and tilted his head back so he could drink some of the water. She then laid his head back down on the pillow and after a minute or so, noticed that he started to breathe easier. The girls lifted him from the floor and helped him to his bed. He lay down and within minutes began to feel much better.

"I'm going to call Bryan," said Monica to no one in particular.

"No," said G-Banks causing the girls to feel relieved that he was okay. However, they knew this was not the end of his medical problems. They also knew from this point on, that someone would have to be near him at all times in case something like this was to happen again.

"Now that we know you're alright," said Tracy with a bit of an attitude, "what is all of those weapons doing in here? You have some explaining to do."

"Tracy, I can't ever recall saying 'I do' to you. You're not my wife, and damn sure not my mother. So stop acting like it," said G-Banks causing Monique and Monica to chuckle. They all loved their father to death, but all knew Tracy could be very overprotective and confrontational when it came to him. They teased her about it all the time.

"No daddy," pouted Tracy. "Tell me what's going on. Please, answer my question."

All the years growing up under his care, he had always forbid them to never answer his private phone or go anywhere near his closet with the giant lock on the door but never telling them why. Now by happenstance, they happened to stumble across what their father had hidden for many years.

"My three angels," he smiled changing the subject. "I'm sorry I've never married. I should have given you three the opportunity to be raised by a mother. Maybe I should have married Amy, Katrina or one of the other good women I've come to know over the years. I believe girls need a mother just as much as a son would a father."

"Daddy," said Monica. "You are more of a daddy and mother to us than we could have ever asked for. Can't you see you've done a terrific job?" she smiled spinning around as if she was modeling her beauty.

"I did do a good job, huh?" he smiled.

"Yes!" chorused the girls as they sat around his bed.

"Tracy," he said. "I'm going to answer your question. But I don't want any of you to think any less of me."

"Daddy, there's nothing you can say that will make us think of you any less than who you are," said Tracy. "We love you and that will never ever change."

"Good," he said while trying to get comfortable on the bed. It was time to tell his girls what he did for many years.

He took a deep breath and said, "I've been a hit man for some very prominent people for quite some time now." He paused to see the effect his words were having on the girls. He thought they were going to break down in tears and ask why as he thought of an answer to give. However, their reactions were something he was not prepared for.

"Daddy is a hit man?" laughed Monique. "I like that!"

"For real, right? Pow, pow, pow," said Monica with both hands pointed as if she were firing two guns.

Tracy was the only one not feeling what she had just heard. She was a bit upset and could not understand why her father would put himself in this kind of position.

"Daddy," she said. "Why are you doing this kind of work? You don't have to do this. You're too intelligent for that. I mean, if you had done it in your youth to feed yourself, fine. But you are a very rich man now, and plus you can't be doing that kind of work in your present condition. You could have died in here a few minutes ago."

"I know," agreed G-Banks. "That's why after I complete these last three jobs I've committed myself to, I'm retiring for good. It was another job after the three, but I may leave that one alone."

He then went into another one of his coughing fits.

"Look at you!" said an angry Tracy. "You can't do anything in your condition, daddy."

"She's right," smiled Monique while handing her father the tall glass of water. "That's why you should let us do those last three hits for you."

G-Banks shook his head in the negative while coughing, before taking a sip of water.

"Are you crazy?!" Tracy asked Monique. "We've never done anything like that, and we're not going to start now. All of us have too much going for ourselves to even entertain that thought. And daddy shouldn't do it either."

"As much as I understand what you are saying," said Monica. "I kind of agree with Monique. Only because you know how daddy is, he's going to do those hits to live up to his word. Like you said Tray, daddy can't do those hits. So he should teach us to do it. I mean, what if daddy happens to go through his illness or something in the process of doing what he does, and it gets him killed? I couldn't bear the thought of that."

The room had suddenly become quiet. The same thought had crossed G-Banks' mind many times since he became sick. But he would never allow his three angels to ever get caught up in the life that he led. Now that same thought of him getting killed while doing a hit had also crossed the minds of his girls as well.

They remained silent, even Tracy, and could not imagine the thought of something like that happening to their father. They wouldn't know what to do if something of that magnitude were to occur. Even Tracy who opposed what her sisters had said, thought about Monica's statement and began to rethink her decision.

"No, no," coughed G-Banks realizing his three girls were seriously contemplating the crazy thought of being hit women. "No, get it out of your minds. The three of you couldn't even kill a chicken if we had to eat it for dinner."

"Daddy," said Tracy as Monique and Monica laughed.

"No for real," he said seriously. "What I do is not for you three to do. As a young boy, I had to do it growing up in North Carolina to survive, just as Tracy mentioned earlier. Before long, I was addicted to the money and the life style as if it was drugs. But none of you have to do any of that. I'm a multi-millionaire now, which means that if any of you choose never to work a day in your life, then you don't have to. All of my money is clean now."

He coughed something terribly before continuing.

"I'm sure I've told you three that my doctor had informed me that I also have heart problems and may have to undergo surgery soon. However, in the event that something should happen to me, everything would go to you three when I am gone."

"Daddy, stop talking like that," said Tracy with tears welling up in her chinky eyes. "I don't care about any money. Like you said, you have money, so please don't do those hits you've mentioned. We love you and we don't want anything to ever happen to you."

"That's right," chorused Monique and Monica.

"Like I said," replied Monica, "we'll do anything for you."

"Anything!" emphasized Monique with her pretty green eyes squinted.

"Look," coughed G-Banks. "I've already committed myself to at least three of the hits, and I'll take care of them myself."

"We can do it daddy," said Monique rubbing her hands as she looked into his eyes. "All you have to do is teach us."

"It's not that simple," he replied.

"I don't care how hard it is," she stated. "Teach us, daddy. Consider it showing us how to protect ourselves. You already taught us everything else."

"Do you know what you're asking?"

"Yes," she answered. "I know what I'm asking."

"You three, all have men I approve of who I am sure will die protecting you," he said still trying to get the thoughts they were having out of their minds.

"But daddy," said Monique, "even you taught us to never depend on a man or anyone for anything. Finances or other. I really would like to learn to protect myself and do what you do."

G-Banks knew his girls would not give up, especially Monique. Tracy was at a loss of words. She still thought of Monica's words of something possibly happening to her father during one of these hits. G-Banks sat thinking and looking at his three girls for the longest twenty seconds before speaking.

"I guess I have no choice," he said. "but to teach you three how to protect yourselves. But let me say this, anything we four say or do cannot be shared or discussed with anyone. That includes Bryan, Barkim and without question, Joe being he's a police officer."

"Daddy," said Monique. "It's only one man that I love and trust more than myself and that's you. I love Joe but I'll never go against anything you tell me or teach me. I would do anything for you. I know a little bit about death before dishonor."

G-Banks smiled to himself while looking at Monique. He knew he would have to definitely stay on top of her, because he knew with her attitude things could get ugly if she wasn't careful. Power can be very dangerous in the wrong hands.

"I'll do whatever," she said, "before I let you risk yourself doing anything in your condition."

"Me too," agreed Monica.

Tracy said nothing. Monique's last statement hung in her mind. She couldn't fathom the thought of anything happening to her father. So yes, if it came to his life, she would do whatever as well to make sure that he was okay.

"Okay," sighed G-Banks. "I'm still not letting you three do those last jobs for me, but if you think you're ready to know what I know then I'll put you three in training. That will mean no Joe, Bryan or Bar-kim for at least two months. Come up with some type of excuse. The first task is self discipline."

He smiled inwardly because he knew the love they had for their boyfriends and could already see the disappointed looks on their faces due to his last statement. He now figured it wouldn't be too hard to discourage them after all.

"Also," he continued really enjoying himself. "After coming home, I want you three to stay in your separate rooms with no television or radio. It'll teach you the true meaning of solitude among other things. We'll also find time to go to the shooting range, but for now we'll go through some mental training. Oh I almost forgot, I'll also have a physical trainer here every morning from Monday to Friday to work you three into shape. I'm talking jogging as well as weight lifting. Nothing too heavy of course."

They looked as if they had already changed their minds. He was delighted to see the long faces. He coughed and asked, "So, you three still want to learn about protection?"

They were quiet for a moment, and then Monique pushed her chest out and said, "Yes daddy, we're ready. I know it's going to be hard, but I'm ready!"

He looked into their faces for a few seconds to see how serious they were.

"Okay," he said. "For starters, bring me the two guns on the floor and I'll show you how to clean, reload and use them."

As Tracy walked over to pick up the two heavy cold feeling guns from off of the thick carpet, he wondered how long would it take before the girls would get tired of all of this nonsense and call the whole thing off. He knew he could break them and make them go back to being the innocent young women they were, but felt his biggest challenge would be Monique because he knew how determined she could be. She had a little tomboy in her and had always tried to follow in his footsteps. He then frowned to himself, because he could actually see a lot of himself all in that girl.

Chapter Fourteen

"Taxi!!!" yelled one of the drug dealers flagging down the cab with his hand in the air as his friend stood next to him wearing a long platinum chain and big circular medallion attached to it that was flooded with diamonds.

"Yo Mike," said the one hailing down the cab. "You can't be wearing that chain when we go to re-up. That shit will bring us too much fucking heat! The cops will be all over us before we even make it up to the fucking Bronx."

"Damn Tone," sighed Mike. "The cops can't be all over me more than you are. You sweating the shit outta me homie. Listen nigga, we good."

"Yo, I'm just try'na make sure we don't get knocked," said Tone. "Especially with this," he patted the brown paper bag full of money stashed in his coat.

"What we need to do," he continued, "is find a much closer connect instead of going all the way up to the fucking BX. The only reason I fucks wit' ya dude, is because the price ain't bad, and his product is half decent."

"Yo," said Mike reaching for the cab's door handle. "We don't have to leave BK soon. In a minute, my man is going to plug us in with his people in the 'ville. The nigga shit is suppose to be good and the nigga, from what I hear, is consistent. That's the problem these days, there's no consistency. One minute a nigga give you something good, and then they got bullshit. I just have to wait 'til my dude get back in town."

The livery cab looking car came to a slow complete stop and waited for the two young men to get inside. The driver could not believe his luck. All day, Drama had been driving around trying to get some money, but the only people that flagged him down were old women with grocery bags. He knew his luck had changed when he saw the two guys flagging him down. He figured they had money. He could tell just from the chain and piece one of them wore.

Mike and Tone jumped inside of the car and were happy to discover that the driver was willing to take them up to the Bronx. It was not often that cabs stopped for young black men. Especially in the heart of Brooklyn. They were even more happy to see that the driver was relatively young himself, because they knew the ride to the Bronx would be a comfortable one as the sounds of Drake's song "successful" came through the car's speakers.

"Where to?" asked Drama revealing two gold teeth as he spoke.

"183rd and Tiebout in the Bronx," answered Tone. "You can get on the F.D.R. from the Brooklyn Bridge and I'll direct you from there."

"I know how to get there," replied Drama. "You'll be there in no time."

"You don't have to speed," said Mike not wanting the cab to get pulled over.

"I got 'chu," smiled Drama pulling away into traffic.

"'My girl love me/ but fuck it my heart beat slow,'" rapped Drake as Mike and Tone relaxed in their seats.

In no time at all, they were on the F.D.R. Drive headed up to the Bronx to re-up.

"Yeah man," said Tone. "We gotta buy a bullshit car and put a stash spot in it, for when we go re-up, son."

"No doubt," replied Mike. "Fuck these cabs, and you know we can't use our shit. My Benz and your Range stands out too motherfucking much."

The sounds of Young Nik's song "Make 'em Mad" came through the speakers as Drama got off of the Major Deegan Expressway at 149th street and the Grand Concourse.

"What's up with that bitch Rhonda?" Mike asked his partner.

"Man," laughed Tone. "Me and the homie Billy Bang ran a train on that bitch last night something serious. Yo, the pussy is wack, but she could suck a main vein out of a nigga's dick."

Drama joined their laughter over the music.

"Word son!" continued Tone excitedly. "I might make that bitch wifey just on the strength of that. No wonder those two fool ass niggas from Queens is warring over that bitch."

"Fuck that," said Mike. "I'm not warring over no bitch."

It was now dark outside as Drama made a left turn on Webster Avenue. He slowed down and turned on his blinkers.

"Pardon me fellas," he said to his two passengers as he turned his body around slightly to see them.

"Do y'all mind if I pull over and take a quick piss?" he asked. "It'll be quick. I been holding it ever since we left Brooklyn."

They figured the cab driver to be cool people. After all, he did stop and pick them up when no other cab would.

"Go 'head homie," said Tone. "Do your thing."

"Thanks," said Drama as he pulled over and put the car in park. He opened the door and they waited for him to get out. Instead, he spun around in his seat facing Mike and Tone raising the most ugliest .45 revolver handgun either of the two had ever saw in their life. The gun had black electrical tape around the handle. Mike and Tone individually shared two seconds a piece of it being continuously pointed in their faces. Being it was dark out, the only light came from inside of the car due to Drama's door being slightly opened.

"Take that fucking chain off!" growled Drama with the gun pointed in Mike's face.

The two of them could not believe their bad luck and fear showed all in their faces as Mike took his big expensive chain and diamond infested piece off from around his neck and handing it to Drama.

"Now, this is what I want y'all to do," ordered Drama. "One at a time, take your clothes off piece by piece and hand it to me. First you," he pointed the gun at Mike.

Mike quickly came out of his clothes and handed them to him as he sat naked in the back seat. Drama took the money from the pockets while at the same time watching their every move.

"Now you!" he ordered Tone.

When Tone removed his jacket, the brown paper bag full of money fell into his lap.

"Bingo!" smiled Drama. "Hand that bag to me."

A frightened Tone did as he was instructed.

Drama quickly looked into the bag and after seeing all of the money it contained, he asked, "How much is in here?"

"Thirty thousand," answered Tone with a pitiful look.

"Okay," said Drama. "Now take off the rest of your clothes and do it slow."

Tone did as he was told, and after Drama rifled through the clothes and took the few dollars out of the pants pocket, he threw their clothes out of the car and said to the two scared drug dealers, "Get the fuck outta my car!"

The two hesitated a moment, and then Mike slowly got out of the car naked, followed by Tone. Drama leaned over the seat with his gun still pointed at the two and closed the car's back door. They went to gather their clothes to get dressed. Both swore revenge under their breath.

Drama pulled away from the scene as if someone was trying to hold his back bumper. He hit Webster Avenue, and after making a turn, found himself back on the Major Deegan Expressway. He roared with laughter when he connected with the F.D.R. Drive on his way back to Brooklyn.

"'It's been a long time coming so now I gotta pop'em/sneak up surprise'em/ snatch'em then hide'em,'" he rapped along with the hot new rapper Berry off of his song "Long Time Coming."

He made it back to Brooklyn in less than 45 minutes and figured instead of going back to Brownsville where he lived. He'd first go to Bedford Styvesant to see his childhood friend who had just came home from an upstate prison.

He pulled up in front of a big brown house on Hancock Street and noticed three guys standing out front. He quickly counted out ten thousand dollars from the bag he took from Tone and Mike, put it in his jacket pocket and threw the heavy chain and diamond infested piece around his neck before getting out of the car. This jooks was like a back in the day robbery, he thought to himself with a smile.

"Who dat?" asked one of the guys standing in the cold.

"It's me, Drama. Yo, where the nigga Bar at?"

"Oh shit, what's going on Drama?" asked one of the guys giving him a pound when he got close.

"Big Bar is upstairs. What's with the gun?" another guy asked pointing to the exposed weapon in Drama's waistband.

"Oh shit," exclaimed a surprised Drama realizing that he was so anxious to see his friend, that he didn't zip up his coat to conceal the weapon on his person.

"I'm giving it to Big Bar," he answered as he zipped up his coat.

"That chain and piece is crazy!" said one of the guys.

"Word!" agreed his two cohorts.

One of the guys sported a dirty looking brown fur coat. He kept touching it as if he were sporting a mink.

"What the fuck is that you got on?" laughed Drama. "Where you get the toilet seat cover from?"

They all laughed, even the guy wearing the fake fur.

"Come on," said the youngest of the trio leading Drama into the house. "Your boy Bar is going to be crazy happy to see you. All the nigga talked about all day was you, and some girl name Tracy."

When they stepped into the living room, Barkim didn't even notice they entered as he watched the Tupac's 'Ressurection' DVD he didn't get to watch in prison.

"What up my nigga?" smiled Drama.

Barkim looked away from the television and couldn't believe his eyes.

"Oh shit!" he yelled standing up. "My boy Drama."

"Damn ," said Drama taking a step back to look at him. "Nigga, you were already a big motherfucker before you went in, and now you went and got bigger. Your chest is fucking crazy!"

Barkim laughed and said, "Man, you act like you a little nigga or something."

He did have a point there. Drama stood 6'1 and was chiseled up in a muscular fashion with Mike Tyson like neck. They gave one another a pound and hug.

"Welcome home playboy," smiled Drama while letting him go. "Yo, I heard you was up there with my boy Askari."

"Yeah," laughed Barkim nodding his head. "I was in there with that nut. That nigga is still the same. With that lightskin prettyboy shit. I use to tell the nigga, brownskin niggas is in now, and that cat Shamar Moore can't even bring that lightskin shit back."

"Shit," laughed Drama. "I don't know what the hell you talking about nigga, I'm a brownskin nigga that never went out of style. So what's up?" he asked changing the subject. "What's the deal with shorty you was writing me about? I thought you would be up in here smashing that out right about now."

"Man," sighed Barkim. "Tracy is the truth! But I don't know what's going on with her. Son, I ain't heard from her in like two and a half months. Everytime I call her crib, her pops tell me she's not home and may not be back for a few weeks. Man, I don't know. It just seems crazy for her to troop the time I had left, and then bounce when I'm two and a half months short. I just hope she's alright."

"Where is she from?" asked Drama.

"She's from outta Long Island," answered Barkim.

"Nigga," laughed Drama, "you let a Long Island chick get your big Brooklyn thug ass open?"

"Yo, she's the truth. Definitely wifey material. But on another note, what's up, you got something for me?"

"No doubt," smiled Drama reaching into his jacket pocket and pulling out the ten thousand dollars and handing it to him.

"That's ten gees," he said. "But I got something else for you too."

First he took off the chain and piece handing it to Barkim, and then took the gun from his waist handing that to him as well.

"It's for you baby boy," he smiled.

"That's what I'm talking about," smiled Barkim. "I can go shopping with the money early in the morning. And this chain and piece is crazy!" he said holding it up before slipping it around his neck. "But you could've got me a better looking gun," he said handing it back.

"An ugly gun for an ugly situation should it occur. Let's get outta here," said Drama changing the subject. "Grab your coat so I can take you to get some pussy nigga. Ain't no sense you staying in the crib thinking about that girl Tracy."

Barkim thought for a moment, looked at his watch and knew he had three hours to be back in the house before the curfew his parole officer had given him.

"Nah," he said, "I don't want no pussy. I want Tracy to be the one to get that first nut. But I don't mind looking at some pussy. Take me to a strip club or something."

After Drama placed the gun back on his waist, they headed out of the house in route to the best strip club in Brooklyn. But no matter how good the girls would look, Barkim had Tracy on his mind something serious.

Chapter Fifteen

G-Banks had first thought that Monique would be his biggest obstacle of getting the girls to change their minds, but actually it was Tracy who had proved to be the more determined one of the three girls.

She would be the first one up in the morning, ready for her physical training and always had some kind of book in her hands. Of course, she was missing Barkim like crazy and wanted to see him on his first day home, but she could not afford the pleasures of any distractions at the moment. Her sisters were doing the same as she, and were depending on her to stay strong. Plus, it didn't hurt that she loved the way the physical training had toned her body.

G-Banks was surprised by their persistence. Everything he threw their way, they overcame it, no matter how crazy or ridiculous it seemed. Also, their shooting had become so accurate, he often wondered if they were perhaps better than he were. He also had them read books such as: The Art of War, Blood In my Eyes, and 48 Laws of Power, among other books. He did a lot of physical and mental training with the girls. However, his health was deteriorating drastically as the days passed by. Some days, he was so bedridden, he could not even move.

The red telephone on his nightstand began ringing and he snatched it up on the third ring. "Hello?" he asked into the phone.

"Hello Mr. Banks. This is Mr. Castellano. How are you feeling these days? I hope you are feeling better," he continued before G-Banks could answer his question. "This fucking guy, Peter 'Pretty Boy' Marcelli is becoming a pain in my fucking side. I'm even hearing some terrible news of this fucking guy disrespecting my own flesh and blood. And these assholes I have around me can't even get close to the guy to even fucking talk to him!"

G-Banks coughed something terribly, sipped a little water out of his glass in his hand and said, "Don't worry about it, I will take care of it today. I already have all the information, and when everything is tooken care of, I'll give you a call."

"Are you sure you're okay?" Mr. Castellano asked very sympathetically. "That cough sounds awful."

"I'll take care of your problem today," replied G-Banks ignoring his question and then taking a sip of water. "You have my word on it."

"Be careful Mr. Banks," warned Mr. Castellano. "You can't judge a book by its cover. This guy is a fucking terror. He already took three of my best—"

G-Banks slammed the phone down in the mobster's ear before he could finish his statement. The last thing he wanted to hear was how dangerous his target was. His philosophy was, if you can be seen you can be hit, and if you can be hit you can be killed. There were no exceptions.

He struggled into a sitting position, stood up from the bed and walked slowly to his walk-in closet. He sifted through the very expensive wardrobe trying to decide what to wear. He settled for a light grey Cashmere three button suit, a white cotton shirt, grey silk tie and a pair of black Ralph Lauren shoes.

After getting dressed and placing his nine millimeter with silencer attach into his shoulder holster, he made his way downstairs. He was coughing badly as he walked slower than ever. The doctor ordered him to stay in bed and drink plenty of liquid, and though he knew he were in no condition to do a hit, he was a man of his word.

"Hey daddy," said Tracy meeting him at the bottom of the stairs. "Where are you going?" she asked.

"I have to go and take care of something," he answered through his coughing.

"The doctor said you need to rest," said Monique walking into the hallway followed by her twin Monica.

"I have three jobs left," he said. "And I'm going to do one of them today. I already gave my word to do it, and everyone knows that Gregory Banks always stay true to his word."

"Well," said Tracy angrily, "you're going to have to break your word for once. You're not going anywhere in your condition, even if we have to go and do it ourselves. So if you feel you have to live up to this crazy word of yours, you might as well just give us all of the information and we'll take care of it. Because daddy, we're not letting you leave out of here in your condition," she said as tears welled up in her eyes.

"No," he coughed. "This is much too dangerous for the three of you."

"Daddy," said Monique excitedly and anxious to practice some of the things she had learned, "you should let us do it. Even you said you trained us pretty well. And we promise, if the job looks too hard or dangerous for us, we'll agree with you and turn back around, and never think about doing this type of stuff again. We'll put this whole hitman stuff behind us."

G-Banks felt terrible as his eyes slightly closed and his legs went weak on him. He knew he were in no condition to go out himself and do the hit. It would be suicidal. He slowly sat on the bottom of the steps and thought hard for a moment before speaking to the girls.

"Okay, this is what I'll do," he said looking into their faces. "I'll give you all of the information on this guy, and see if you're ready to do this job. Before you leave here, we'll come up with a plan on how to take this guy out. If any of you began to feel nervous, let me know and I'll handle it from there. You three understand?"

All three young women smiled, happy to know that their father was not going to put himself in harm's way. He could barely stand up on his own.

"Yes daddy," Monique smiled sweetly. "We understand."

They gathered around their father and received all the information on the wanted man, and after coming up with their plan, they went over it four times to make sure there would be no mistakes doing their first hit. This was a very dangerous job, so everything had to go according to plan.

"Okay ladies," coughed G-Banks. "It's time for you three to go and get dressed."

They helped him to his feet and led him back upstairs to his bedroom. They then went to shower and dress.

After showering and dressing, they walked into their father's bedroom. He was lying in bed. When he looked up and saw his three girls, his mouth dropped open. They were absolutely gorgeous!!! They looked as if they had stepped off of the pages of a magazine that was dedicated to supermodels.

Tracy's hair came down her back and her Chinese like eyes were mesmerizing as the black Dolce& Gabanna dress hugged her body like a glove. Her perfectly round ass and breast stood at attention. She had a very small waist making her ass look as if you could sit a drink on top of it without worrying about spilling a drop. The twins were equally as beautiful, as they stood there with bright smiles and their pretty green eyes sparkling. Their bodies matched Tracy's, and they wore an identical pink Baby Phat pant suit by Kimora Lee Simmons. Both wore their hair pulled back and pinned up exposing the expensive Fred Leighton diamond earrings in their ears. All three young women clutched matching Coach bags, and Tracy wore her Gucci Envy Me perfume and the twins wore Dior Me, Dior Me Not by Dior. They almost smelled as good as they looked.

"How do we look, daddy?" smiled Monica spinning around.

G-Banks was stuck with his mouth open marveling at their beauty. He weakly pushed himself out of bed before answering her question.

"All three of you," he said, "look very beautiful and radiant. You are sure to steal the attention from any woman in your presence."

"Arrr," smiled Monique, "Thank you daddy."

"Now let me pick out something nice to go with the outfits you're wearing," he said walking slowly to his artillery closet. After opening it, he grabbed three .40 Caliber handguns with silencers attached, three small bottles of poisonous liquid and three surgical scalpels.

"Here you go ladies," he said handing the weapons to the girls. "You know I love you three with all my heart and you also know you don't have to do this, right?"

"Yes daddy, we know," sighed Monique as they put their weapons inside of their bags. "And we love you too. That's why we're doing this."

She then kissed him on the cheek and Monica and Tracy did the same.

"Don't worry," said Tracy. "We'll be fine."

They then exited the room and down the stairs.

When they got out of the house, the three of them got into the chauffeured Maybach car. G-Banks watched them from his bedroom window and shook his head, wondering had he done the right thing as the car pulled away from the house.

"So, what did Bryan say when you told him that it will be awhile before you could see him again?" Tracy asked Monica making small talk as they headed towards their destination. They were all nervous but fought hard to hide it as they talked 'girl talk', as if they were just heading out for lunch or something.

"He took it quite well," answered Monica. "Actually, too well if you ask me. If that man is sleeping around on me with one of those nurses in that hospital, I will break his neck."

Tracy and Monique laughed but knew she was serious.

"When I told Joe," laughed Monique, "he damn near cried. He acted as if I was leaving his ass for good. I'm telling you, I got that man pussywhipped!"

They all laughed.

"I wish I could've spoken to Barkim," said Tracy. "I know he was probably like, 'damn this girl just broke out on me when I had only two months left.' That's how he talk," she laughed causing her sisters to laugh as well.

"I didn't even see my baby on his first day home," she pouted. "I was suppose to be there waiting for him."

"Well just be glad you weren't the first woman he saw," laughed Monique, "because if they say is true, he would've had your coochie black and blue after doing all that time."

"I wish!" laughed Tracy.

They talked about everything, to keep their minds off of the job that loomed ahead.

"Your face looks real good," Monica stated to Tracy. "You've been using that stuff you told me about?"

"My face always looks good," Tracy stated matter of factly. "But yes, I've been using the stuff I told you about. It's called, 'Beanie Genie' made out of boiled Kenyan coffee beans made into a lotion. Something used in Africa, but a beautiful young sister name Nyakio Kamoche Grieco is making moves over here with it. It's all different kinds. I just bought the whole Nyakio Kenyan Coffee and Sugar Body Scrub."

"When we get home," said Monica, "you can show me where I can order it from."

"Me too," said Monique.

"Shoot," said Tracy. "When we get back home, I'm going to see my baby Barkim. This morning, daddy said we can resume our regular lives. I can't wait to see Barkim, and I purchased this nice long dress and—"

"Girl," laughed Monique cutting her off. "That's something you wear to an award show. I saw the dress. It's nice but not for the occasion. Beautiful dress but not something you want to wear to go and give your man some booty."

They all laughed, gave each other high fives and agreed.

The chauffeur had finally pulled up in front of the big Italian restaurant. The three girls exited from the car and all walking by looked at them in admiration as they walked into the well known establishment.

"I'm thinking about getting my hair wrapped later in the week," said Tracy moving her hands dramatically with each word spoken to Monique and Monica. She learned that acting played a big part in doing hits or robberies. She was on stage and would have to perform an Oscar award performance to get what she needed to get done. Everyone looked on at their entrance inside of the restaurant. Their sexy walk alone made the Italian men drool, and their women gave the three girls envious stares. These three young women were more than gorgeous. They were stunning!

"Your name please," said the Italian headwaiter standing near the door with a list of names for reservations.

Tracy gave the man an annoyed look for interrupting her talk with her sisters concerning her hair.

"Nicole Smith," she said with attitude as the twins scanned the restaurant trying to scope out their target.

"Excuse me ma'am," the headwaiter said scanning the list. "I do not see a Nicole Smith."

"What do you mean you don't see a Nicole Smith?!" yelled Tracy making a scene which caused everyone in the restaurant to look on. "I am thee Nicole Smith!"

Mr. Peter 'Pretty Boy' Marcelli sat at his usual table. He looked on fascinated at the sight of the three beautiful young black women. His left hand held a gun under the table, and ziti dropped from his fork in his right hand as he looked at the most beautiful women; black or white, that he had ever saw in his life.

"I bet she's a good fuck," he said under his breath as he stared at an angry Tracy arguing with the headwaiter. "A fucking animal in the sack!"

His eyes had then settled back on the twins, and his heart began to beat something fierce. He quickly looked across the table at his blonde hair date. Moments ago, she was very attractive; that is until Tracy, Monique and Monica entered the restaurant.

"Victoria," said Mr. Marcelli to his female companion. "I want you to get lost. If ever I should feel like seeing you again, I'll give you a call," he dismissed her.

His eyes went back to Tracy, Monique and Monica.

Victoria huffed, stood from the table and stormed pass the three beautiful black women. She could not believe Peter Marcelli would do something like this to her. She was the daughter of the mafia boss; Mr. Castellano. She now felt awful for betraying her father for the handsome mobster who had robbed her father of nearly half a million dollars. However, all of the women loved Mr. Peter 'Pretty Boy' Marcelli, and Victoria was no different from the rest.

It was a piece of cake for Mr. Marcelli to land Victoria into his bed; the hard part was keeping her out of it. However, she was already a distant part of his memory, as he stared at the three beautiful young black women. He longed for the desire to taste them and relax in their circumference. He made sure his gun was in place on his waist, ran his hand through his shiny black hair, stood up and quickly apporached the headwaiter and the women he had his eyes on.

"Hey, hey, hey, what's the problem here?" he asked revealing a mouthful of beautiful white teeth.

"I have everything under control, Mr. Marcelli," said the waiter looking frightened by the mobster's presence.

Tracy smiled inwardly, because she knew they had found the man they were looking for. She pouted her lips and threw on her sexiest look as she gazed into the mobster's eyes.

"This man here doesn't want to let my friends and I enter," pouted Tracy. "Maybe it's because we're black. But I'll have you know that I love Italian food and Italian men even more."

Mr. Marcelli's mouth went cotton dry at the last part of her statement.

"My father," she continued, "is a professional basketball player, and of course, his babygirl should not be treated in such a manner."

"Mr. Marcelli," the headwaiter said quickly. "They are not on the list, sir."

"Relax Jimmy," said the mobster. "They're friends of mines, and they can dine with me."

"Very well," said the waiter moving aside.

"Ooh," squealed Monique excitedly. "You're so handsome. I love Italian men as well, and wouldn't mind if I did a little dining of my own" she smiled seductively while eyeing his crotch area.

"Me too," agreed Monica looking into his light brown eyes.

He caught an instant erection at that moment that just would not go away. He couldn't understand it. He and Victoria had sex the entire morning, and now looking at these three beautiful girls, it was as if he hadn't had sex in months!

"Let's say we exit this dump," smiled Tracy, "and create our own little party. I have daddy's car out front and it's big enough inside for anything."

"Anything?" smiled the mobster.

"Anything!" chorused the girls.

At this point, the handsome mobster would probably give up his left testicle to be with the beautiful black young women. There was no hesitation when Monique put her hand in his and led the way out of the restaurant. He glanced at the beautiful sight of her perfectly rounded ass switching from side to side.

It was now dark out, and the nightlife was just beginning. However, to Peter 'Pretty Boy' Marcelli, something just did not feel right. When they reached the Maybach, he quickly let go of Monique's hand and drew his nine millimeter from his waist surprising the three girls.

"What is this, a set up?" he asked looking around very suspiciously.

"Oh my God!" said a frightened looking Tracy as she moved closer to her sisters. "You have a gun. I thought you were a nice man. Please, don't tell me we've picked up a street thug," she said looking terrified with her hand over her heart next to the scared looking twins. The acting lessons their father gave them, they knew was paying off when they noticed the mobster relax a bit.

He slowly opened the car's door and peered inside. His gun followed everywhere he looked. The black female chauffeur was genuinely frightened when she turned around in her seat and saw the gun the mobster held in his hand pointed in her direction.

Satisfied that he was maybe overreacting, Mr. Marcelli put his gun away, looked at the girls apologetically and said, "I am very sorry ladies. I did not mean to frighten you. And no, I am not a street thug. Actually, I'm a successful businessman who had been robbed before who refuses to let it happen again. So, I just take precautionary measures. So," he paused, "shall we start this party?"

They waited for a moment, and then Tracy was the first of the trio to speak.

"Come," she said taking his hand into hers. "I must have you. I confess, I love bad boys. You just don't know how wet you make me. My Italian stallion."

He laughed, and his ego was as big as his appetite for the three young women at this moment. They all got inside the car and got comfortable as it pulled away from the curbside.

"So," he asked Monica as he rubbed her thigh. "What do you do for a living?"

"I'm an accountant," smiled Monica.

"Really?" he asked surprised. "I thought you were living off daddy. So, let me ask you something. Let's say, I have over two million dollars in cash stashed away. It's not really clean money, if you get my drift. But if I wanted to go legit with it, would it be difficult?"

"Well," smiled Monica, "anyone who has such a large amount of cash is definitely not in the mainstream of society. In that situation, you would be forced to borrow money in order to build your credit worthiness. In your case, that would be nearly impossible since it appears your money was not obtained legally. To justify where those funds came from is a problem. If you want to deposit over $10,000 in the bank or any other financial institution, the IRS wants a paper trail on where that money has come from. Many years ago, a similar rule has been implemented for money orders exceeding $3,000 because money orders are often used to launder money—"

Monica held his attention talking, as he rubbed her thigh moving his hand closer and closer to her private area. He was so occupied trying to get his hand into her panties that he didn't even see when Tracy poured him a glass of wine from the small bar located in the back of the car and mixed a little of the poison liquid into his drink. She then passed him the glass and inserted her tongue into his ear as she openly massaged his hardness.

He removed his hand from Monica's thigh and downed the drink in one gulp before tossing the glass to the car's carpeted floor. He then tried to kiss Tracy on the lips but she slightly turned her head causing the kiss to land on her cheek instead.

Monique leaned over and unbuttoned his shirt.

"This is what I call heaven," slurred the mobster as the girls laughed. He wondered why his words seemed to sound slurred. He only had one drink. And for some odd reason, the girls laughter seemed to go on and on, and sound slower and slower. He began to feel very dizzy and his eyes started seeing six women instead of three. He lazily reached down for his gun but it was already removed by Monique. He then passed out and the girls quickly began undressing him.

"Stop right here!" Monique yelled to the chauffeur.

The chauffeur stopped in front of a dark alley and put the car in park. The girls did not worry or question the loyalty of the chauffeur. Valerie was no spring chicken and had been with their father from the very beginning. Her loyalty had proved to be unquestionable. She was considered to be the only one from G-Banks's early past that he trusted since allegedly breaking away from his childhood friends, the Chicken Thieves who he grew up with.

Monique opened the car's door and the girls dragged Mr. Marcelli into the dark alley. They leaned him up against the wall, and Monique and Monica pulled their scapels from their purses.

"I guess it's true what they say about white men," laughed Monique grabbing hold of the mobster's penis with her gloved hand, "Either they are all small, or 'Pretty Boy' here was just lacking in this department."

She then grabbed his balls, and with two swift motions of the scalpel, Mr. Marcelli's bloody sack was in Monique's hand. She then stuffed it into his mouth as instructed, and Monica used her scalpel to slit his throat.

All three young women were walking back to the car when Tracy spun around, took aim with her .40 Caliber in hand and placed two perfectly shots to Mr. Marcelli's forehead.

Chapter Sixteen

"I don't know why Drama didn't tell me that he took this fucking chain from niggas in the 'Sty!" cursed Barkim angrily.

"Man, you know how Drama is," said his cousin Boo. "He don't give a fuck who he rob. If you not peoples, the nigga's taking that shit. The only reason I got wind of who it was is because them niggas be in my projects a lot."

Boo was from Marcy projects, and Mike and Tone lived two blocks away from him on Hart Street.

"So, you giving the chain and piece back?" asked Boo.

"Hell no!" answered Barkim angrily. "What I look like giving that shit back to them after they tried to murder me yesterday in broad daylight?"

Barkim was standing on the corner of Bedford Avenue and Gates Avenue talking to a guy he knew from upnorth when he noticed two guys getting out of a blue Range Rover wearing baseball caps pulled down to their eyes walking towards him. He saw the nine millimeter in one of the guy's hands and he took off running, not waiting to see if they were coming for him or not.

It was definitely confirmed when he heard the rapid gunshots and bullets hitting parked cars in the direction he was running in. He ran top speed zig-zagging from time to time so the shooter could not zero in on his back. He was in good health, so the cause of his fast heart beat did not come from his stamina but the fear of being shot.

Barkim heard no more gunshots as he reached Halsey Street, and was relieved when he looked behind him and no one was chasing him. He slowed his pace to a steady jog and headed straight home on Hancock Street. Now his cousin Boo was filling him in on who the guys were who was trying to murder him, and why.

"Mike was the only one in the 'sty with that chain and piece," explained Boo. "That's how he knew his shit when he saw you wearing it."

"Well," continued Barkim pulling the .45 revolver from his waist as he sat on the couch in his living room, "wherever I see those niggas, it's on! I wish I had this shit on me yesterday."

"Yo man," sighed Boo. "I feel you but this ain't the eighties anymore. You can't walk around with a gun on you everywhere you go. Nowadays, niggas kill niggas off of information. Majority of niggas that get killed now is because somebody set them up. That's how the game goes. You my cousin, so you know anything I find out, I'm pulling your coat to it."

Barkim looked up at the ceiling and sighed loudly.

"This fucking dude Drama," he said angrily. "He's out in Brownsville without a care in the world, and I'm stuck in the 'sty warring with two motherfucking clowns!"

"Damn Bar, you spoke the nigga up," laughed Boo as Drama and Barkim's little brother Gee walked into the living room.

"What up?" smiled Drama sitting down.

"I'll tell you what's up nigga," answered Barkim angrily. "Those two lames you took that chain and piece from tried to murder me yesterday."

"Word?!" responded Drama standing up.

"Yeah. Boo told me who they are and where they live."

"Oh okay," Drama said relaxing and sitting back down. "We just find 'em and wash them niggas up. What else is good?" he asked as if the situation with the chain was not even a problem.

"Where is John and 'em at?"Barkim asked Gee while ignoring Drama's question. He couldn't believe his friend had put his life in danger. Beef with gangsters was the last thing a person needed after just coming home from doing a state bid. He had too many other important things to do besides get into shoot outs, get shot or kill someone. He really had his mind set on staying out of prison, but he was not letting anyone do anything to him, that was for sure.

"John is in front of the house with Camron," answered Gee.

"Come on y'all," said Barkim standing up and leading the way out of the living room.

When they got in front of the house, a lightskin guy approached Barkim giving him a pound.

"Yo Bar," said John, "what's good?'

"Ain't shit," answered Barkim. "Yo, you know what I need you to do? I need you to find out everything you can on those niggas that tried to do me dirty. And make sure—" he stopped mid-sentence when a black R8 Audi with dark tints pulled up and parked in front of the house.

"Who the fuck is that?" asked Barkim to no one in particular as he slowly reached for the .45 revolver in his waistband.

"I don't know," answered Drama also reaching for his gun. "But that car is sick!"

When the car's door opened, they expected to see a guy step out of it. Instead, Tracy emerged from it looking as gorgeous as ever. She wore a black mink coat and you can see the nice Gucci boots she sported.

"Change of plans," smiled Barkim handing the gun off to Drama. As he walked over to his girl, the rest of the guys present looked on with their mouths open not believing how good Tracy looked.

She laughed at their facial expressions before giving her man the biggest kiss and hug he'd gotten since coming home.

"Damn baby," smiled Barkim. "You had a nigga stressed the fuck out and going crazy wondering about you."

"Were you worried and concerned enough to keep your dick in your pants until you saw me?" she smiled.

"Hell yeah," lied Barkim. He got some from a stripper Drama introduced him to, but even then, his mind had been on Tracy.

"Lyer!" laughed Tracy. "Anyway, I'm here now. So no cheating."

"Let's go inside," said Barkim grabbing her leather gloved hand and leading the way towards the house.

"Damn!!!" exclaimed Drama when Tracy and Barkim got close to him. "Do you have a sister, an aunt, a young looking grandmother?"

Everyone standing near laughed, including Tracy giving a cute little laugh.

"Actually," she said, "I have two sisters, but unfortunately, they are both in relationships. I'm sorry."

"Don't be sorry," said Drama. "A boyfriend never stopped me from getting what I want. Next time you come, bring a picture with you. As good as you look, I have to meet somebody in the family. No disrespect to my boy Bar, but damn you're beautiful."

Barkim and Tracy laughed as they entered the house walking pass Drama, Gee, Boo, John and Camron.

Barkim and Tracy entered his bedroom. She sat on the bed and looked around the small bedroom as he took off his coat and hung it in the bedroom closet.

"When I pulled up," said Tracy, "I noticed you had a gun in your hand. What's that about after just coming home from prison? You know you can go back carrying that thing around."

"It's not my gun," lied Barkim. "My man Drama was just letting me see it right before you pulled up. And I'm definitely not carrying no hammer around with me."

"I like that chain and piece you have on," she complimented changing the subject.

"Thank you," smiled Barkim. Any thoughts of returning it back to Mike and Tone now was definitely out of the question.

"Drama gave it to me as a coming home present," he said.

"Are you ready for my present?" she smiled.

"Of course!" he laughed. "Why wouldn't I be?"

Tracy took off her long mink coat revealing she only wore her black Gucci boots and red and black teddy under the mink. Barkim smiled broadly as she spun around modeling her perfect body for him. He quickly walked over to a small radio in his room and after pressing a button, the sounds of Jamie Foxx's song "Why" came through the speakers. He walked back to the bed with the biggest smile on his face.

"You like?" she smiled taking the coat completely off, throwing it to the floor as she looked into his eyes.

"I love," he smiled.

Tracy straddled him, taking his shirt off. She kissed his forehead and eyelids. She then kissed his cheek and nibbled on his earlobe; first the right one, then the left one.

Barkim squirmed and sighed loudly.

"Baby, are you okay?" asked Tracy.

"Yes," he whispered. "But you better stop."

"Or what?" she smiled devilishly.

She then kissed him on the right side of his neck. She gently moved her soft wet lips to his, and sucked on the lower lip and then the top. They kissed slowly, stopping in between each peck, and then the kiss became more intense.

While still kissing him, she unbuttoned his True Religion jeans, and planted soft kisses from his big chest to his six pack abdomen. When he slowly slid the pants completely off, she admired the Roc-A-Wear boxers he wore, and of course it was something big peeking out at her. Something she had been dying to see for far too long! She was not disappointed as she licked her lips before placing her mouth over Barkim's hardness. She licked and sucked as she looked up into his eyes.

"Ooh baby," sighed Barkim. "That shit feels so good."

She massaged his hardness as she continued licking and suck-ing.

"Baby I want you," she said while raising up and straddling her legs back over his lap proceeding to come down on his hardness. "Oooh!" she squealed.

"Are you alright?" he asked.

"Yes baby, I got this!" smiled Tracy. She slowly attempted to come down again as she closed her eyes, licked her lips and softly bit her bottom lip. When she had it all the way in, she began to rise up and down faster and faster. With each rise up, she let out sweet soft sighs of pleasure mixed with just the right amount of pain.

Barkim held his hands on her hips helping to control the move-ments. His eyes were filled with gleam as he kissed any and every part of her body he could touch without disturbing the flow of their love making.

"Give it to me baby," moaned Tracy.

He flipped her over and began to eat her like a man starved.

"No!!!! Stop!!!" begged Tracy really not wanting him to stop at all.

"Ooh baby," she moaned. "Oh my God, that feels so good. So, so good."

He came up and inserted his hardness back into her giving her what she wanted. She let out a surprising, "Oooh shit! Baby, give it to me. Give it all to me!"

"Is this what 'chu want?" asked Barkim moving up and down and in a circular motion faster and faster.

It felt too good for her to answer.

After a moment she screamed out, "Yes, yes, yes!"

He kissed her aggressively grabbing her face. They made uncontrollable, hot, passionate love until Barkim was ready to cum.

"I can't hold it any longer," he breathed heavily. "I'm ready to cum. Damn baby, I'm trying to...to...hold...Oh shit, are you ready baby?"

"Yes!" screamed Tracy as they came together. After falling over one another, they laughed while trying to catch their breaths. They then just lay in bed not saying anything to one another. Tracy had her back to him and he looked down at her shapely ass.

He kissed the back of her neck and said, "I love you baby."

When she didn't say anything back, he looked over her shoulder and discovered that she was fast asleep. He smiled to himself feeling that he had indeed put that work in. He kissed the back of her head and knew he was in love. He then layed back and stared at the ceiling in deep thought. His parole officer wasn't sweating him as of yet, so he figured when Tracy awakened, they could perhaps go to one of the many restaurants he heard about when he was incarcerated. He couldn't wait to get his driver's license, and then it would really be on.

Chapter Seventeen

Joe smiled broadly as he sat at his kitchen table watching the beautiful Monique cook his breakfast. She only wore a red bra, red panties and black high heels.

He was so happy to have her back into his life. Those two months of her absence had proved to be pure torture. He had become so depressed during that time, he was labeled as one of the biggest assholes in the department at the precinct he worked. He began treating criminals or those arrested like animals, planted drugs in cars, and even walked around with an attitude towards his peers. Now with Monique back in his life, everyone was happy to see him as his usual nonchalant self.

"Baby, I miss you," he smiled.

"I know," said Monique. "You've mentioned it at least ten times since yesterday."

She then turned around and placed his egg omelet on a plate before carrying it to him and sitting across from him.

"What was that story about that I saw on the news a few days ago?" she asked. "Something about an Italian man being killed and dismembered."

"Oh," said Joe taking a sip of his coffee. "That was a guy named Peter 'Pretty Boy' Marcelli. He was tied to the mob."

"I've heard that much on the news," Monique said sarcastically with her hand on her hip. "Tell me something I don't know."

"Well, we believe Mr. Marcelli was killed by Mafia boss, Mr. Castellano. And it seems that Mr. Marcelli was even hated by his own people to the point that no one is willing to step forward with any information. There are no real leads. All we have to go on is," said Joe pausing to take a sip of his coffee, "he had sex before he was killed. Apparently, there were a woman's juices dried up on his testicles that some sick bastard stuffed into his mouth. It was a very gruesome kill-ing. I wonder who would do something like that. This world is sick."

"Do you think it was more than one person?" she asked on the edge of her seat.

"I would say so," answered Joe taking a forkful of egg omelet into his mouth. "Only because the slashings of his body looks as if they were done from different angles as if more than one person had parti-cipated. The guy's neck was also slashed and he was shot in the head."

Monique knew the dried juices found on his testicles had to be-long to Victoria; Mr. Castellano's daughter. She was also sure the young white lady had run back to her father after hearing about the demise of Mr. Marcelli and how he was killed.

"Somebody must have really wanted him dead," she said. "I must say, police work sounds very dangerous. You just be very careful out there."

"I will. You are so, so sexy," he smiled while putting his fork down.

"Well," she smiled standing up from the table. "Let me take my sexy self upstairs and get dressed. I have to get home and make sure my daddy is alright."

"Tell Mr. Banks I said hello," he said picking up his cup of coffee.

"I will," she replied before heading upstairs to Joe's bedroom to get dressed.

After dressing and kissing Joe goodbye, Monique jumped into her blue Vanquish Aston Martin and headed home. She had the rap-per Twister's old song "Hope" featuring Faith Evans playing through the speakers and she sung along as she drove. She was proud of any rapper or singer out of her hometown Chicago who had made it big, or who were just representing the Chi to the best of their ability.

After pulling up in her driveway, she got out of the car and wondered who the old beat up Buick belonged to that was parked out in front of the house. She had to admit, she was very curious to find out the answer. She used her key to open the front door, and was greeted by loud laughter and conversation coming from the living room.

"We had a ball!" laughed Barkim as Monique entered the living room. "We went to—"

"Hey," interrupted Tracy seeing her sister enter.

Barkim and Drama turned to see who it was she was greeting.

"Barkim and Drama," smiled Tracy, "meet my loving sister, Monique. Monique, this is Drama and my baby," she smiled seductively, "Barkim."

"Damn!" exclaimed Drama standing from the sofa and approaching Monique. He took her hand into his hand and kissed it.

"When your sister said you looked good," he said, "that was definitely an understatement. You're gorgeous!"

"Why, thank you," smiled Monique biting down on her bottom lip flirting with him.

"Hello," interrupted Barkim with his hand outstretched. "I've heard so much about you. It's finally nice to meet you in person."

"Same here," she smiled. "I've heard a lot about you as well."

"But I didn't hear enough about you," said Drama looking her up and down causing her to blush.

"She already has a man," interjected Barkim. "And he's a cop!"

"My sister has such a big mouth," smiled Monique. "Drama, I think you're cute. And I like the name Drama."

"Because she's a drama queen," laughed Tracy causing her sister to give her a look.

"And I think you're very beautiful," Drama smiled back. "So, tell that cop boyfriend of yours to take those handcuffs off of you, so you can really be free to enjoy life's pleasures."

"Oooh," squealed Monique. "You're going to get me into trouble."

"Sweet heart," flirted Drama, "it's not trouble that I want to get you into."

"Whose raggedy car is that, that's parked out front?" asked Monica walking into the living room.

"Mines," answered Drama.

When he turned to see who the voice belonged to, it forced him to do a doubletake.

"Damn!!!!!" he said rubbing his eyes causing everyone to laugh. "Twins! Beautiful twins!"

Monica shook her head with a smirk on her pretty face and asked, "Is that your car?"

"Yeah that's my war wagon," answered Drama. "I know it doesn't look like much, but that 'raggedy car' keeps my pockets looking pretty good."

"Well you have to move it," she said. "Because my fiancé normally parks there and he should be on his way here now. So, if you don't mind."

"We're about to leave," he said. "I just came to pick my boy Bar up."

He then turned back to Monique and said, "Beautiful, ditch the pig and make a come up."

Monique only smiled.

Barkim kissed Tracy, said his goodbyes to all and was just about to leave when G-Banks walked slowly into the living room. He looked as if he had aged ten more years since Barkim saw him last.

"Norris, is that you boy?" asked G-Banks holding his hand out to be shaked.

"Hey Mr. Banks!" smiled Barkim shaking his hand. He noticed the lack of strength in the oldtimer's handshake, and he felt sorry for the old gangster.

"How are you doing?" he asked. "It's very good to see you, Mr. Banks."

"It's good to see you too," smiled G-Banks. "Especially out here on the outside. I hope you have plans on staying out and doing the right thing for yourself. As for myself, I can be doing a lot better, but the old man never complained. Who's your friend here?" he asked motioning towards Drama.

"Oh, that's my friend Tymell," he answered using Drama's government name.

"How you're doing?" said Drama holding out his hand. "You can call me Drama."

"No, I'll call you Tymell," said G-Banks causing all to laugh as he weakly shook his hand. "Listen, you and Norris here will get a lot further in life using common names as opposed to those crazy street names. I say that because a lot of successful people fear street guys. And though fear can at times work to your advantage, it can also very well work against you. Just name me one street thug that lasted in the streets for over twenty years being feared. It doesn't happen. Not even for half the time I've just mentioned. Being loved can take you much further than fear if administered right," said G-Banks giving the two young men words of wisdom.

"When I was on my way in here," he continued, "I heard what Monica was saying concerning your car. Disregard what she said. Only because Tymell, you strike me as someone doing illegal activities from time to time. And if that's what you do, then that's the best kind of car you can drive. Forgive me if I am wrong on assuming how you acquire your income, but if I am correct, then let me say that only dumb street niggas buy houses, cars and the like with their illegal gains. Save the showing off for if you are ever fortunate enough to learn the many tricks of turning dirty money clean. The biggest problem our people have is that we know the price of everything and the value of nothing," he said walking away leaving Barkim and Drama open mouthed.

"Norris," he continued while walking slowly, "I would like to have a few words with you in my study. Please follow me."

The two men exited from the living room.

"Pops is a very smart man," said a very impressed Drama to Monique, Monica and Tracy.

"I still say you're in dire need of a new car," laughed Monica causing everyone else to laugh as well.

$$\$\$\$\$\$\$$$

"Have a seat Norris," said G-Banks sitting behind his big desk as Barkim sat across from him.

"Listen," he began. "I know you're just coming home from prison and it's going to take you some time to re-adjust to what's happening out here in society, but if you need any help, don't be afraid to ask me. I know some good people. Okay? But what I called you in here for is to talk to you about Tracy. That's my little African princess, and I don't ever want to see her hurt. Now she has everything that she can ever wish for, however, things weren't always this good for her. She's been through a lot as a child and I want you to understand that. So, if you have any intentions of hurting her emotionally, mentally, physically or whatever, I suggest very strongly that you leave her alone now. All three of my girls had been through a lot of bad things, but Tracy had it the worse. So I'm asking you as a man, how do you truly feel about my daughter?"

"I love Tracy," said Barkim sincerely. "And I will never hurt her in any way. She knows things about me that I have never shared with anyone and vice versa. I feel very strongly—"

$$\$\$\$\$\$\$$$

"You ready to go?" Barkim asked Drama with a smile after entering back into the living room. They said their goodbyes to everyone and headed back to Brooklyn.

"I almost forgot," said Monica to her sisters after locking the door behind Barkim and Drama. "Daddy wanted to talk to us."

Tracy and Monique followed her into the kitchen where G-Banks sat drinking coffee and reading his newspaper.

"Yes daddy?" asked Tracy as they entered the kitchen.

He looked up from his paper with a smile and said, "I'm very proud of you three. Everything you've put your minds to, you have accomplished. The three of you have brought me more happiness than I ever knew existed. You are my daughters and I would do anything for you. You know I love you three more than life itself. But I think it would be very wise for you all to visit Chicago and see your mothers."

Tracy sucked her teeth as Monique and Monica looked away.

"Wait, wait, wait," G-Banks held up his hand. "First, listen to me. I know you all do not care whether you ever see your mothers again, but it would be a terrible mistake to not allow yourselves to at least bring some kind of closure to that part of your lives. Trust me, I'm speaking from experience."

"Daddy," said Monica, "we understand everything you are saying, but you're the best mother and father we could have ever wished for.

We don't need to see those women. You've showed us unconditional love from the moment you let us into your home and heart. And we love you."

"I know," he smiled. "And you don't have to go to Chicago. I'm not forcing you. I just thought you three should have some kind of closure to that part of your lives. Instead of maybe later regretting that you hadn't," he said standing up and picking up his newspaper.

"Oh yeah," he continued before walking out of the kitchen. "I had put an envelope in each of your rooms for that last job. I hear everything was done well."

"Daddy," said Monique. "You know you don't have to give us any money for that. We only did it for you."

"I know," he smiled. "But the money came as a bonus from Mr. Castellano to you three as a token of his appreciation. There were no witnesses, so I have to admit, the job was well done. Who knows? Maybe I'll consider letting you all do one of the other two jobs. But right now I'm not sure about that. For now just think about what I said earlier about visiting Chicago. I'm sure you know it's not the same Chicago and Cabrini Green you all left when you were children. Things changed drastically and your mothers moved to different apartments. I have the information if you should need it."

He then walked slowly out of the kitchen and headed up to his bedroom.

"So what's up?" asked Tracy. "Y'all wanna go back to the 'Chi or what?"

"Look at you," laughed Monica. "Sounding like Barkim."

"We may as well go," replied Monique thinking about what her father had said. "Only because daddy really wants us to go. He just isn't saying so."

"Why do you think daddy never married?" asked Tracy changing the subject.

"I asked him already," said Monica.

Tracy and Monique looked at her surprised.

"Why didn't you tell us?" asked Monique.

"More importantly, what did he say?" asked Tracy.

"He told me to mind my business," laughed Monica. "Then he said he never had the time or patience to be in a committed relationship and it would distract him from his job. He said we're enough, a handful, he don't need no relationship. And Tracy already acts like his wife."

Monique joined her twin's laughter as Tracy shook her head.

"Do y'all want to have a little fun while we're out in Chicago?" asked Tracy changing the subject with a mischievous grin on her pretty face.

"Fuck yeah!" answered Monique. "Revenge is a dish best served cold."

Monica only smiled, knowing that she would be down with whatever her two sisters wanted to do. After all these years, they were finally going back to the windy city, but this time they were ready for whatever!

Chapter Eighteen

"I had the nigga!" fumed Drama as he paced the living room in Barkim's mother's house.

"All those gunshots and nobody got hit?!" asked Barkim sitting on the couch not believing the news he received.

"Nope," answered Boo. "I heard them niggas saw y'all as soon as y'all came in the projects. They were just acting like they didn't see y'all. And when y'all got close, that's when they started shooting at y'all."

"Something told me they knew what time it was," said Barkim thinking about the way things had unfolded in their attempt to kill Mike and Tone yesterday. "That's why I started shooting as soon as I saw one of them little niggas walking on the side of the building."

"What y'all need to do is give them boys their money and chain back," said Boo. "Innocent people might mess around and get killed the way y'all shooting. Y'all already had like six shootouts on six different occasions and nobody got hit."

"I ain't giving shit back!" said Barkim angrily.

"Word," agreed Drama. "I'm not wit' taking shit and giving it back. Fuck that!"

"Yo Drama," said Barkim, "you still got the stash spot in your car, right?"

"No doubt," he answered.

"Then let's roll," replied Barkim standing up and placing his .45 revolver in his waistline before zipping up his jacket.

"Boo stay here," ordered Barkim. "I don't want them niggas to know we're family."

"Niggas already know," said Boo standing up and putting his nine millimeter in his waistline as Drama did the same.

"You know how word gets around," he continued.

The three young men walked out of the house and when they got in the old car, Drama pulled hard on each side of the dash board until it gave way exposing a big square hole.

They placed their guns inside of it and Drama snapped the dashboard back in place. After starting the car, they were on their way to handle their business.

"Yo," said Boo, "why you don't go to one of those electronic places and get a proper stash spot put in?"

"Because it wouldn't work," explained Drama. "Yo, I stay up on all the latest shit. The police got this new device they hook up to your battery, and every electronic device you installed pops open."

Barkim didn't say anything. All of this was new to him and he was impressed that Drama stayed up to date on whatever the police were doing. He sat back and took in all of the knowledge Drama possessed.

They drove around Bedford Stuyvesant and decided to go through the block where Mike and Tone lived. As they drove down Marcy Avenue, they saw a beautiful lightskin girl with a body that made all three of them do a double take.

"Stop the car," said Boo. "Let me holla at shorty real quick."

Drama laughed and kept driving.

"I know her," said Drama. "Shorty's a hoe, and she's only sixteen years old."

"Clinton Dannemora!" exclaimed Barkim causing them to laugh. "Drama, knowing you, you probably still hit that."

Drama only laughed confirming that he did.

"You a dirty dick nigga," laughed Boo.

They got their weapons out of the stash spot, and when they reached Hart Street they noticed four guys standing around on the corner as they slowly drove by trying to get a good look at their faces. The four guys looked back at them as well trying to see who was in the car.

"Is that them?" asked Barkim with his gun in his hand.

"I'm not sure," answered Boo. "I didn't really see their faces."

"Drama, pull around the block again," ordered Barkim.

When they pulled around the block for the second time, they were surprised to see Mike, Tone and another guy with the four guys they initially saw. They had their guns drawn waiting to ambush the car.

"Oh shit!" said Drama noticing what awaited them. He looked in his rearview mirror and saw two cars behind him in traffic and could not reverse.

"Yo!" panicked Boo. "I'm getting out shooting!"

The cars behind Drama began blowing their horns for him to move.

"No, don't get out shooting," instructed Barkim. "Just stay calm. Drama, drive through real fast and duck down low. Roll all the windows down."

Barkim and Boo stuck their guns out of the windows and began firing as Drama pushed his foot down on the gas pedal and slid down low in his seat.

Mike, Tone and the young boys also began firing at the speeding car coming in their direction. Neither crew took perfect aim as they crouched low and fired their guns hoping their bullets hit their targets. Bullets entered parked cars, the side of houses and only God knows what else.

Boo looked through the back window when they were in the clear and saw one of the guys on the ground holding his leg.

"One of them got hit!" he yelled excitedly.

"Who?!" asked Barkim in the same excited tone. "Mike or Tone?"

"Nah," answered Boo. "It was a little nigga that got hit."

"Damn!" cursed Barkim as Drama made a left turn hitting Dekalb Avenue.

"Drive back to the crib," ordered Barkim.

"Hold up," said Drama pulling over to the curb. "First, let's put the guns back in the stash spot."

After stashing their weapons, they headed back to Hancock Street where Barkim lived.

"Yo, we gotta get them niggas," said Barkim after briefly reflecting on what transpired moments earlier. "I'm not wit' walking around Brooklyn looking over my shoulder."

"Don't sweat it man," said Drama while turning on the radio. "We gonna get them niggas."

The sounds of the hot new female rapper Young Nik's song "Make 'em mad" came blasting through the system.

"Make 'em mad, make 'em mad, make 'em mad," rapped Drama along with the song as Boo sat in the back seat bobbing his head still a little shooken up from the shootout.

Barkim looked out of the passenger's window in deep thought. He knew if he gave the chain and piece back the beef with Tone and Mike would still be on. Unbeknownst to Boo and Drama, he already tried squashing the beef through a mutual friend he knew from when he was locked upnorth. But egos were involved and they just could not come to an agreement. Barkim's friend Nitty from Lefrak had told him that not only did Mike and Tone want their money and chain back, but they also wanted him to set up Drama for the embarrassment of robbing them and leaving them in the Bronx. Nitty respected Barkim when he said "Fuck them, the beef is on" because he too could never set up any of his peoples. Despite the griminess of the game, some still lived by the code and possessed loyalty.

"Damn!" cursed Barkim as they pulled up in front of his house. His luck just couldn't get any better.

"What's up? Your mom's home or something?" asked Drama.

"Nah," answered Barkim. "Look at this nigga."

Standing on his stoop stood his parole officer, Mr. Jonathan Marshall. A black man only on the surface, who made it his first priority to send a parolee back upstate to prison for the stupidest reasons. If a parolee missed his curfew by minutes, this man would try to violate him and put him back behind bars.

"Who the fuck is that?" asked Drama.

"That's my punk ass parole officer," answered Barkim as they parked and got out of the car.

"Hey Mr. Houston," said the P.O. looking at his watch. "I've been waiting here for about twenty minutes now."

"So, what's the problem?" asked Barkim confused. "My curfew ain't for another two hours."

"I know," smiled the P.O. "I just wanted to let you know that if you don't have a job soon then I'll be forced to violate you."

"Mr. Marshall," said Barkim trying to remain calm. "I told you three days ago that I start work Wednesday, which is tomorrow."

Barkim remembered back in the days, when the thug Pappy Mason had faced allegations of having a parole officer killed. He didn't know if it was true or not but as he looked at his asshole smiling P.O., he wondered if he had the balls to do the same to this prick.

$$\$\$\$\$\$\$$$

The pretty brownskinned girl with short hair stood over the stove cooking two kilos of cocaine in a big black pot. Angela was considered to be somewhat of a street chemist when it came to cooking cocaine into crack making sure everything came back. She learned the trade watching her sister on many occasions cook. Eventhough her sister only cooked up a few grams to get high, Angela always watched very closely until she figured she had it down pat. She didn't get high but knew she could make some extra money doing it for the local dealers that didn't know how or didn't have the patience to do it. She started off with her ex-boyfriend's half an ounces, and not long after was sorted by almost every dealer in the neighborhood. For the dealers, it meant no more buying cooked up product with no idea of what was added in the product they purchased. She was paid $300 dollars for every brick she cooked, and this afforded her to sport the latest wears and handbags.

The dealers in the neighborhood got no bigger than the two dealers presntly sitting at the table watching her cook. Mike and Tone always purchased and had their cocaine cooked in New York before sending it out of state. They had just come back from Atlanta and could not believe niggas had the audacity to try and kill them on their block.

"Is Little Jimmy alright?" asked Angela as she cooked.

"Yeah he's cool," answered Tone sitting behind her playing with a triple beam scale placed in front of him. "The bullet went straight through his leg. The other one was a graze wound."

"Damn!!!!" cursed Mike pounding his fist on the table. "This punk motherfucker Barkim keeps getting away."

"To be real with you," said Tone, "I don't really care about that nigga Barkim, the money or that fucking chain. I just want that nigga Drama for dissing us like that. You know the word is in the streets now how that nigga did us. I don't know how he thought we wouldn't find out who he was. Money talks baby, that motherfucking money talks."

"But we still should've got the chain back when Nitty said he could get it back from Barkim if we squashed the beef," said Mike missing his chain and piece. "And the beef still could've been on after we got it back. Fuck Nitty."

"Nah," said Tone dismissing Mike with the wave of the hand. "Nitty's cool and we don't need that beef with him, Snoop and Shameek and 'em. What's up with that nigga Boo?"

"I talked to the nigga Skeeda," answered Mike, "and he said Boo is the nigga Barkim's cousin. That explains how the nigga Barkim know who we are. Being Skeeda's from Marcy too, he asked me not to fuck with Boo, but fuck that! He's rolling with his cousin so he's getting it too."

Angela stood over the stove cooking up the cocaine listening intently to everything Mike and Tone were saying. It was hearing the name Boo that caught her attention. She knew Boo. In fact, she had a crush on him since they were kids and he still came around often to chill with her brother.

"Word, fuck that," agreed Tone. "We gonna wash that nigga Boo ass up too when we see his ass."

"Don't sweat it," said Mike leaning back in his chair. "Before we jet to Connecticut, we'll put a plan together soon to get all 'dem niggas."

"The first one is done," announced Angela carrying a huge aluminum pan with three giant sized circular compressed crack boulders that looked like giant cookies stacked on top of one another.

"Push that scale over so she can sit that on the table," Tone instructed Mike.

Mike followed the order.

Angela sat the pan down and headed back to the stove to cook up one more brick. Mike's eyes followed Tones' as they looked at her round shapely ass as she put more water in the pot and began cooking again. They then looked at one another and bust out laughing.

"What y'all laughing at?" smiled Angela slightly turning her head to the side as she expertly mixed the baking soda with cocaine.

"Nothing," answered Tone with a smile. "I was just thinking that maybe we need to run this operation like in that movie 'New Jack City' where all the girls work for us butt ass naked. You know what I'm saying? You down for that or what?"

Angela sucked her teeth as the two thugs laughed.

"I'm not getting naked for no one but my man," she said with a playful attitude. "Y'all better get Donna and them dumb bitches y'all got bagging up strip naked."

Mike and Tone looked at one another smiling as if they were really considering doing what she had just suggested. They all made small talk until Angela was finally done cooking up their product.

"Here," said Mike handing her a thousand dollars. "Whatever's extra, get something nice that you think I would like to see you in, or come out of."

"Thanks," smiled Angela taking the money and walking out of the kitchen towards the front door being followed by Tone to close and lock it behind her. He pulled out his nine millimeter just in case someone tried to rush in as he let her out.

"Take care," he said before closing the door and locking it after she left.

Angela stuffed the money into her tight jeans pocket and quickly walked down the street pulling out her cell phone to try and make contact with Boo to inform him of what Mike and Tone had in store for him.

Chapter Nineteen

The girls were totally in for a surprise when they went back to Chicago. The area where they had grown up as children was just not the same. Stranger's Home Missionary Baptist Church was now boarded up. A lot of the high rises were no longer there, the New City YMCA was gone, and the affordable stores where most bought their food and other things were also gone. The store owners just could not afford the rent and were forced out. Cabrini Green was totally different. Only a handful of buildings remain, surrounded from all sides by new condominiums and booming retail stores. Twenty percent of the condos had been set aside as affordable housing; a third was public housing, and the rest were selling up to $850,000 a piece. The twins and Tracy's mothers were fortunate enough over the years to stay and move into different apartments.

Like many years ago, standing on the side of the now boarded up church stood a group of guys talking and wearing the latest hood wears. However, walking by was a whole different class and ethnic groups.

"Damn!" said a darkskin brother stepping away from his friends when he saw the three beautiful young women he'd never seen in the area walk by.

The rest of the guys had then looked in the direction where their friend had stepped off in and damn near tripped over themselves to press the other two young women.

"Hold up a minute!" shouted the darkskin brother as the girls stopped and turned around. Two friends of his also approached, leaving the rest of the guys to go back to where they were standing and wishing they were the ones who saw the beautiful girls first.

"Where y'all from?" asked a lightskin guy wearing expensive clothes, jewelry and his long hair in cornrow braids.

"We're from here," answered Tracy but stealing glances at the darkskin guy talking to Monica. He looked so familiar but she could not place him. It had been too many years ago.

"But we left Chicago when we were younger," she continued. "So, we're just coming back to visit."

As the darkskin guy and his caramel complected friend so-called layed their game down on Monique and Monica, Tracy didn't hear a word the lightskin guy was saying to her. She nodded her head to everything he said as she tried to remember where she knew the darkskin guy from that was talking to Monica. Then it hit her like a ton of bricks!

Tracy quickly glanced away and said to the lightskin guy, "I see a whole lot has changed around here. Are the gangs still out here warring?"

"No," smiled the lightskin brother. "Those days are gone. But you still didn't tell me your name."

"Oh, it's Tameeka," lied Tracy. "What's yours?"

"I guess you didn't hear me when I said it to you the first time," smiled the brother. "My name is B-Hi. Back to your question, niggas is always gonna die, but it's not like it's used to be. What's really sad is these white folks are taking all this shit from us. They got an eleven year plan to raze and rebuild this whole area because this is like the most valuable land in Chicago."

Tracy looked around and saw a Starbucks, a gourmet grocery, rows of identical condos, and could see they were owned mostly by white weathy owners. The blacks were peing pushed out. Most of them were already put out and had to move to areas that were even worse than what Cabrini Green had been. She could see what B-Hi had been saying.

"They already knocked down most of the buildings," continued B-Hi.

"I see," said a surprised Tracy looking around not believing that white folks were destroying or changing what she once considered home.

"So, where are you living now?" asked B-Hi changing the subject and trying to get to know her better.

"I'm in New York," she answered. "But like I said earlier, I'm from here. I lived on the dark side," she said referring to the reds.

A car was parked near the curb blasting the instrumental to Fifty Cent's song "Window Shopper" as a local rapper from the whites, named 40 Cail Slim, ripped the instrumental to pieces sounding just as good as the G-Unit rapper himself.

"You look as if you are doing pretty well for yourself," smiled Tracy pointing to the jewelry he wore. "So, I know you're not worried about them tearing any buildings down."

"Actually I am," replied B-Hi. "Rich or broke baby girl, this is our life. Right on the side of this building, we're here. You know what I'm saying?"

"I hear that," smiled Tracy with her New York City accent.

"Let me get your number?" he asked. "It would be a pleasure to take you out to dinner before you leave the 'Chi."

"I would really like that," lied Tracy. "But I'd prefer you give me your number, if that's okay with you."

"For sure," he smiled pulling a pen and match book cover from his pocket. As he wrote his number down, Tracy looked and saw the other two guys give Monique and Monica their numbers as well.

"Here you go," said B-Hi handing the number to Tracy. "Take care of yourself, and make sure you give me a call."

"I will," she smiled while walking away.

"That boy game is sooo weak," laughed Monique as she and her sisters got away from the young men and headed towards their destination.

"It changed a lot around here, right?" asked Monique as they walked and looked.

"Yes," agreed Tracy and Monica.

"Monnie, what did that boy you was talking to say his name was?" asked Tracy.

"His name is Damien," Monica answered.

"I knew it," frowned Tracy. "Y'all don't remember him?"

"No," chorused the twins.

"Remember we was kids," Tracy reminisced, "and my mother let that boy that sold drugs in the building rape me?"

Monique and Monica's mouths dropped open in surprise as they both stopped walking.

"I got his number right here," said Monica angrily fishing the small piece of paper out of her pocket.

"What do you want to do?" Monique asked Tracy with her pretty face screwed up in an angry mask.

"We'll have a few words with him before we leave Chicago," answered Tracy as they continued walking.

As the girls walked on, they could not believe what had happened to the building that they once called home. 624 on W. Division Street was now an empty lot. Tracy's mother, as well as the twin's mother was relocated to the low rises and they lived in the same building as one another once again. Some considered the area to now be horrendous.

"You know there's a Chanel store a few blocks away from here now, right?" asked Monica changing the subject that brought them back to a lighter mood.

"Yes," smiled Monique. "You know we have to make a stop there before we leave."

When they got to the low rise building, a skinny lightskin guy stood out front selling drugs as if he had a license to do so. He looked at the pretty girls he never saw before and wanted badly to say something, but the small line of customers kept him occupied. The girls were grateful for that, because not only were they all in satisfying relationships but also did not want to be bothered anymore. They decided to see Tracy's mother first.

She took the small piece of paper with her mother's information on it that her father had given her, and the three proceeded to their destination.

After Tracy knocked on the door several times, it swung open and there stood an old woman with gray hair peering over her glasses.

"May I help you?" she asked while looking over the three girls.

"Uh...uh...yes," stuttered Tracy. "I was told that my mother now lived here, and I was wondering if she—"

"Tracy?" interrupted the old skinny woman with her hand over her mouth and peering intently over her glasses. "Oh my God, you're beautiful!"

"Ma?" asked Tracy in surprise. She knew it had been a very long time, but her mother could not have aged so much in that time. But she could see the resemblance in the old lady's face. She could not believe it.

"Of course not dear," smiled the old lady. "Let's try grandma and you would be correct."

Tracy was completely at a loss of words. She never knew her biological father or anyone from his side of the family, and her mother had claimed not to have any living relatives.

The old woman understood what Tracy was going through and knew what she had been told concerning her family. She really felt sorry for the beautiful young woman in front of her and her heart went out to her.

"Child," she said, "I know what you've been told. As you can see, that wasn't true. I am alive and well. Come on in."

When she opened the door wider, Tracy, Monique and Monica entered the small and spotless apartment. It was new furniture and the place smelled fresh. Tracy looked up at the living room wall and saw her childhood picture hanging there. She hadn't seen that picture in so long, she looked at it as if it was a stranger as if she didn't know the little girl.

"Look at you," smiled her grandmother. "You look just like your father, child."

"Where is my mother?" asked Tracy as she sat down on the black leather couch followed by the twins.

"Well," smiled the old woman sitting across from her. "To answer your question, I would have to start from the beginning. I know your mother told you that her parents had passed away. But of course, that wasn't true. My husband and I just did not approve of your father being with your mother because he was a heroin addict with nothing to offer her. The child could have finished school and became something of herself. She was always so smart, but she was so in love with your father. When my husband John and I had it out with her, she left home never to be seen or heard from again. She was only sixteen years old at the time. We were so worried but it was nothing we could have done. We later found out that she was pregnant with you, and your father had died from a drug overdose. And instead of coming back home, she decided to stay away and raise you on her own. But if we had known how bad she had gotten so involved in drugs, my John and I would have came and got you and for sure had her committed to a rehab. Sadly my husband; your grandfather passed away from a heart attack two years ago and never got the chance to see you or your mother; his daughter again. I went through so much after losing my John, but after hearing from your mother again about a year ago, I again felt alive with something to live for. Unfortunately, she was in the same place where she is now. But receiving her letter meant so much to me," she said with her hand over her heart.

"Where is she?" asked a surprised Tracy.

This was all too much for her to take at one time. She was confused about the whole situation and did not know what to do or think. She first had it in her mind to come to Chicago and give her mother a piece of her mind for the ill treatment she received as a child, but now her mind was all over the place and she didn't know what to do.

"She's in the Danbury Connecticut Federal Penitentiary, for transporting drugs for some guy the police had been watching," the old woman continued. "When I first went to see her, the child looked like death. But now she's back to her radiant beautiful looking self," she smiled. "You know, sometimes those places can be a blessing in disguise. When she told me what she had done to you as a child I could not believe—" a few tears escaped from her eyes as she tried to continue.

Tracy and the twins walked over and put their arms around the old woman and said comforting words to her.

"It's alright," said Tracy rubbing her shoulder.

"No child should have to go through what she had put you through," the old woman continued while shaking her head no. "It tore me apart just to hear about it. And it's really hurting your mother today, but we have to live with our nightmares that we create. Just wait until I tell her that I've seen you. And you are so beautiful," she smiled through her tears. "What have you been doing? Tell me about yourself."

Tracy filled her in on her achievements in life, and some of her hobbies. She told her about G-Banks and how he was the best father they could ever had wished for. You could see the love in her eyes when she expressed her love for him and her sisters; Monique and Monica. Her grandmother smiled and sat silently listening to everything Tracy was saying until she finished.

"This Mr. Banks," smiled the old woman, "sounds like a very good man. He sounds like an angel."

"Oh no, he's definitely no angel!" said Tracy causing the twins to laugh. "But he's a very good man and we love him to death. Well, that's about it."

"I know it's all so soon and everything," said the old woman, "but I would like to get to know you, if that's possible. You're my only grandchild."

"Of course," said Tracy standing up as the twins and her grand-mother did likewise. "I would like to get to know you also."

"Here," she said taking a card with her number on it out of her bag. "Take my number and call me whenever you want."

"I will," smiled the old woman taking the number. She then kissed Tracy on the cheek and gave her a firm loving hug.

"You girls take care of yourselves and stay in touch with me," she smiled kindly.

"Okay," the girls said in unison as they headed for the door.

"Wow!" was all Tracy could say when she got in the hallway after her grandmother closed the door. She didn't know what to think or say, so she remained quiet in her own thoughts.

The twins were also quiet as they wondered what awaited the two of them. They took the stairs to the next flight up, and knocked on the apartment door. Monique thought about turning around and not seeing her mother but then something told her to just get it over with. She expected Derrick to open the door, but when her mother Clurisa stood in the doorway it took her aback.

Clurisa also wore a shocked expression on her face. She looked much better since the last time the twins saw her, but she looked much older. They thought about Tracy's recent encounter but knew this was not their grandmother. Her hair was graying and she wore bags under her eyes as if she hadn't slept in days.

Without saying anything, Clurisa opened the door wider so the girls could enter the small apartment. The tears fell from her eyes as they all entered walking pass her.

As soon as they stepped into the livingroom, their eyes fell on Derrick. He sat in a wheelchair with his head tilted to the side as if being stuck in that one position. Only his eyes travelled to their faces. He had a look of surprise in his eyes when his eyes fell on the twins. He actually had a look on his face as though he had so much to say to them but he could not speak.

"What happened to him?" asked Tracy being the first one to speak.

Clurisa looked around nervously, licked her lips and said, "He was shot several times by one of those young fools outthere who claimed my husband was having sex with his little sister. Now why would he do that? That don't explain why they robbed him for his money after shooting him. I didn't and still don't believe that accusation not one bit. Not even one bit."

All three girls looked away in disgust that she was still deceiving herself that Derrick was a good man. Tracy shook her head and looked at Derrick with an unreadable expression.

"They had paralyzed him from the neck down," she continued, "and he's in a strokelike state. He can hear you, but he cannot speak."

Monique looked at how pitiful Derrick looked with his head to the side sitting in that wheelchair, and wanted to laugh but held her composure.

"Anyway, you girls look terrific," said Clurisa not knowing what to say or where to begin as she searched for words. "I'm...I really...I'm really sorry that we had not become a better family. But I tried. I mean, I did miss you two since the day you've ran away from home.

Derrick just felt that I should not...I'm really sorry. I've really worried about you two. But I knew you two would be better off with Mr. uh, Mr. Banks. I see the two of you have turned out well. I'm happy for you. I do know what you two were going through. I'm not stupid. It's just that...things are never easy to say or deal with. I hope you two understand. I've stopped drinking," she said licking her lips and nervously rubbing her hands together. She had known this day would one day come, but no matter how she prepared for it, she now did not know how to deal with it. So, she tried to do the best she could.

"I've been clean for three years now," she continued.

"I'm proud of you," smiled Monica.

Monique stood next to Tracy with an unreadable expression on her face.

"Do you girls want something to drink?" asked Clurisa.

"No," answered Monica and Tracy.

"Yes," answered Monique speaking for the first time. "I'm thirsty!"

"Oh...oh...okay," stuttered Clurisa. "I'll be right back. Let me get you something cold to drink."

As soon as she walked into the kitchen, Monique quickly walked over to Derrick. With all her strength, she slapped him upside the head. WHAM!

"Stop it!" said Monica through clenched teeth as Tracy tried to subdue her laughter.

Monique smirked as she began to punch Derrick's big head from side to side.

Monica quickly rushed over and tried to pull Monique off of Derrick while also looking towards the kitchen hoping her mother hadn't heard the punches to Derrick's head.

"Stop it!" she said pulling on Monique's arm.

Monique snatched her arm out of her sister's grasp.

Spit drooled from Derrick's lips as his eyes desperately pleaded for help. The blows felt as if he was being pounded with a sledge hammer, and he could not move to escape the thunderous blows.

Tracy laughed so hard at the scene in front of her, that her stomach had started to hurt.

"I said stop it!" Monica told her twin sternly as she successfully pulled her away from Derrick.

"Here you go baby," said Clurisa walking back into the livingroom carrying a glass of soda with ice in it.

"Thank you," said Monique taking the glass and gulping down the soda. "I needed that. I could go for round two now."

"Oh, you want more?" asked Clurisa reaching for the near empty cup.

"No, no. I was reffering to something else," said Monique causing Tracy to roar with laughter once again.

"Anyway," said Monica. "We still love you. And maybe we'll come back to see you soon."

"I love you girls too," said Clurisa as the tears fell from her eyes.

Monique looked away and walked towards the door being followed by Tracy. She was not so forgiven. She thought about the past and was glad to not have grown up around her mother and Derrick.

Monica was a bit more compassionate and forgiven. She approached her mother and gave her a kiss and hug before pulling away, and catching up to her two sisters.

As soon as they stepped into the hallway, the girls looked at one another as if to question their next move.

"So, what now?" asked Monica.

"I say we go back to our hotel," suggested Monique, "take a shower, get some rest, and then get in touch with our bad boy friend Damien."

"Let's go," said Tracy anxious to see the drug dealer again, but this time it would definitely be on her terms.

Chapter Twenty

"Yo man, she just called and told me what they were saying," said Boo pacing the floor and running his hand through his hair.

"You act like you scared," joked Drama.

"I'm not scared of nobody," Boo replied angrily. "I'm just saying, it's really on now. I ain't letting nobody kill me."

"Fuck them niggas," said Barkim standing from the couch and looking at his watch. "I gotta go and see this punk ass parole officer."

"Where's grandma?" asked Boo.

"Her, my mother and Gee went food shopping," answered Barkim. "I can't wait to get on my feet and get my own place. "

"I thought your shorty was holding you down," said Drama.

"She is, but I can't live off no one. I have to get my own shit. Tracy just plugged me in with a guy her father knows that has a construction company. That's what's up. It'll definitely keep my P.O. off my ass. I have to go see him now. Let me get outta here before I fuck around and get violated."

"Yo," said Drama standing up and slipping on his jacket, "I'm riding wit' you. Boo can stay here. I'll drive you down there and chill in the car 'til you finish. I could buy some sneakers downtown while I'm waiting."

"That's cool with me," smiled Boo kicking off his brown and beige Timberland boots and grabbing the t.v. remote. "Yo Bar, if your girl Tracy calls, I'll let her know you had to go see your P.O. I'll be here waiting on grandma, Auntie Jean and Gee to get back from food shopping," he smiled rubbing his stomach. "See you when you get back."

"Come on," Barkim said to Drama.

The two exited the house and jumped into Drama's old Buick. When he started the car, the sounds of the new hot artist from Lefrak; Billy Bang, song "Why you gotta go so Ham" came blasting through the speakers. Drama put the car in drive and pulled off heading towards Downtown Brooklyn.

$$\$\$\$\$\$\$$$

"Come on son," said Tone putting a black nine millimeter in his waistline. "It's time we take that nigga Barkim off the map. Then we'll get Drama and that nigga Boo. You sure that nigga Barkim go to the parole building downtown today?"

"Yeah," answered Mike. "My man said he see the nigga there every Tuesday at the same time in parole. Come on, let's get outta here. But it don't make no sense for both of us to be strapped down there. I'll drive, and when we see the nigga you pop 'em."

"Whatever," said Tone walking out of the house being closely followed by his partner Mike.

The two of them jumped inside of the black Range Rover and hit Dekalb Avenue heading towards Downtown Brooklyn.

When they reached Flatbush Avenue, they saw Donna and her friends, who they hired to bag up their drugs, standing in front of Juniors restaurant. Mike pulled over and said, "I'll be right back. Let me tell Donna and 'em to be at the crib tomorrow at three to bag up."

"And we have to get some more dope down to the 'A'," he said before jumping out of the truck and approaching the girls.

It took him two minutes to give the order to Donna and her friends to be at the house before coming back to the truck. He got inside and turned the music down.

"They said what's up," he said pulling off into traffic and heading in the direction of their destination.

"I hope you told them they have to get butt ass naked so nothing come up short," said Tone bobbing his head to the song 'In the club tonight' by a rapper named Midnite Blu from Lefrak Queens.

The two of them were a bit nervous as they headed towards the parole building. They hoped everything would go as they planned it.

"Just like clockwork," smiled Tone as they pulled up in front of their destination.

"What's up?" asked Mike looking around the area and not seeing anything.

"There go the nigga Drama's car," answered Tone pointing. "Yo, he's getting out now."

Drama stepped out of the car, stretched his legs and arms and was about to get back into the car when Barkim came hurrying out of the parole building looking upset.

"Oh shit son!" said Tone excitedly. "We got both of them niggas! Just drive pass slowly."

"That fucking P.O. is an asshole," complained Barkim walking to the car. "I was upthere all that fucking time and that motherfucker tell me to come back when—"

"Boom! Boom! Boom! Boom!" the shots rang out.

"Yeah motherfucker!" yelled Tone jumping out of the truck firing his weapon.

Barkim and Drama tried running for cover. Barkim ran behind a red jeep but caught a bullet to the right side of his chest.

"Oh shit!" cursed Drama ducking behind a parked car as Tone ran towards him. He never thought that his black cell phone would one day save his life as he pulled it out of his pants pocket.

Thinking the cell phone in Drama's hand was a gun, Tone quickly ran back to the Range Rover and jumped inside as Mike quickly pulled away from the scene.

"Damn!!!" cursed Drama getting up off of the ground and walking towards Barkim to make sure he was okay.

"Fuck!" he cursed before frantically dialing 911 on the same cell phone that saved his life moments earlier, as his friend lay on the ground with blood pouring from his chest.

A crowd of people began to form and parole officers ran out of the building to see what was happening as Drama cursed out the police dispatcher for taking so long to obtain the whereabouts of his friend bleeding to death. He hung up on the 911 operator and cursed himself for not thinking. He knew he should've gotten Barkim to the hospital himself.

He carried and half dragged his friend to the car and sat him in the passenger seat, before running around the car and jumping in the driver's seat. He could hear people cautioning him to not move Barkim until the ambulance arrived.

"Shut the fuck up!" cursed Drama under his breath as he raced to Brooklyn Hospital hoping and praying that his friend would live. He couldn't picture losing his best friend. No, not like this.

"Ahhh," moaned Barkim in pain holding his chest as the blood poured over his hand, shirt and the car seat.

"You gonna be alright," comforted Drama in hopes that he was right. "What's up man? Talk to me."

"Ca-ca-call my girl Tracy," said Barkim barely getting the words out as he felt the burning sensation the bullet had caused.

Drama didn't see the logic in calling Tracy, so he ignored his friend's request. It was nothing she could do, he thought as he whipped around traffic. His friend's life was now in God's hands.

Drama pulled up in the emergency area of the hospital and jumped out of the car.

$$$$$

"So tell me Mr. Damien," said Tracy with an evil glare in her eyes and a devilish smile, "how many women or should I say children, had you raped in your lifetime? Wake up Damien, I know you can hear me."

Damien shook his head from side to side and tried to focus on the present. He still was seeing a little blurry. All he remembered was getting a phone call from Monica telling him that she and her two sisters were down to see him and him alone, before leaving Chicago. She told him that he was the cutest of his friends and wouldn't mind sharing him with her sisters for a sexcapade he would never forget. She told him to meet them at a hotel and gave the information so he would know where to come. Damien knew the freakiness some women possessed and was down to entertain the ladies. So he set out on his mission.

After meeting up with the girls and registering the room, Damien came back to the rented car with the biggest smile on his face. He thought of the many ways he was going to fuck these chicks. The girls seemed a bit tipsy as they drunk out of one of the Moet bottles. He flashed the room key and they stumbled out of the car giggling.

As they entered the room, Monique handed Damien an open bottle of Moet and watched as he drunk deeply from the poisoned bottle, as Tracy and Monica passed the good bottle back and forth to one another.

Damien had the biggest smile on his face because he knew this was going to be a fantasy fulfilled. But only after two minutes of hugging, kissing and feeling on the girls, he began to feel drowsy and funny. He never knew the Moet to be so strong. He then looked at the laughing girls one last time before passing out.

"Damien," smiled Monique. "Snap out of it."

It took him a moment to regain focus and when he did, he did not like the position he was in. His mouth was duct taped, his hands were handcuffed above his head to the bedpost and his feet were spread apart tied tightly to a two foot piece of wood placed between them.

"Oh," smiled Tracy pointing to the piece of wood placed between his feet. "I saw this on a movie I think was called 'Misery' or something like that. If you didn't see it, you are going to love this!"

Damien looked down at his nude body. His eyes then travelled to the serious faces of the three girls all wearing rubber gloves and staring down at him. For some reason, they just did not look attractive to him anymore. His eyes desperately questioned them as to what this was all about.

"Look at me," said Tracy stepping forward. "I still don't look familiar to you, Damien?"

He looked real hard at her and for the life of him he just could not place where he knew the beautiful darkskin girl in front of him.

"Let me refresh your memory," she continued. "I was a little ass girl back then living in the 'Green' with my crack addicted mother. You use to sell drugs to her or take advantage of her weakness and…it was me who had to pay for it. One day you came up to our apartment and gave my mother some cracks to rape me. I was only a baby then, Damien. Now do you remember me?"

Damien's eyes got as wide as saucers as he remembered the long ago incident. He now recognized the beautiful darkskin girl standing in front of him. He made sounds trying to say he was truly sorry and that he was young and stupid at the time, but the duct tape silenced his every word.

"We should've brought a gun with us to blow his perverted brains out," said Monica.

"Let the show begin," Tracy smiled sinisterly. "Being old Damien here never seen the good movie 'Misery', I say we bring the movie to him!"

She pulled a hammer from her Clutch bag and Damien nearly fainted at the sight of it. His eyes opened wide in fear. He tried to brace himself for the blow to come when he saw Tracy's hammer held hand swing in a high arc. It came down with such tremendous force.

"Crack!!!!" The sound of the hammer connecting with his left ankle was sickening. The bone shattered in three different places. Damien bounced in pain all over the bed as the handcuffs subdued his upper body. He had never felt pain like this in his life.

Tracy walked around the bed and with all her might swung the hammer again connecting with his right ankle.

"Crack!!!" This blow was worse than the first. The bone protruded from his skin. The pain was so unbearable, he passed out.

"Wake up Damien," laughed Tracy. "You're missing the best part of the movie."

Monica walked to the bathroom and returned with a pail of cold water. She threw the water in his face with hopes of bringing him back to consciousness.

When he came back to, Monique pulled a hypodermic needle from her bag. She walked closer to the bed and grabbed Damien's arm. With the other hand, she took the needle full of Succinylcholine and injected the poison into his vein. Damien's eyes shot wide open in fear as the poison kicked in.

When injected, Succinylcholine is a fast lethal drug with a terrifying twist. It causes paralysis but does not alter the level of consciousness. It suffocates you so you maintain consciousness while suffocating. Damien was awake but couldn't move. The drug paralyzed his body but not the terror he was going through. This was hell!

Tracy's cell phone began ringing and she pulled it from her bag. She wondered who could be calling her at this time of night as she answered the call.

"Hello?" she said into the phone. "Oh, how are you doing?...Can I call you back?...Where is he?...Is everything okay?"

"What?!?!" she then yelled into the phone causing Monique and Monica to stare at her.

"When? Who did it? Where is he?" she asked into the phone.

Monique and Monica looked on hoping and silently praying that the call wasn't concerning their father G-Banks. They wore very worried expressions on their faces as they watched their sister's every move and what she said into the phone.

"We have to get out of here," announced Tracy to her sisters as she put her cell phone back into her bag. "I have to hurry and get back to New York!"

"What happened?" asked a worried Monica.

"Barkim got shot in his chest," panicked Tracy walking towards the door forgetting about the dead Damien sprawled on the bed. "They said he is in critical condition."

Monique and Monica felt their sister's pain but were relieved to learn that the call was not about their father. They all knew they had to be by his side now more than ever.

As Tracy and Monica walked out of the hotel room, Monique pulled a book of matches from her pocket and lit the whole book. She then threw the lit book on Damien. The bed and Damien both went up in flames. Monique knew they couldn't afford to be careless. The burning of the body would cover up any puncture wound by the needle.

Monique looked around the room one last time before catching up with her sisters.

Chapter Twenty One

"I don't believe this shit!" fumed Detective Cornwell as he sat at his desk eating a stale donut and sipping from a cup of warm coffee.

He was a fat white man with thinning hair. He had been on the police force for seventeen years now and was considered to be one of the station's best homicide detectives.

"We got two bodies back to back," he continued talking to his white Italian partner, Detective Russo. "And we can't seem to come up with a fucking witness on either case!"

"Yeah, and it's not like these cases are linked to some niggers," shot back Detective Russo in a low tone as to not let the non-white officers in the station hear his racist remark.

"These were two respectable businessmen," he said meaning white. "I mean, first we get the body of Mr. Marcelli. We both know he was a mobster, but I tell you John, he was a good fucking guy. He was from the neighborhood, you know? And I really liked the guy. But what bothers me the most is the way they killed him. Those animals didn't have to cut his throat, cut off his balls and shove them in his mouth before shooting him in the fucking head," said the officer sounding like a mobster himself.

"Here is where these two bodies tie in," he continued while sitting on his partner's desk. "Both of these men were murdered by someone very professional. Or maybe even, a gang of professional killers. The only difference is, the second guy Mr. Bader was a well respected businessman. He also was connected to some very powerful people, but he was no gangster. And just like that, he's dead. With two gunshots to the back of his head execution style. I swear to you John, I'm going to catch the man or men who'd done both of these heinous killings."

Detective Russo was justifiably angry, but he was way off base thinking it was a man or men who did the killings; even the murder of Mr. Bader. Actually, Monique did that hit alone. She had to practically beg her father to let her do it. She wanted to do the hit by herself for two reasons. One, to keep her father's word to the people who paid to have the hit done, and also to test her skills of the many things she had learned. Doing hits was like a drug and she had definitely become addicted.

Mr. Bader was a thorn in the side of his business partners for a number of years. For a long time he had manipulated and stole millions of dollars from the multi-million dollar corporation he was a part of. Despite the investigations his partners conducted, Mr. Bader was smart enough to cover his tracks and tamper with the paperwork. However, one of his partners had gotten fed up and decided to take matters into his own hands. He paid G-Banks handsomely in advance to handle the problem. When he recently called and found out how sick G-Banks were, he thought more of his money had went down the drain until he picked up the newspaper one morning and learned that his partner/associate Mr. Bader had indeed met his unfortunate demise.

Monique donning all black with her hair pulled back into a ponytail and holding a black nine millimeter with silencer attach, crouched down low in the hallway of the big expensive mansion when she heard Mr. Bader's car pull up in the four car garage. Her father had taught her all about alarms, so it was no problem for Monique to get through the so-called best security system that money can buy.

Mr. Bader punched a few numbers into his new alarm system with a smile before opeing the door with his key. He entered the big house and sat his briefcase on the floor before resetting the alarm. He picked up his briefcase and loosened his tie as he headed towards the kitchen area.

"I need to start working this shit off," the fat white man smiled as he patted his bulging stomach as he sat his briefcase down in the kitchen and opening the well stocked refridgerator. He reached for the left over meatloaf and was dead before he could touch it.

"Pap! Pap!" the nine millimeter spit.

Mr. Bader's body fell forward into the open refridgerator as his legs slid from underneath him. Monique quickly made her get away, not leaving any clues behind.

"I'm telling you John," said Detective Russo, "we need to look into all of Mr. Bader's business dealings, as well as whether the guy was banging someone else's wife or something. Because this guy didn't appear to have any enemies."

"We're going to look into all of that," Detective Cornwell assured his partner.

"But right now," he said standing up and putting on his jacket, "we need to make a run."

"Where to?" asked his partner standing up as well.

"Just come on," he answered leading the way out of the station house.

They got inside of the blue unmarked police car and drove towards the Italian restaurant in a small section of Brooklyn called 'Little Italy.'

"So how's the family?" asked Detective Cornwell as he maneuvered through traffic.

"The wife is fine, but my daughter," Detective Russo answered with a bewildered look on his face and throwing his hands in the air in frustration.

"What happened?" asked his partner while quickly glancing away from the road.

"My kid," he answered shaking his head in disgust, "I think she's at that age where she's being influenced by them fucking niggers! She plays that rap crap all day long, and get this. One day last week, one of those fucking moolies had the fucking balls to even call my

house asking for her! Can you believe that shit? The balls of that nigger!"

"I'm saying Tony, Christina is a grown woman now. What is she
now, twenty one? She can make her own decisions."

"No, no, no," replied Detective Russo quickly while shaking his
head from side to side as his face turned a beet red. "No nigger is
marrying into my family!"

"How do you know it was a black guy that called the house?"
laughed his partner but understanding why his friend was upset.

"Because I've never heard of an Italian named Fruitquan," he
answered causing his partner to laugh even harder.

"But what's good for the goose," smiled Detective Cornwell, "is
also good for the gander. You've been my partner going on what now,
twelve years? And Tony, we've fucked our fair share of black women.
Those working in the station, all the way to the street walkers."

"Yeah John," he looked over sadly at his partner, "but fucking
was all it was. But I could never marry, introduce my family to or get
serious with a nigger bitch. I'm sorry John, but I just cannot do it. And
besides, what we men do isn't suppose to be done by our women.
They are never suppose to fuck niggers!"

"Leave that to us huh?" smiled his partner.

Detective Russo did not answer.

They had finally pulled up in front of the Italian restaurant. Detective Cornwell gave his partner an understanding look before exiting
the car. They then entered the restaurant.

"Detective Cornwell," said the detective holding out his hand for
the head waiter to shake. "And this here is my partner Detective Russo. I'm the one you talked to this morning over the telephone."

171

"Oh yes," smiled the head waiter shaking the cop's hand. "How may I help you?"

"Well, I was hoping that maybe you can help me with some kind of information to go on in regards to the murder of Mr. Marcelli. I want to bring his killers or killer to justice."

"I wish I can help detective, but I did not see any crime take place. However, I did see Mr. Marcelli enter the restaurant with a very beautiful blonde. They must've had a fight, because after she stormed out of here, he exited the establishment with three very beautiful black, and rude may I add, women. I think I've mentioned that to another officer."

When Detective Russo heard the work black, he turned up his nose.

"Was this on the day of the murder?" asked Detective Cornwell.

"Yes," answered the head waiter. "When Mr. Marcelli left with the three women, it seemed to me that they were going to have some fun, if you know what I mean."

"Yes, I know what you mean. Did you see anything else that looked out of the ordinary?"

"No," answered the head waiter.

As an afterthought he said, "Oh wait, I do remember one of the girls saying uh...something about her father being a professional basketball player."

"Great," said Detective Russo sarcastically. He didn't want to hear anything else about another black person today. He headed back towards the car.

"Thanks for the information," said Detective Cornwell. "If I have anymore questions or if you remember anything else, give me a call."

He then exited the restaurant and joined his partner in the car.

"What is it?" asked Detective Cornwell starting the car and glancing over at his partner.

"Just thinking," answered Detective Russo. "You know, maybe we shouldn't put so much energy into this shitty case after all. We have no leads, and it's not like Mr. Marcelli was an angel. We have nothing. Do you know how many hookers in New York alone we would have to question concerning old 'Pretty Boy'?"

"That may not be such a bad idea," smiled his partner.

"And do you know how many NBA basketball players with spoiled teenage daughters there are running around spending daddy's money?" asked Detective Russo.

"Well," replied his partner pulling into traffic, "we'll just have to keep our eyes and ears open. Plus if we don't solve these cases, it's not like we can't pin the bodies on a nigger. The best way to clean up the books. I mean, we've done it before."

"Yeah," smiled his partner cheering up. "You're right about that. And guess who just came home from prison on appeal?"

"Who?" asked his partner curious to know.

"The drug kingpin Supreme Justice," he answered. "The same guy that took a shot at you before going to jail."

"Really?" smiled Detective Cornwell as he drove to the station.

Chapter Twenty Two

"I told you," laughed Tone, "it was a matter of time before we got them niggas. If that nigga Drama wasn't holding I would've got his ass too."

He and Mike stood around a bunch of their young soldiers.

"You think the nigga Barkim is dead?" asked Mike.

"Hell yeah," smiled Tone. "I hit that big nigga square in his chest. Who the fuck wanna be that big anyway? Now the nigga gone' be in his casket all squished the fuck up."

Everybody laughed at Tone's joke.

"Yo," said one of the young boys standing around, "That new Fifty Cent joint is crazy. I forgot the name of it, but he's dissing everybody. He got at Jada again, Fat Joe, Ja-Rule and a whole bunch of other niggas."

"What the fuck is he still dissing Ja-Rule for?" laughed another young boy. "He already took their whole team down."

They stood in front of Mike's house. The young boys stood around he and Tone awaiting their next orders while smoking their blunts. They all stood around and made small talk until Tone's cell phone began ringing. All stood quiet giving their boss respect.

"Oh word!" laughed Tone into the phone. "My nigga! We're on our way."

"What's up?" asked Mike seeing how excited his friend was. "What's good?"

"Let's ride out," he said walking to his car. "That was the nigga Speed on the phone. He said he has a little present for us down in Gowannas Projects. They holding one of our enemies down there."

"That's what's up," said Mike walking to his new truck and adjusting his gun. "Let's roll."

Mike and Tone jumped in the truck and the rest of the young boys headed for their cars ready to ride out. The truck pulled off leading the way followed by the gang of young gunners in different vehicles.

"Who you think it is?" asked Mike as they headed downtown Brooklyn.

"I don't know," answered Tone examining the nine millimeter in his hand. "But I got something for whoever it is."

"Well let's get it over with," said Mike turning onto Bond Street. "We have to get back so we can have Donna and 'em bitches bag that work up. Yo, we need to tell those bitches they have to start bagging up naked 'cause we been taking losses. Son, they'll go for that shit."

Tone laughed.

They pulled over to park and the young boys following them did the same.

Tone got on his cell phone and placed a call. After talking into the phone for a minute, he hung up and led the way up a dark side street. Up ahead he could see a car with the headlights on and three guys standing over someone. Tone quickened his pace and within minutes he and his crew were also up on the car.

After giving the three young men a pound in greeting, he smiled widely as he looked down in the heavily bleeding face of the young man lying on the ground in between the car's door. Tone grabbed the guy off of the ground and punched him in the nose so hard you can hear the bone break with a loud crack. The hard blow forced Boo to fall back into the car. Something told Boo not to come down to Gowannas, but when his man Speed told him he had a plan to make big money he didn't hesitate to take the trip. He been set up and now hoped Mike and Tone would spare his life.

"That's that nigga Boo?!" asked Mike excitedly pulling his gun and running up to the car. Without hesitation, he and the young boys opened fire on the car hitting Boo in the head and other parts of his body. Even Tone pulled out his gun and shot Boo in the back before kicking the car's door closed.

A young boy ran up to the car handing Tone a big red metal canister. Tone opened the top and approached Boo's shot up body. He poured the gasoline from the canister all over Boo and the car seat. He then lit a match and tossed it. Boo and the car went up in flames. First Barkim and now his cousin Boo. They wanted Drama next.

Mike pulled three thousand dollars from his pocket and handed the money to Speed. The young men smiled, laughed and talked as they went their separate ways.

"Someone call an ambulance!" yelled a spanish man running out of his house and trying to save an already dead Boo from the burning car.

$$$$$$

"You're still not going to tell me who shot you?" fumed Tracy. She couldn't understand why Barkim would not answer her questions about the shooters. He was experiencing bad pain from the gunshot wound, but nothing like what his heart was feeling after hearing about what his enemies had done to Boo.

Tracy looked at Barkim with an angry look on her face. She look even more gorgeous when she's upset, thought Barkim as he grimaced from the pain in his chest. It felt as though someone was sticking a screwdriver through it.

"You don't need to know," said Barkim. "This is a street beef between thug niggas and we're going to handle it the thug way. I'm sorry I can't do things your way. But us street niggas don't do things the suburban way. This is Brooklyn baby; ain't no calling the police."

176

"Who said anything about calling the police?" asked Tracy with an attitude. "I would just like to know who shot my man, that's all. Is that too much to ask?"

For the last three months she had been visiting Barkim in the hospital hoping and praying that he would be okay. The doctor said the bullet nearly missed his heart, and had it been an inch in either direction he would had been dead.

"Tray," said Barkim using her nickname, "if I told you it's not like you would know them. You can't do nothing for me with this situation. I don't need you to start asking questions in the streets and getting hurt. This is Brooklyn, not Long Island so be easy and let me handle it. They shot me up and killed my cousin? It's on."

"You don't think I can handle myself?" asked Tracy.

Drama and Barkim's little brother Gee bust out laughing as they sat in plastic chairs a few feet away from the hospital bed. Barkim would've laughed as well but the pain in his chest was unbearable. To the young men in the room, Tracy looked as though she couldn't handle a street beef if it came with instructions. They wanted to tell her this, but didn't want to hurt her feelings.

Tracy wanted to let her man know that she were no slouch when it came to putting in dangerous work, but she was sworn to secrecy by her father, G-Banks.

"Ma, I know you can handle yourself," lied Barkim causing Drama and Gee to laugh again. "But listen baby, I got more important things for you to do. Like bringing some clothes uphere for me so I can have them when they let me out of here this week. I'll handle the street shit. And those fucking police keep coming here try'na question me like I'm a snitch or something. I'm from the old school, I ain't with that telling shit. These niggas killed my cousin Boo," he said sadly.

Drama and Gee sadly dropped their heads and felt the pain as well. The whole family was taking his death very hard.

177

"I know baby," said Tracy rubbing his face. "And I know the police keep trying to question you. My sister's boyfriend Joe is a cop out here in Brooklyn, and he told me you were being questioned."

"I know that nigga was try'na get you to convince me to tell, right?"

Tracy's smile answered his question.

"And my punk ass P.O.," he continued, "wanted to violate me and send me back to jail because I got shot! That uncle tom piece of shit. I'm getting tired of his ass."

"Why don't you change parole officers?" she asked.

"It's not that simple," he answered. "I'll have to complain to his supervisor and all kinds of shit and that can take forever."

"You said you wanted to move, right?" she asked.

Not knowing what she was getting at he asked, "What do that have to do with anything?"

"Well," she explained, "if you move that would most likely change your parole officer being you will be in a different location."

He hadn't thought about that and now wondered where and how he would be able to afford to move out of his grandmother's house and into a place of his own. He hadn't gotten on his feet yet since coming home from prison.

As if reading his mind, Tracy comforted him.

"Stop worrying about if you would be able to make your way. You're good. I got 'chu," she smiled using his ghetto slang.

"There's some nice houses out in Queens," she continued. "I'll see about one before you get out of this hospital. That's if you don't mind from time to time me staying with you."

"I insist you move in with me," he smiled back.

"We'll see," she said while backing away from the bed. "I'm starving. I'm going to get us some food. I know you're tired of this stuff they're feeding you."

"Word," he smiled.

"I'm going with you," said Gee quickly, wanting to ride in her expensive Jaguar. He hoped people he knew would see him in the car with the dimepiece. He would definitely be in someone's conversation. "I'm starving too," he said.

"Y'all can just bring me something back," said Drama reclining back in his chair and glancing through a Robb Report magazine.

Tracy and Gee exited from the hospital room.

Once inside the car, Tracy put on the new Alicia Keys cd while making small talk to get to know Gee a little better. Within minutes they were laughing and talking as if they knew one another for years.

"Who shot my baby Barkim?" she asked after she was sure he was comfortable.

Gee looked out of the tinted window not wanting to get her involved in his brother's beef but decided that it wasn't that important to keep the info to hisself. I mean what can she do, he asked hisself. The streets were already talking about Barkim getting shot and Boo being killed; and even threw names out as to who did it. There would be no retaliation until Barkim got out of the hospital or if Drama happened to run into those fools.

"It was two dudes from the 'sty named Mike and Tone," answered Gee. "They making money out here. They suppose to be some big niggas in the game."

"Let's drive through there before we go to the restaurant," suggested Tracy.

"Nah," said Gee not wanting to betray Barkim's trust. "We don't need to go through there."

"I won't tell Bar," smiled Tracy. "Plus, I got tints on my windows. Nobody can see us in here. And we're not going to do anything. We don't even have to stop. We can keep on going. Pleasssse," she said in that voice of hers that made men do whatever she said.

"Alright," said Gee not seeing any harm in doing what she suggested. He just wanted to get to the restaurant so he can eat. He gave her the directions and she quickly headed towards the destination.

Gee wondered had he done the right thing giving her information Barkim did not give. He figured it was no big deal and shrugged it off. He just hoped she'd never mention it to his big brother Barkim.

They drove through the block and as usual, Tone and Mike were standing around with a group of young boys talking shit and laughing. A few girls stood around the ballers also. They all turned and looked at the expensive brand new Jaguar slowly driving by and wondered who was inside of the luxury car.

"That shit is tight!" said Tone excitedly as those standing around agreed.

"Yo," said Mike, "that's the next joint I'm copping. Yo, y'all niggas watch and see."

Gee filled Tracy in on who was who; even the girls and what they did for the two thugs and how they moved. Gee knew a lot about Tone and Mike because people were talking about them now more than ever before.

Tracy drove slowly by, soaking up the information like a sponge. She watched how Gee relaxed when they were out of the area. He leaned back in his seat and enjoyed the sounds of Jadakiss, as Tracy drove to the restaurant with Mike and Tone on her mind.

Chapter Twenty Three

Monica hoped her suspicions were wrong. She just could not get rid of the feeling that something was not right. It had been nagging at her since she left the house this morning. She hoped everything and everyone were okay. She stopped in her tracks. She could not believe what she was seeing. As she walked the hospital's corridor standing directly in front of her was Bryan and a nurse. The two were smiling and he touched her hand softly with every word spoken. The brownskin petite nurse blushed as Bryan poured on the never ending compliments.

'What the fuck is this?' Monica thought angrily to herself as she approached the two. When Bryan noticed Monica standing before him, he looked as though he was caught with his hand in the cookie jar as he limply dropped the nurse's hand to the side.

"Monica," he stuttered. "Let-let-let me explain. It's not what you think. I was just-I was just," he said at a loss for words. He was busted and knew it.

"What the hell is this?!" asked Monica. "And who the hell is she?!"

"She's just-she's just," he stuttered.

"Excuse me," said the frightened nurse hurrying off back to her station. She knew she had no wins in a fight with the angry Monica.

"So, this is what you have to do whenever you receive one of your emergency patient calls?" asked Monica with her pretty eyes piercing his.

"No," answered Bryan nervously as he fumbled for words. "I just…Well, she thought I was…Monica, we were only talking. It went no further than that. I swear," he replied honestly.

The nurse was just one of many that the doctor occasionally flirted with. But it never went further than that. He was in love with Monica, and only flirted with women to ensure himself that he still had it. However, looking into his lady's angry face, he hoped he would be able to explain himself out of the situation and retain the trust in their relationship. He knew he had work to do, because Monica was totally pissed off. She was heated and wanted to slap his face so badly but couldn't bring herself to do it.

"You actually think I'm just going to stand by and go for this shit?" asked Monica using language she rarely used. She wanted to punch him in the face.

"But I can explain," pleaded Bryan. "I was only—"

His conversation was cut off by the ringing of Monica's cell phone. She held her left hand up to his face cutting off his lame excuses. She spoke into the phone after looking at the caller ID.

"Hello?" she said into the phone. "Moe, why you sound like that?"

"What?!?!?!" she yelled into the phone. "Noooooooo!!!! Please don't tell me what I think you're saying."

She was presently in a state of denial and did not want to hear what she had just heard. The tears instantly fell from her eyes.

"What's going on?" she asked into the phone. "It's not making any sense."

Bryan looked on very concerned and hoped that everything was okay.

"Daddy is dead," cried Monique on the other end of the phone. "I can't believe this, I can't believe this," she repeated over and over again.

"Moe, tell me daddy is okay," sobbed Monica. "Please tell me you're just playing….I know you don't play like that. Oh my God!!!!"

"What's wrong with Mr. Banks?" asked Bryan able to put the pieces together after listening to Monica and watching her break down. He wanted to know what was going on as well as comfort her, but she paid him no mind as she talked and pushed him slightly out of her way.

"I'm on my way!" she cried into the phone. "Did you call Tray yet?"

"No," answered Monique. "I'm about to call now. Daddy is dead, Monnie. He's dead!" she wailed through the phone.

Monica heard nothing Bryan was saying to her and when he went to hug her, she pushed him back and stormed out of the hospital to see what was happening with her father. She forgot all about the incident with Bryan and the nurse. That was so unimportant right now. She had to hurry and get home.

She got inside of her white BMW and rushed to the big Long Island home hoping and praying that somehow she perhaps had heard her sister wrong. 'Daddy is not dead', she thought over and over as she maneuvered through traffic. She then wondered where in the hell was Tracy.

$$$$$$

Tone and Mike's eyeballs damn near popped out of their heads when they saw the expensively dressed beautiful chocolate dime-piece emerge from the XJ8 Jaguar. She wore a diamond ring on her middle finger and a diamond bracelet that was blinding.

Tone and Mike remembered seeing the same car drive by no longer than a week ago, but had no idea, until now, that the beautiful young woman was the driver and owner of the vehicle. They wondered who her man was and what she was doing in the area.

Tracy took long sexy strides towards the corner grocery store where they exited from. The two thugs stood there and watched her approach. They could see she had a nice ass from the way her long mink coat danced around her thighs with each step she took.

"What's good baby?" asked Tone as she got closer.

He and Mike had just purchased their empty crack vials from inside of the Arabic store on Broadway. Unknown to them, Tracy had been following the two ever since they left the block.

"I've finally been blessed to see the mysterious beautiful woman behind the wheel of that Jag," smiled Tone. "What's your name?"

"Kim," lied Tracy with a smile.

"Like LiL Kim?" asked Mike not noticing how corny his line sounded.

Tone looked away embarrassed at his friend's choice of questions, but Tracy acted as if his question had actually amused her.

"Something like that," she smiled while checking out the area. She wanted to kill the both of them now but was disappointed by the many people walking by on this cold day.

"Who's your man?" asked Tone taking over the conversation again. "I don't ever recall seeing you and if I was your man, I would never let you outta my sight in fear that another nigga may scoop your pretty ass. So tell me, who's the dumb nigga?"

"Well, if you was my man you wouldn't have to worry about me being out of your sight," smiled Tracy with her hand on her hip causing her coat to slightly part showcasing one of her shapely thighs. "Because I am a very trustworthy woman, and I would ride for my man 'til the end."

"And to answer your question," she continued, "I have no man at this present time. Now isn't that something?" she smiled.

"No doubt," said Tone with an ear to ear grin.

Looking at her car and appearance, Tone figured her ex-man to be maybe a big time drug dealer. But it was the poor fool's loss and Tone's gain, he thought to himself with a smile. In his lifetime he had some very pretty girlfriends, but could never recall having someone as gorgeous as the darkskin cutie that stood in front of him. Just the thought of how jealous and envious people around his way would be if he showed up with Tracy and the Jaguar caused him to want her even more. He knew he would definitely have to step his hustling game up now, because without a doubt, every nigga in Brooklyn that was getting any real money would be out to snatch her away from him.

"Can I get your number?" he asked pulling out his own cell phone.

"I'll take your number instead," she smiled taking her cell phone from her bag. "I'm never home and it's not often that I answer my cell phone because my ex-man blows my phone up trying to get back what he had. So when you call me, just leave a message and I'll call you back."

"Oh okay," said Tone. "My number is 718-931-3131. Make sure you call me."

"I'm saying, what are you two doing now?" she asked.

"We about to head back to my crib," answered Tone. "I gotta call up my homegirls so they can come over and bag up some of our shit. Just a lil' something we leave here when we head outta town."

"And you trust those girls you got doing it?" she asked with a raised eyebrow.

"Yeah," he answered. "They're cool. They been doing it for us for the longest."

Tracy gave him a look as if that made no difference.

"I hope they are not friends with one another," she said knowing they were because Gee already put her on. "Because I wouldn't trust girls in packs to do anything. That's when the scheming starts. Especially if they're friends!" she emphasized the last word of her statement.

G Banks

Miz

"My ex-man," she continued, "had five girls who were friends bagging up his stuff, and they was stealing big pieces of rocks and he didn't even know it being that he was copping so many keys at a time. And he said it was easy for them to steal because you can never say for certain what the coke is suppose to come back to. Anyway, he found out they was stealing from him because they made the mistake of selling product to one of the same people he sold weight to."

Tracy didn't know what she was talking about. She had saw a girl say those same lines in a movie she once watched, and hoped Tone and Mike did not see the same movie.

Mike looked at Tone as if to say 'I told you so.' The seed of doubt was planted, and he wondered where would Donna and her friends sell their product if they had indeed been stealing while bagging up the drugs.

"That's why I say we should 'New Jack City' them bitches!" said Mike angrily.

Tone hoped he wouldn't expound any further about their business. The last thing he needed was Tracy to think he could not handle his operation successfully. He wanted to show that he was just as smart, if not smarter, than her ex-man.

"I'm not doing anything right now," said Tracy. "I'll bag up with y'all. That's if you two balling ass niggas are not scared to get your hands a little dirty for a few hours."

"You'll bag up with us?" asked Tone surprised.

"Yes," answered Tracy matter of factly as if he asked a dumb question. "I used to bag up with my ex when he first started selling drugs. Despite my looks and how I occasionally talk, I'll have you know that I am not new to this. Plus, it will give me a few hours to get to know you better," she smiled, and flirted with Tone openly looking down at his dick print through his jeans.

"I love the sound of that," smiled back Tone.

186

"Yo I like her," laughed Mike. "You can tell she's a down ass bitch."

"Excuse me?" asked Tracy with her lip upturned looking at him as if he had just disrespected her to the utmost.

"You don't know what to say out'cha mouth," said Tone angrily to his friend. "Can't you see I'm talking to her?"

"I didn't mean it like that," apologized Mike. "I'm just saying, she's mad cool."

"I'll take your words as a compliment," smiled Tracy easing the tension between the two friends. "Come on, let's get this show on the road," she said walking back to her Jaguar.

"Kim, didn't you want to get something from the store?" asked Tone.

"No," smiled Tracy slightly turning around. "I pulled over because I saw what I wanted. And it wasn't inside of the store."

Tone laughed before jumping inside of the Range Rover.

Mike pulled away from the curb and Tracy followed closely behind them thinking of her next move.

After pulling up in front of Tone's house, they went inside and sat at the kitchen table. Mike sat four big plates down with a pack of Gem-Star razors in front of Tone and Tracy. He then pulled five pans from the kitchen's cabinet with giant sized cooked cracks place on each one. He sat them on the table and took a seat.

Tracy looked at the huge crack rocks and didn't know what to do or where to begin. She didn't remember anything about the drug game she was exposed to as a child back in Chicago. She took off her coat and sat back down in her chair.

"Damn!!!" said Tone and Mike in unison after seeing her body for the first time. Their mouths dropped open causing Tracy to smile showing her pretty white teeth.

"Nigga, you got a winner!" Mike said to Tone.

"Word," he agreed.

"Let's get this over with," he said getting back to the business at hand.

"Hold up," said Tracy reaching into her black Dior bag. "Let me get my chewing gum."

Instead of chewing gum, she came out of her bag holding a black nine millimeter with silencer attached. Both boys looked at her in surprise not moving.

'Pap! Pap! Pap! Pap! Pap!'

She opened fire hitting Tone directly in his forehead killing him instantly. Her second shot hit Mike behind the left side of his ear but he was still alive. He managed to stand up and stumble out of the kitchen towards the living room.

"Oh shit!" he cried holding his ear and trying to make it to the front door.

Tracy stood in the hallway and took perfect aim. She squeezed the trigger and three shots were perfectly placed in the back of Mike's head.

She calmly walked back to the kitchen, slipped on her coat and exited the house leaving the front door partially open.

On her drive to the hospital to visit Barkim, her cell phone began ringing and she answered it as she turned onto Dekalb Avenue.

"Hello?" she said into the phone. "Oh, what's up Moe?...Why do you sound like that?...What's wrong?...I won't be home until later...No, tell me now...What?!?!" she screamed into the phone.

"No, no, no," she cried shaking her head from side to side as the tears fell from her eyes.

"Oh God, noooooooooo!!!" she wailed into the phone as she pulled the car over to the curb not knowing what to do. As the tears rolled down her face, her forehead began to get hot and her heart ached like never before. She just could not believe that her father was dead.

Chapter Twenty-Four

"If anyone had a motive to have Michael Boney and Tony Myers killed, it would be you," pointed the fat white homicide detective standing next to Barkim's hospital bed as his black partner looked on with an angry scowl on his face.

"I don't know what you're talking about," replied Barkim truthfully.

This was the second time hearing about the death of his two enemies, Mike and Tone. Drama was the first to tell him the news and let him know that he didn't have anything to do with the incident, even though he wished it was he that caught the two gangsters slipping. Now the police were questioning him about the double homicides.

"Do you know I can send you back upstate Mr. Houston?" asked the black detective speaking for the first time since entering the hospital room. "And I wouldn't want to do that, so just cooperate with us here."

"No disrespect detective," said Barkim angrily, "but I don't have shit to tell you about those two niggas. Shit, I don't even know them. But let me tell you something. When I was upstate I used to really utilize that bullshit ass law library, so I know what y'all niggas can do and what y'all can't do. So, let's stop playing games here. You're only fishing, so don't come in here threatening me about being violated on parole. I don't know shit about them two dead niggas, and that's real. Y'all ain't got shit on me and you know it."

"Not yet," responded the black detective.

Then looking at his watch he said to his white partner, "Come on, I have to get out of here. We have a funeral to attend."

The two detectives had then walked out of the hospital room after leaving a card on the small table on the side of Barkim's bed. The black detective looked so familiar to Barkim but for the life of him he just could not place where he knew the cop from. He threw it out of his mind and figured the officer to be someone that arrested him many years back or something.

"What up?" asked Drama walking into the room two minutes later. "Those pigs just left outta here?"

"Yeah," answered Barkim. "They're still trying to question me about those two birds, Mike and Tone. Anyway, you brought my clothes so I can get the fuck up out of this hospital?"

"Yep," he answered holding a plastic bag containing a Champion sweatsuit and a pair of Nike sneakers.

"Yo, get rid of that chain and piece you took from them birds," ordered Barkim. "We don't need to get caught with that shit. I talked to Tracy earlier. You know the funeral is today, right? Damn, that's fucked up that the oldtimer died from heart failure like that. He was a good man."

"He seemed real cool," agreed Drama glad that he had the opportunity to meet the oldtimer.

"More than you'll ever know," said Barkim remembering the first time meeting him in the upstate prison's visiting room.

"Yo," he said, "you can take me to the crib and wait for me to get dressed. I'm going to the funeral. I'll call Tracy on the way and you can leave me at the funeral."

"Nah," said Drama, "pops was cool. I'm going to the funeral too to pay my respects to him."

"Aiight," said Barkim getting out of the hospital bed and began putting on his clothes.

"Damn," laughed Drama, "I'm gonna miss seeing you in that hospital gown with your ass hanging out."

"Man, shut the fuck up!" laughed Barkim glad to finally be leaving the hospital, but saddened to know that within the next hour or so, he would be seeing G-Banks for the very last time.

$$$$$$

"Oh my God!" cried Monique as the tears fell from her eyes.

"It's okay," comforted Tracy rubbing her shoulders and kissing the top of her head.

The twins were surprised to see Tracy being the strength of the family. They knew the death of their father was eating Tracy up as well, but somehow she remained strong letting them know their father would want them to remain unbroken despite his demise. He always said, he didn't raise weak women so Tracy represented him as best she could. They all tried to remain strong, but it was a very hard thing to do. To not break down? It was easier said than done.

Monica ordered the maid to take the rest of the week off with pay, and she herself did all of the chores around the house to stay busy. She needed to stay occupied. She knew had she not stay busy, she would go crazy because she couldn't handle her father's death at all. She washed clothes, dried them and scrubbed floors that were already clean. Her boyfriend Bryan continuously called and even stopped by the house regularly, but she just was not up to seeing him or talking. She would just leave him sitting in the livingroom while she found some more chores to do.

Monique was also taking the death of their father pretty hard. She could not eat, and all she did was cry as if she would not be able to find her way in life without the guidance of the only man she had come to know as her daddy. Her boyfriend, Joe the cop, would come by and try to comfort her as best he can but it was nothing in the world like losing someone you loved with all of your heart.

Tracy was also going through it big time, but knew she had to stay strong. She made all of the funeral arrangements and after locating her father's phone book, she contacted all of the people she figured to be his friends or associates who did not know about his death.

192

His lawyer, Mr. Shapiro was handling his estate to have everything put in the three girls name; even the two houses in San Diego, California. They had only visited the houses twice. It was now theirs but they felt so much more comfortable in the big Long Island home they grew up in.

"Everything is going to be okay," said Tracy taking a step back from Monique. "Now, go and get dressed. We have to get to the funeral."

"I don't think I can see him in that casket again," sobbed Monique.

"You have to see him for the last time," she said while giving her sister a hug and then a gentle push towards the staircase.

Yesterday at the wake, things were horrible for the girls. They could not bear the sight of seeing their father lying in that casket. Monique fainted, Monica walked out of the huge church, and Tracy stood in front of the casket not being able to bring herself to look inside of the casket at her decease father. But she knew to bring some kind of closure, she and her two sisters would have to be strong and look in that casket today, because it would be the last time they would ever see him again.

Tracy already had on her long black dress. All she had to do was slip on her shoes and grab her purse and coat. She entered the kitchen and gently pulled an already dressed in black Monica away from washing clean dishes.

"Come on Monnie," she said using her sister's nickname and leading her to the kitchen table to sit down. "It's going to be okay. Daddy would want us to remain strong. You know what he would say, right? He would say, 'if those tears doesn't make us richer, than you better stop those damn tears,'" she said in a deep voice trying to imitate G-Banks.

Monica smiled through her tears. It was her first time smiling since learning about the unfortunate demise of her father.

"It's going to be very hard for us but—"

"Ding-Dong," the front door bell interrupted Tracy mid-sentence.

"Now who can that be?" she asked standing up and taking Monica's hand to stand as well.

They walked together hand in hand, and when Tracy opened the door, Bryan and Joe stood there.

"We thought we'd escort you ladies to the church," said Joe.

"Come on in," invited Tracy opening the door wider. "Hey Joe, Monique should be down in a minute."

The two men entered the house and Bryan put his arms around Monica but she did not respond to his embrace.

Monique had then descended down the stairs dressed in black and they headed out of the door to get to the church on time. They knew this was going to be a hard day for them all.

They rode in silence until they reached the big church and saw the heavy police presence and the crowd that were trying to enter.

"What are so many police here for?" asked Bryan as the driver pulled up in front of the church.

"I have no idea," replied Joe. "But I'll find out."

The girls said nothing.

When they entered the big church and sat in the seats that were reserved for them, they looked around noticing some very prominent and powerful people. There were a few celebrities, senators, judges, black businessmen that looked like gangsters, a lot of women crying; most of whom the girls remembered who had a relationship with their father at one time or another, a few Chinese businessmen, Italians that looked like mobsters, and a few others.

"Wow!" exclaimed Joe looking around. "Now I see what the police presence is all about. I'm surprised I didn't hear about this in my station."

Actually he did. He just had no idea that it was G-Banks's funeral that was being talked about.

"Shhh!" shushed Bryan wanting to hear what the mayor of the city had to say as he stepped behind the podium flanked by two police officers.

Tracy turned around in her seat and was glad to see Barkim and Drama searching for their seats.

"Over here," she waved to them as she made room next to her for her man and his friend. She was glad she made the funeral invitation only, because had it been open to the public it would have been ridiculous and no room to move.

"I've known my good friend Mr. Gregory Banks for quite some time," said the mayor.

The girls had the privilege of meeting him years back when their father invited him to their home before he became mayor of New York City.

"Mr. Banks was a very good, kind, generous and thoughtful man," continued the mayor. "He had done a lot for his community by opening many businesses for those in the city to find work. I remember the first time I had met this great man—"

Tracy, Monique and Monica were astonished and amazed at what the many people had said concerning their father. There were people who talked about the money he'd donated to save their businesses, homes and families. There were those who talked about what he did for education, and even a prisoner's advocate group spoke of how he had recently donated thousands of dollars and expressed his concern for rehabilitation as opposed to only punishing and getting rich off of young black and latino men and women.

G Banks   Miz

Everyone knew Mr. Banks to be a good man but only knew pieces of him. Very few knew of his days with Frank Matthews and the
chicken thieves, a few knew of him being a hitman, most knew him to
be a very good businessman, and all knew him to be very stern. His
life was like a puzzle that only his three daughters could piece together. The world knew nothing of the perfect father he had been to
them growing up. The father who took them to Disney Land, the mov-
ies, dinner, put them in private school and always joked around with
them. Like when Monique and Tracy was fifteen years old and he
would catch them in their pajamas watching television with their hair
looking a hot mess and ice cream on their faces, and would come in
with a smile and a camera snapping pictures making them scatter like
roaches full of laughter. Or when Monica was always late getting up
for school and he poured water on her bedsheet while she slept.
Upon waking up, she knew she peed in the bed being her underwear
was wet as well, only after washing up and entering the kitchen to find
her father, her sisters and even the maid laughing at her. That's what
life was like for the girls living with their adopted father. The girls
touched his heart like no one had ever and he loved them to death as
they loved him.

Bishop Damon Sessions had then stepped up to the podium and
gave one of his spectacular sermons. Most of those in the church
cried, screamed and some even fainted after realizing they would
never see G-Banks again.

The casket was open and after the bishop preached his sermon,
everyone stood to view the body for the very last time.

Tracy, Monique and Monica cried and screamed as they looked
into the casket at their father. Barkim, Joe and Bryan had to hold the
young women firmly as they cried and nearly fell to the floor.

It was then that Barkim and Joe had caught eye contact for the
very first time. Barkim's heart began to beat like a drum as he recognized that Joe was the same detective that came to the hospital to
question him only hours ago. He then remembered the detective telling his partner that he had a funeral to attend.

Joe quickly looked away and attended to Monique. He knew all along who Barkim was, but due to the unfortunate demise of G-Banks, he also knew it was not a good time to inform Monique and Tracy that he was one of the detectives working on the case sent to question Barkim about the murders of Mike and Tone.

Drama stood up and made his way towards Monique. He wanted to comfort her and let her know things would be okay. He knew the man trying to console her was her cop boyfriend, but he did not care about any of that. Because whatever Drama wanted, he always went after.

Chapter Twenty-Five

It has been four months now since G-Banks's departure from here, and Tracy really wished she had her father with her right now. She had visited Barkim many times in prison, but never felt as nervous as she did today as she sat in the visiting room across from her biological mother, Darita, at the Danbury Federal Correctional Facility located in Danbury, Connecticut.

Darita looked at her daughter with tears of joy and pain in her eyes. She was very happy to see Tracy, but felt horrible at the terrible memories she had put her child through. She was truly hurting inside for her actions.

Darita looked like her old beautiful and radiant self before the drugs, but her teeth were still a bit yellow from the many years of neglect when she was using.

Tracy sat close to her grandmother but did not feel a real connection with her either. She wondered what she was doing with these people. She felt no kinship. Only her father could make her feel better in such a situation. But he was no longer here to protect her and give advice on what to do. Maybe she should've asked Monique or Monica to come along, she thought to herself. She didn't even know why she agreed to come in the first place. When her grandmother asked her over the telephone, she accepted the invitation not even thinking whether she was ready to see her mother or not. And Barkim was still on parole so he couldn't come with her.

Tracy sat in the big uncomfortable visiting room full of strangers not knowing what to do or say. Though the visiting room was big, it was not crowded at all. There were mostly females and of course children visiting the incarcerated women. The only males in attendance were sons, a couple of brothers, maybe a father, and the male c.o.'s stationed at their respective post.

Tracy immediately noticed the difference between this place, and the men's jail where she use to visit Barkim. The women's visting room was damn near empty as opposed to the very crowded men's visiting room in the men's prison. Women visited men in droves, but these women received very few visitors, especially from men. It was unfair. The men definitely needed to step it up, thought Tracy as she looked around at her surroundings.

"So, how have you been doing?" smiled Darita. "You are looking very very good. You're still beautiful."

"Thank you," replied Tracy nervously. "I'm doing okay. I've completed college...um, everything is going good."

"She looks just like her father, doesn't she?" smiled her grandmother asking Darita but looking at her.

Tracy felt like a mannequin in a department store window the way the two women stared at her with smiles. She began to fidget with her hands and could not wait for the visit to be over. She seriously doubted that she could do this again. She only came because her grandmother had practically begged her and she didn't want to disappoint the old woman. She knew the old lady had already been through a lot with losing her husband, and once she promised to accompany her grandmother, she knew she couldn't go back on her word.

"That girl looks just like her biological father," repeated the grandmother to Darita.

"Yes she does," smiled Darita.

Her mood had then changed to sadness as she looked at her beautiful daughter with tears falling from her eyes.

"I'm sorry baby," she began talking about what had been troubling her. "I'm truly sorry for the horrendous way I treated you when you was a child. You were always my pretty baby, and I never thought hitting rock bottom would cause me to do the things I had done to you. Being in here has been a blessing in disguise for me. I wasn't arrested, I was rescued. And since I've been in here, I have done a lot of thinking and I can say, that I've changed to become a better person. The person I was before the drugs. Just wiser now. My life had become a nightmare. You don't understand—"

Tracy could not believe her ears. This lady sitting in front of her actually had the nerve to talk about her life being a nightmare. Tracy wanted to yell at her and mention the countless nightmares she had growing up as a child in Chicago. She wanted to let her know her self-esteem as a child was so low she couldn't even bare to look at herself in the mirror. That is, until G-Banks, the man she had come to love as her father; erased the nonsense from her mind by loving her unconditionally and teaching her that black was the most beautiful color one can be. Growing up, she did hear the little boys in school say how pretty she was but she was no fool. She figured half correctly that they were only trying to get into her panties. It was G-Banks who took the time to show and teach why black was so beautiful and why she had the right for her self-esteem to be as high as anyone elses. To deny what he said, was to deny his love, and his love as a father was enough to convince her that he was right.

"At night," sobbed Darita, "I always look at the photos I have of you. I even—"

"Please," interrupted Tracy holding both hands to her ears not able to take anymore.

"I'm sorry," she said while standing up and trying to pull herself together. "It was good seeing you and everything, but I shouldn't be here. I can't do this. I'm very very sorry, but I just can't."

Darita's face dropped and she began crying uncontrollably.

"Honey," said the grandmother to Darita, "understand where the child is coming from. She's been through a lot. Maybe this is all too soon. Things take time."

Tracy was grateful her grandmother understood. She came along way in life and was still mourning her father's death and was in no mood to go down memory lane with her biological mother. Going back mentally was too painful and looking at Darita brought back the painful memories.

"Tracy baby," said her grandmother, "you can go and wait in the car if you'd like and I will be there in a second."

Darita stood up with tears falling to the small visiting table looking pleadingly at her daughter for forgiveness and a hug. The hug she could get, but the forgiveness part, Tracy wasn't sure of.

Tracy nervously hugged her, and Darita hugged her back tightly not wanting to let go.

Tracy felt so confused. She understood her mother's pain but her mother was the one that made her life a living hell. Didn't she deserve not being forgiven? Didn't she deserve to be in jail? These questions were going through Tracy's mind but she had no answers. She just didn't know. She would definitely need more time.

"Please forgive me," cried Darita holding her tightly. "I'm sorry for everything I've done. Please forgive me baby."

Tracy pulled away and quickly exited the visiting room. She desperately needed air and time to think. This was way too much for her to deal with at the moment. She had recently lost her father a few months back and just did not possess the strength or energy to deal with this mother/daughter situation. Not right now.

After getting processed out of the facility, Tracy walked outside and began to instantly feel better. The chilly November cold hit her face as she walked towards her car. This had been a terrible day for her so far, and she had just wanted to hurry up and drop her grandmother off at the airport to go back to Chicago so she can get home, take a hot bath and call Barkim over. That's exactly what she needed to clear her mind, she thought. Just the thought made her smile. She was so into her thoughts, she didn't even hear the voice calling out to her from behind.

"Hey beautiful, hold on a minute!" yelled the darkskin brother behind her but she didn't hear him.

She was still smiling when she reached her car. She then felt a strong presence behind her. Tracy quickly spun around with her small fist balled up ready to swing with everything she had. She and her sisters were taught to defend themselves with their hands so she was ready for whatever.

"Whoa sweetheart," said the chocolate brother holding up both hands and moving his chin out of knockout range in case she swung.

"I didn't mean to startle you," he continued. "Basically, I just wanted a few minutes of your time."

Tracy relaxed a bit and looked in his face as her heartbeat began to beat regularly again.

"My name is Kevin Jones," he said holding out his hand, "but my friends call me Flavor."

She hesitantly shook his hand. She shook it to be polite but had no intentions of really getting to know the brother. However, out of curiosity she asked, "And why would anyone call you Flavor?"

"Because women say I'ma sexy muh'fucker," he smiled causing her to laugh.

"I'm a male exotic dancer," he explained. "Anyway, when I saw you in that visiting room, I have to admit that your presence lit up the dreary atmosphere."

"I bet you say that to all the girls," smiled Tracy.

"Only the pretty ones," he smiled back. "Not to get into your business or anything, but you looked as though you were going through some serious things in there. Is the woman locked up your sister or something?"

"No, she's...she's," stuttered Tracy not knowing how to answer the question. "Well, let's just say she's suppose to be my mother."

"Oh okay. I just came from seeing my mother as well. I don't know if you're up to sharing your problems with me but if it involves your mother, trust me, I can relate. Me and my moms went through a hell of a lot. But what can I say, you only get one mother."

"And one father," Tracy said sadly.

"That's true," replied Flavor.

Tracy was already in a relationship and wasn't with playing the field, but she did enjoy the brother in front of her conversation. He seemed very easy to talk to, and wasn't too bad on the eyes, she thought; with his wavy hair, deep dimples and athletic build.

"When I was young," continued Flavor, "my little brother and I had to fend for ourselves. Because my moms was never around and I never knew my pops. Yo, we was fucked up, excuse my language. But we lived in a two bedroom rat infested apartment with no heat and sometimes no water. I raised my little brother the best I could. I made sure he went to school and everything. The little nigga is taking his bar exam to be a lawyer now," smiled a proud Flavor.

"That's great," smiled back Tracy.

"But it all came with a price. To make sure he was good, I had to drop out of school to get a job. And then my moms got trapped off by the Feds just for fucking with a drug dealer. I didn't even know that shit was a crime. So, she's locked up for being his girl and spending the money he'd give her. I could've just said fuck her for dissing me and my little brother, but I couldn't be like her. I love her regardless, and come to check her to show her what love is really about. I think she's beginning to understand."

"You're a hell of a guy," said Tracy admiring his strength and out-look on things. She wished she possessed that same strength.

"So, what made you become a stripper?" she asked.

"I said dancer," laughed Flavor causing her to laugh as well.

"Nah," he continued, "jobs are hard for a black man to find. So instead of throwing a brick or selling one risking the chance of going to jail, I'd rather shake and pull what my momma gave me."

"You're funny," laughed Tracy. "So, are you from out here in Connecticut?"

"Nah, I'm from New York. The Boogie Down Bronx."

"Okay," said Tracy thinking. "I just got my boyfriend a job. Maybe I can help you. Would you be interested in doing construction? I have a few connects to get you hired and in the union."

"Word?!" asked Flavor excitedly. "Hell yeah, I'm down for that. Here I am about to ask you if you wanna become a stripper because you have the look, and I'm the one getting a job offer. That's crazy!"

When he said stripper in reference to Tracy, she tilted her head back and gave a very displeasing look.

"Please don't take that as any form of disrespect," said Flavor noticing the look she gave him. "I'm simply saying you are very beautiful. That's all. One day, can I take you out to dinner to get to know you better?"

"Tempting," smiled Tracy, "but I'm okay. As I stated earlier, I have a man that I'm very much in love with and can't see myself having dinner with another man. But you can give me your number so I can have someone call you about the job. Because taking off your clothes for a living is not good. You can catch a cold....or something else you may not want."

Flavor laughed and without even going into his pocket, he extended his business card with his name and number on it.

Tracy took it and put it in her purse.

"Are you ready child?" asked her grandmother walking up behind her.

"Take care," said Flavor walking away and getting inside of a blue Honda Civic.

"Yes I'm ready," answered Tracy opening the passenger's door for her grandmother. She then walked around to the driver's side, got in and started the car.

She noticed her grandmother staring at her with a smile.

"What?" she asked.

"Child," said her grandmother, "I saw that look in that young man's eyes when you two were talking. But that's nothing," she waved her hand through the air dismissing it. "When I was your age child, I had men open like a twenty four hour grocery store. On my worse day."

Tracy laughed pulling away from the Federal women's prison while making small talk with her grandmother. She was really beginning to warm up to the old woman.

After dropping her grandmother off at the airport and promising to give her a call, Tracy headed home. She thought about what the guy Flavor had said in reference to his mother and that made her think about her own biological mother. She wondered if she had what it took to one day be able to love, forgive, and most of all, accept her mother. She didn't know the answer, but did agree with her grandmother, it would definitely take time.

She pulled out her cell phone and dialed Barkim's number hoping she would be able to reach him. After the phone rung twice, he answered.

"What's up baby? How was the visit?" asked Barkim.

"Tiring," sighed Tracy. "I'll tell you all about it when I see you. Where are you?"

"Just driving around with Drama. Why, what's up?"

"I have a surprise for you," smiled Tracy. "So, drop Drama off somewhere and meet me at the house. Baby, I want you to lick me nice and—"

"Drama is about to get drpped off at the corner right here," he interrupted making her laugh. "I'll be there in a few."

"Okay baby," she said snapping her cell phone closed.

"It may not be a bad day after all," she smiled to herself as she hurried home.

Chapter Twenty Six

"Oh yes, yessss! That's my spot right there," moaned Monique lying on her back with her thick lightskinned thighs spread apart. She had never gotten her pussy eateded this good in her life. With her eyes glazed over and her mouth slightly parted, she had her hands on the back of his head pulling his face into her.

"Ahhh yes," she moaned with her back arched as she began to climax. "Oh, oh, ohhh shit! Yes, yes, uh, uh, ohhhhh!" she yelled out as she came.

Drama kissed his way up to her breast licking and kissing her nipples as his dick became rock hard again. He threw her legs over his broad shoulders and entered her slowly.

"Damn," he sighed. "You're so wet and tight."

"Yes," moaned Monique gyrating her hips meeting him thrust for thrust. "Give it all to me baby."

She needed not instruct Drama. For he vowed if he ever gotten the chance to make love to Monique, he would put it on her so good she would name her first child after him even if he wasn't the father. He was glad to have not listened to Barkim when he warned him not to get involved with Monique. Because of her cop boyfriend. An asshole cop at that. But he didn't care anything about that. He would've made his move at G-Banks's funeral had not Barkim seeing what was about to transpire warned him to chill out.

"Chill the fuck out!" whispered Barkim in his ear. "Now is not the time for that shit. You see her cop boyfriend right there, right? Don't disrespect Mr. Banks's funeral by causing a scene. And stop thinking with your dick for once."

The words from his friend were enough to make him chill for the remainder of the funeral. So he really thought that he missed his opportunity to get close to the beautiful Monique, but luck had it that when he called her house today to see was Barkim over there, it was she that answered the phone. She said she was the only one home and they began flirting from there.

"So, you're there all by yourself, huh?" asked Drama.

"Yep! Just little ole' me," giggled Monique. "And I always get bored when I am all alone."

"You don't have to be alone," he said while standing at a pay-phone. He didn't know how he forgot his cell phone and left it in the house. Normally that was something he always remembered to take out the house with him. He knew of too many thugs who'd gotten killed at a payphone so he constantly looked around making sure no one crept up on him as he talked.

"I know I don't have to be alone," smiled Monique knowing he liked her. She liked him as well but wasn't ready for anything deep with him. She was also tired of being in a relationship with Joe. She wanted to just do her and enjoy life without being attach to any man. She began to feel this way after her father's death. She liked Drama's thug persona and just wanted to have a little fun with him.

"I'm saying ma," said Drama trying to make his move. "I'm not doing anything at the moment either. I'm suppose to go to club Perfections in Queens tonight but I'm good now. Maybe I can swing by your place and keep you company for a little while."

"That would be nice. Guess what I have on," teased Monique enjoying every minute of playing with Drama's head.

"What?" he breathed hoarsely.

"A pink teddy...black high heels...and strawberry flavored lip gloss."

There was silence on the other end of the phone.

"Hello?...hello?" asked Monique. She then laughed after realizing that the fool dropped the phone and was already on his way to her house.

"I hope the poor boy doesn't get into an accident," she laughed hanging up the phone.

Within 45 minutes, Drama was ringing the doorbell with his beat up car parked out front. She looked out of the window and laughed before opening the door for him to enter. As soon as he stepped into the house, he knew Monique was playing games with him because she wore nothing she described over the phone. There were no teddi, black high heels or lip gloss. She wore a pair of tight blue jeans that showed off her curves, a light blue tee shirt with a picture of the late singer Left Eye on it, and a white pair of ankle socks. But she still looked sexy. Drama could have cared less if she wore a snokel coat with reebok pumps as he stared into her pretty green eyes.

"Drama I was only playing with you," laughed Monique. "You know I have a boyfriend."

"Fuck him," smirked Drama coming closer towards her. "I came all the way out here to Long Island. At least you can give a nigga a hug."

She smiled, figuring what can a hug hurt as she allowed her arms to circle his body. She felt every bulging muscle in his back and felt very comfortable and safe in his huge arms.

Drama rubbed her soft back with his strong hands and enjoyed the feel of her soft hair against the side of his neck as she tilted her head to the side. He then lowered his head and his lips met hers. They were caught up in the moment and their tongues playfully danced together as their hands began to move freely getting to know one another's bodies.

His tongue explored the sweet insides of her mouth as she began to get wet between her legs. At this moment, she wanted him so badly and allowed herself to give into his touches. She couldn't even remember leading him to her bedroom. They undressed and when she removed his Roc-A-Wear boxers, she was greeted by a hard on that looked as if nothing could make it go away.

Monique let her freaky side come out. She gently grabbed his manhood, stroked it and kissed it all over. She then grabbed his balls and let her tongue dance over the hairy sac. Drama leaned his head back and moaned loudly as she loved his inflamed genitals with her lips and tongue. She enjoyed the musky smell of his man balls and the humid taste of his love muscle; taking it between her lips and sucking fervently, dabbing the pee hole with the tip of her tongue.

Drama's passion contorted face told her how much he was enjoying what she was doing to him. He then pulled out of her mouth and motioned for her to stand up. When she did, he slowly led her to the bed and kissed every part of her body. He rained damp kisses all over her breast before sucking one nipple and then the other. His tongue had then explored her rib cage and her belly button.

"Ahhh," moaned Monique softly.

By the time Drama placed his face between her legs, her body was overwhelmed with passion. The instant his tongue touched her clitoris, she was shrieking with pleasure. When his mouth licked and sucked her womanhood, she moaned, groaned and thrashed around on the bed like an animal in heat. Monique could not take it anymore.

"Fuck me," she breathlessly pleaded. "Please, fuck me Drama."

He positioned his well defined body above hers and slowly entered her.

"Damn baby," he moaned, "you're nice and tight. You like that?" he asked grinding into her.

"Yes," moaned Monique. "I like that. Give it all to me."

Giving it to her he did. They made love until they were both satisfied and spent.

Drama then looked over at Monique and breathlessly said, "Baby, I think I'm in love."

"Drama, don't fall in love with me," she said seriously. "It was only sex. Good sex I may add, but let's not talk of that love word. We both know that I'm presently involved with Joe, and this sex that you and I just had wasn't suppose to happen."

"Are you happy with the cop?"

Monique smiled and thought for a moment before speaking.

"Most of the time," she answered. "Joe is a good guy. He just acts like an ass on occasion but what man doesn't? Anyway, I don't want to talk about him right now," she smiled running her freshly done nails across Drama's chest. "You're here now, and that's all that matters. So, let's just have some fun with no strings attached. Is that okay with you?"

"Aiight, aiight," answered Drama surprised that he had been shot down even though nicely. He was really trying to lock Monique down and thought he had done so after the encore sexual performance. Any other girl he had put it on like that would get so open it was almost certain they would want more of him all to themselves. But not Monique. Her statement hit him harder than a slug of whiskey and hurt his ego more than he cared to admit. He wanted all of her to hisself and trying to get her hooked seemed to only have him more open for her. He knew she was wifey material but he would have to deal with her on her terms, for now.

"You wanna go out tonight?" he asked propping himself up on one elbow.

"Where to?" she asked looking into his eyes.

"I had plans to go to Perfections tonight. Have you ever been there?" he asked.

"No, I'm not the club type. But you mentioned earlier that it was in Queens. So, at least it's not a far travel."

"No, it's not far at all. Do you want to go with me?"

"Well, tonight I'm not doing anything so I don't mind. How are we getting there?"

"I'm driving," he answered.

"Boy," laughed Monique, "you couldn't take me to a frankfurter stand in that thing you call a car."

It seemed she couldn't stop laughing at his beat up car.

"Okay, okay, enough about my car. You got your shit off. You don't have to keep getting rec on my car."

"I'm sorry," she smiled. "We can take my car and you can drive, okay?"

"Word?!" asked Drama excitedly anxious to get inside of the expensive car and behind the wheel.

Later that night, Drama and Monique arrived in Queens at club Perfections and parked the car. When those who knew Drama saw him getting out of the blue Vanquish Aston Martin with the green eyed dime piece on his arm, their mouths dropped open.

Walking to the entrance of the club, people spoke to Drama with respect and admiration as most wondered who the cutie was holding onto his arm. They pegged her to be a celebrity or something but had no idea who.

"Hi Drama," a few girls called out.

"What up Drama?" said a few guys standing out front.

"I see you have a fan club," smiled Monique.

"Nah it ain't like that," he smiled back.

"I'm kind of hungry," said Monique. "Let's go to a restaurant when we leave here. We're not staying here long, are we?"

"Nah we're not staying long. The party tonight is for my boy Rondu from Brownsville. His coming home party. I just wanna show my face. Then we can hit the restaurant and anywhere else you want to go," he smiled.

He was excited as he showed Monique and the car off tonight. It definitely made him want to step his game up a thousand notches. He also thought of how to make Monique his because she was by far the best looking woman he had ever been with; and possessed what most women her age didn't possess these days. CLASS!!!

Chapter Twenty Seven

Monica exited from her car and wondered why she allowed herself to come back to the hospital after catching Bryan talking to that nurse months back. But Bryan practically begged her to come. She was still a bit upset and would not have come but it was something very important that she had to talk to him about. Even though she was upset with him, they still were having sex. Days after they last had sex, Monica began to feel queasy and nauseous and when her period did not come, she knew what time it was. She took the at home pregnacy test to be sure, and as sure as Sunday comes before Monday, the results of her test came back positive. She didn't know whether to be happy or disappointed. Because although she loved children, she was not sure if she was ready for motherhood and didn't know the first thing about raising a child.

She entered the hospital and got on the elevator that just so happen to open when she reached for the button. After pressing her floor, she looked down at her perfect figure before shaking her head.

"Pretty soon I will have more chins than a chinese telephone book," she laughed at her own joke as the elevator went up to her floor.

She stepped out of the elevator and the first person she saw was a handsome Jamaican brother with long dreads coming down his back. He was brownskinned, muscular and showed his pearly white teeth when he smiled. She then looked down at his crotch area and had to do a double take. Why did men that she find attractive only popped up when she was already involved with someone, she thought.The timing was all wrong and despite still being angry with Bryan, she was still very much in love with him and wouldn't let no one come between what she and her man shared.

"Hey gal," the dread called out to her.

Monica walked by him very quickly on legs that suddenly felt as if she were walking on rubberbands. She could not explain the attraction she had for the handsome dread but she did know she had to get as far away from him as possible. Trying to completely ignore him, she approached the nurse's station and the heavy set nurse sitting behind the desk recognized her immediately.

"Hello Ms. Banks," smiled the nurse. "Doctor McCray's been waiting on your arrival. This way please," she smiled while getting up from her chair and leading the way to an office down the hall.

When they got in front of the wooden door the nurse rapped her knuckles on the door in some kind of code and smiled at Monica again before walking away. The door opened and Bryan invited Monica in after giving her a kiss.

When she entered, she noticed the candle lit office and the huge blanket on the floor in the spacious office. On the blanket sat seafood, wine and fruits among other treats. The Isley brothers's song "Between the sheets" played softly from a small portable radio sitting on the desk. The office curtains were drawn giving the room a romantic feel to it.

"I'm very happy you've come," smiled Bryan after locking the door. He assisted her taking off her coat and then motioned for her to sit down on the blanket on the floor. She could smell the Echo Davidoff cologne he wore as she sat on the blanket and removed her Crocodile d'Orsay pumps. She got comfortable folding her small feet under her legs.

"Honey," said Bryan sitting down next to her and taking her hand into his, "I love you and I know you're still upset with me. But again, I apologize for my foolishness. It will never happen again. That I promise you. You are my life, and you mean the world to me. And the reason I've asked you to come here today," he said taking a small black velvet box from his white doctor's jacket, "is to ask you, will you marry me?"

Monica held her hands to her lips and nodded yes as the tears fell from her eyes. She let Bryan slip the ring on her finger and kiss her passionately. She loved this man and hoped he would forever be in her life.

"Now let's eat," he smiled.

"No wait," she said causing him to sit his glass of wine down and look into her eyes, "I have something very important to tell you."

"Baby I'm pregnant," she blurted out.

"We're having a baby?!" he asked so excited that he almost knocked the food and bottle of wine over.

"Yes," laughed Monica.

"Baby, thank you, thank you, thank you," he said kissing her face all over making her laugh and squirm in his arms.

She enjoyed the attention he gave and loved the time spent with her man.

After their romantic brunch, Bryan went back to work as Monica prepared to leave the hospital with the biggest smile on her face. She walked down the long corridor and was about to turn the corner when she heard a woman's voice call out to her from behind.

"Excuse me miss, can I please have a word with you?"

Monica turned around and saw a petite nurse hurrying towards her. As the nurse got closer, she realized it was the same nurse that Bryan was talking to months earlier.

"Now what in the hell do she have to say to me?" Monica said under her breath as the nurse approached her apologetically.

"I'm really sorry for stopping you like this," said the nurse, "but I want you to know that there is absolutely nothing going on between Dr. McCray and I. I respect myself enough not to get involved with another woman's man. We black women have to start looking out for one another. You know what I'm saying?"

"Yes I do," smiled Monica in such a good mood that she decided to hear the woman out. Normally, she would've dismissed the nurse with the wave of the hand and kept going about her business but after the romantic brunch with Bryan, she was feeling extremely good not letting anything sour her mood.

"Gurl," continued the nurse with a smirk, "Dr. McCray doesn't want me or any other person in this hospital. He's just a flirt. But I've noticed he stopped ever since that last incident. I can tell he really loves you. And I would never disrespect anyone's relationship. I don't care how fine he is. My momma didn't raise no fool, chile."

Monica noticed the country accent in the woman's voice.

"Are you from the south?" she asked.

"Yes," answered the nurse. "I'm from Tennesse. I came up here about seven months ago. I was doing nursing back home as well."

"Oh my God!" she squealed after spotting the engagement ring on Monica's finger. "That ring is soooooo beautiful!"

"You like?" smiled Monica holding it up so she can get a better view of it. "He just proposed to me."

"Wow! That is wonderful. Gurl, I am really happy for you and Dr. McCray."

She looked in the nurse's eyes and could see the sincerity in her words and that made her smile even wider.

"Thank you," she said. Then looking at her watch she said, "Well, it was a pleasure talking to you but I really have to run. Maybe we'll talk again sometime."

"I understand," said the nurse. "I would like that. You take care."

"You too," said Monica walking away and pressing the button for the elevator.

She couldn't wait to get home and tell her sisters the good news that they were going to be aunties as well as now being engaged to

Bryan. Just thinking about it, she could see their smiling faces and the thought made her smile. But then she got a little sad because the one person she wanted to share her good news with was now deceased. Tears began to well up in her eyes and with the back of her hand she wiped them away before they can fall. Things had truly been hard emotionally for she and her sisters since the death of G-Banks. She thought about what he would say had he still been alive and given the news that he was going to be a grandfather. She could hear his voice now.

"'Look here, if it's a boy I want my little man with me at all times. But if it's a girl, keep her with you. I've had enough of raising girls,'" she pictured him saying with a smile.

Monica laughed outloud to herself as the elevator door opened. She stepped inside of the elevator and along with two old white women and a black nurse stood the handsome Jamaican brother she saw when she first entered the hospital. Their eyes met and Monica smiled politely to return his, but strangely enough she now felt nothing for the man as the elevator door closed and descended down to the hospital's lobby.

G Banks   Miz

Chapter Twenty Eight

"A yo Gee," laughed Barkim as the five guys standing around also laughed, "you're a funny motherfucker!"

They were standing near the corner of Lafayette and Marcy Avenue across the street from Tompkins Park. Children ran up and down the Brooklyn blocks as guys and girls walked the avenue. It was winter time but the weather was nice so a lot of people were out as if it were spring.

"So, what happened when the bitch saw you and your man together?" asked Barkim.

"The bitch looked puzzled," answered Barkim's little brother Gee. "She didn't know I knew son. I don't give a fuck. We could both fuck the bitch. I ain't never beef with a nigga over a stinking ass bitch."

"There go your homeboy," said Drama to Barkim changing the subject as he nodded his head in the direction across the street at a guy named Paul who was pushing himself in a wheelchair.

At one time, Barkim and Paul had been the best of friends. That is until Barkim went to prison and Paul wasted no time getting at his then girlfriend, Lena. He lied and did everything possible to betray his friend telling Lena that Barkim was only using her and had other girlfriends she knew nothing about. He convinced her that he even told Barkim not to do her like that but he did it anyway. Being young and naïve, Lena fell for the bait hook, line and sinker. Barkim was really hurt being betrayed by two people that he really thought were in his corner. When he told Drama about it over the phone, his friend really felt his pain. So one cold winter night, Drama and Boo took it upon themselves to settle the score with Paul. As Barkim sat in his jail cell, Paul was coming out of the corner grocery store when two figures in black wearing baseball caps pulled over their eyes ran up on him opening fire leaving Paul paralyzed from the waist down. For some reason, he knew Barkim had something to do with him being shot and he hated him for it. When Barkim received word of what happened to Paul, strangely he didn't feel no enjoyment of what happened to someone who betrayed him. Instead he felt nothing.

"That ain't my boy," said Barkim in reference to Paul as they watched him push himself in the wheelchair. "I wonder if he still gets pussy."

"That nigga wasn't getting too much pussy anyway before Coach Drama sat his punk ass on the bench for life," laughed Drama. "That's why he pressed that bitch you had in the first place. Faggot ass nigga. I should go and tip that nigga chair over," he said as everyone laughed knowing that he would do it.

Paul looked at Barkim and his friends with his face screwed up as he pushed the wheels on his chair. He wished all kinds of illnesses on the boys across the street laughing at him.

Five minutes later, an unmarked police car pulled up to the curb in front of where they were standing. Being that none of them were dirty with drugs and guns, no one ran.

Joe and his white partner exited from the police car and slowly approached the small group. Barkim hated the coincidence of Joe working in the same area where he happened to live. He also wondered what the two detectives wanted to talk to him about now. He hoped it wasn't about Mike and Tone again, because he knew nothing and even if he did he would never say anything to a police about it.

"What's up Bar?" asked Joe as if they were hanging buddies.

The three guys hanging with Barkim, Drama and Gee looked at him as if to question why the detective addressed him by his street name. Joe knew the code of the streets and knew speaking to Barkim in public addressing him by his street name would make him look as if he were a snitch. He did not like Barkim and did not hide that fact, so he didn't care what came of it.

"What's going on Joe?" asked Barkim unaffected by the cop's silly game. "What brings you and your partner around?"

"Well," began Joe to Barkim but standing in front of Drama looking in his face, "I was just in the area and felt the need to pull over and warn this clown here that it's a very poor health hazard to speak to my woman. Because believe me, I can become his worse mother-fucking nightmare, if you know what I mean."

Drama didn't say anything. He just stood his ground and looked directly back into Joe's eyes. If he weren't a cop things could have gotten very ugly. Because he didn't back down from anyone.

"Why are you approaching us with this shit?" asked Barkim in Drama's defense. He just hoped his friend remained quiet and let him handle it.

"Because I know what time it is," answered Joe still looking in Drama's face trying to intimidate him and get a reaction so he could lock him up and do him dirty while having him in custody. "I saw how this sucker was looking at my lady at Mr. Banks's funeral. Plus, I saw his beat up ass car parked in front of her house."

"You know he takes me to see Tracy," explained Barkim. "Yo, that's all it's about."

"For his sake," said Joe backing away, "I really hope so."

"Joe," smiled his white partner digging in his pants pocket and playing with the small brown paperbag full of crack vials that they had took earlier from a twelve year old wanna- be drug dealer, "I say we search these guys and see what we can find. You never know, we may even find some cracks."

Joe smiled knowing what his partner had in mind but had to de-cline the offer. He knew the Banks family would have a fit if they found out he had set Barkim or any of his friends up to go to prison.

"No let's get outta here," he said walking back to the car with his white partner following behind.

Once he got back in the car, he looked out of his window at Dra-ma and said, "Don't forget what I said. Take my warning very serious-ly, Drama."

The car then pulled away and rode off down Lafayette Avenue.

"Damn man!" cursed Barkim angrily at Drama. "I told you don't fuck with shorty! But you don't listen! Now we gotta worry about that lame ass cop breathing all over us. First my parole officer, and now this nigga."

"Don't sweat it playboy," smiled Drama as if it was nothing. "You and Tracy is about to move in together in a new house somewhere so that takes care of the parole officer. And just relax, I'll deal with punk ass Joe the cop."

"Anyway," he continued looking at his watch, "I gotta bounce and hit these little niggas off with some work that I got pumping on New Lots Avenue. What I really need is some good dope. Somebody who can hit me consistently with good shit. Until then I have to do what I have to do. These little niggas should be finished cause I hit them off last night."

Barkim shook his head from side to side and bit his tongue of what he really wanted to say. Instead he asked, "You're still moving bullshit ounces nigga? When I went upnorth you were still moving the same shit. And that was mad years ago. Don't you get it? If you're not rich by now it's not going to happen."

Drama thought about what his friend had just said and knew he was right. He'd been selling small amounts of crack since the mid-nineties and still moving the same amount of drugs in the year 2011. He wasn't with working a bullshit minimum wage job but knew Barkim was right. He was risking his life of going to jail or getting killed for nothing. Plus, after that night of showing out with Monique and her expensive car, he stayed away from club Perfections and any other club. He knew he couldn't go back in bullshit after showing out big. Monique bought so many bottles of Moet Rose, he started handing a few out to people he knew. He looked at his beat up car parked near the curb and knew he would either have to step up his game or leave the game alone altogether.

"You're a bad muh'fucker Drama," smiled Gee as the other three guys nodded their heads in agreement. "This nigga's about to get arrested for stealing a nigga's bitch! A cop's bitch at that."

Everyone laughed except Barkim because he knew the situation was very serious and could easily get out of hand. He partially felt responsible because it was he that took Drama out to Long Island to the Banks residence. Drama was his best friend and he just didn't want anything to happen to him. But what could he do now?, he thought as he looked at a laughing Drama as if he didn't have a care in the world.

"Man y'all niggas is crazy," laughed Drama. He then gave them all a pound before walking to his car.

"I'll be back," he said over his shoulder. "I gotta go and collect that rent money."

He then jumped in his beat up car and made his way down Lafayette Avenue. As he made a right turn on Tompkins Avenue he thought about what Barkim said and knew it was time for him to take his game to the next level. But how?

Chapter Twenty Nine

"What's up baby?" said Drama into the phone as he sat on his bed. "I really need to talk to you about something very important. It can be profitable to you as well."

"Talk to me baby," said Monique on the other end of the phone. "What's going on?"

Drama had been up all morning thinking. He was tired of the way his life was going. His money wasn't right, his living conditions sucked and he hated the car he was pushing. It was definitely time for a change. He didn't know if Monique could help him or not but it didn't hurt to see. Even if she lended him a few thousand dollars he would be cool with that. As they say, a frank beats a blank.

"It's a lot going on," said Drama, "but I need to talk to you in person. Can I come see you?"

"Actually, I am not home but I can come and see you. Give me the address and I can be to you in like the next hour and a half."

"That's cool," said Drama. "We really need to talk."

He gave her the address, hung up the phone and hoped all worked out well. As soon as he stood up from the bed and put on his Polo goose, his ten year old twin little brothers bombarded their way into his room with a thousand questions.

"Can we hang out with you today?" asked Ronald.

"Can you buy me a pair of sneakers?" asked Donald.

They just kept asking questions before Drama could even answer one. He looked at the two and smiled. He loved them boys and wished he could do more for them.

"I would let y'all hang with me today," he said, "but I have so much to do. Here, take this," he said pulling money out of his pocket and giving them fifty dollars each. "When I get right I'll take y'all shopping."

"Thanks," said the boys in unison with big smiles on their faces. They took the money and were out of his room just as fast as they entered.

Drama laughed, grabbed his keys off of the dresser and headed out of the room. Once outside, he saw his workers sitting on the benches in the Vandyke projects in the Brownsville section of Brooklyn.

"Yo, yo, yo," said Drama walking up to the five young boys. "What's good?"

"Ain't shit," said the chubby youth who appeared to be the leader of the pack as the rest also greeted Drama.

"Y'all finish with the work y'all had?" asked Drama.

"That shit been done," said a slim lightskin youth handing over seven hundred dollars.

Drama put the money in his pocket without counting it. He was tired of the small change he was making. Something had to give and give quick. He sat on the bench and talked with them for at least an hour while they smoked their morning blunts. He didn't smoke and only drink occasionally. He always wanted to be more on point and alert than the rest of the drug dealers and thugs in the streets.

"Oh shit," said a brownskin youth inhaling the blunt and looking at a message on his phone. "My man just text me and said he got that purple on deck."

Drama shook his head. He didn't understand how drug dealers were putting messages through their phones like that. These weren't throw away phones either. He knew the police can very easily pull up phone records and messages. He even saw guys in crowded shopping areas advertising the drugs they were selling! That really blew his mind. Because anyone can be a detective. These guys were begging to go the the penitentiary, he thought.

His phone began ringing and looking at the caller id he saw it was Monique. Just the call he been waiting for.

"Hey sexy," he smiled into the phone. "Where are you?"

"I'm where you said to meet you," she answered.

"Okay I'll be there in a second," he said hanging up his phone and standing from the benches.

"Come on y'all," he said to the group of young boys, "walk with me over here."

They walked out of the projects and when they got to Lavonia Avenue, Drama saw Monique sitting in a black Range Rover parked under the train trussel.

The boys posted up on the sidewalk as Drama walked up to the truck. He opened the door for her to get out and when she did, the young boys couldn't take their eyes off of the cutie that looked like she stepped out of a magazine.

"What's going on baby?" she asked after kissing him.

"Let me get straight to the point," said Drama. "I don't like asking people for nothing but shit is twisted for a nigga right now."

As he talked, Monique's eyes were on the five young boys. Drama took it that maybe she were a little frightened and thought he should had left them in the projects, but Monique's mind was somewhere else with it.

"Anyway," continued Drama, "I was hoping you can help me out with a few thousand to get on my feet and I can give it back to you with something extra."

"I have a better idea," said Monique looking into his eyes. "Why don't you make me a silent partner in your little empire and that will give you the opportunity to be as big as you want to be in this game? Let me make a few calls and maybe I can get you whatever you want and need. And remember, I said silent partner. That doesn't mean I have no say so; it means you keep quiet and my name never comes up to anyone."

Drama laughed. She didn't.

"Let me find out you know about the streets a lil' something," he smiled. "Yo, I wish I had a good dope connect and we would really be good. But shit niggas is selling is weak and when you get something good it's not consistent."

"First let me say I know a lot about the streets," said Monique, "because I had a good teacher and also I'm originally from Chicago. I'm no dummy. Don't worry about product, I said I would handle it."

"Okay," said Drama not really believing too much of what she was saying. He couldn't picture her knowing anything about the streets. Yes, he knew her father was very strong with politicians and the like because he saw the powerful at the funeral, but the streets were different, or so he thought.

"What's up with those guys?" she asked looking at the five young boys.

"Oh," answered Drama. "They're cool. They're workers and shooters. I try to get them a little money so they won't be out here killing each other for pennies."

"Those two are your shooters right there," she said pointing at the chubby one and a very darkskin one.

"I see weakness in the other three," she said matter of factly.

Drama looked and knew she was right. Because everyone knew the three she spoke of lived off of the strength of the two she picked out. But how did she know that?, he thought.

"Oh you're talking about Lunch and Slave," said Drama. "They get busy."

"I take it they're called Lunch and Slave," she said, "because Lunch is chubby and Slave's complexion is so dark."

"You're half right," he laughed. "We call him Lunch because he's always ready to eat. And we call the other one Slave because when he was little, everytime you saw him he was always going to the store for someone."

Monique laughed.

"Okay," she said. "I will call you within twenty four hours and we'll take it from there."

"Cool," said Drama. "At least let me take you to get something to eat."

"Come on," she said.

After opening the truck's door for her, he walked around to the passenger's side.

"Yo," he said to the young boys, "I'll be back to hit y'all off. I'm going to get something to eat."

"Yo, can I come?" asked Lunch.

"Tell him yes," laughed Monique. "And tell Slave to come also."

Drama invited the two and told the rest that he'll be back. They got in the Range Rover and headed to Olive Gardens.

Chapter Thirty

"My baby just made it happen real big!" smiled Monique.

"Which one of your babies?" laughed Monica.

"Both of them," she bragged as Tracy shook her head from side to side as if to say her sister was crazy.

"Remember the mayor gave us his personal phone number and said to call anytime?" asked Monique but finishing her statement before they could respond. "Well, I gave him a call and took him up on his offer."

"What offer?" asked Tracy and Monica in unison wondering what she were up to.

"The offer he made to us at daddy's funeral," she answered. "That if he can help us with anything for us to not hesitate to reach out to him."

"What did you reach out for?" asked Tracy sternly.

"Let's just say," smiled Monique, "that I've convinced him that someone in a high position in the police department has been doing a very lousy job and things can be much better if he allowed the right person to take over."

"Soooo," she dragged out the word, "a few things had been set up and arranged and all went according to plan, so my Joe will soon be New York City's first black police commissioner!" she smiled. "Boy! A lot of strings had to be pulled for that favor there."

Her two sisters stared at her open mouthed not believing what she had just said or pulled off. They knew then Monique had completely lost her mind.

"And what else did you do?" asked Tracy after getting over the initial shock.

"Now the good part," smiled Monique while sitting back in her chair and putting her feet up on the table. "Drama and I, my other baby I may add, had a little meeting of the minds a few weeks ago. And let's just say, he's going to be a bigger drug dealer than any of these guys that thinks they're balling," she laughed before continuing. "Daddy had a lot of connects in his private phone book and I'm talking some illegal ones as well. You'll be very surprised by the many important people who know us as his daughters and is more than willing to assist us in whatever endeavors we choose to partake in. Anyway, the phone call and the meeting worked out well, so I gave Drama enough money to do his thing on a major level. And you just have to meet his two gunners. They're not smart as us, but they get busy and are so cool. Especially Slave. That boy will do anything for me. They killed some big guys in the streets and got Drama's name ringing bells in every borough."

"Are you crazy?!" asked Tracy not believing what her sister had done.

Monica simply laughed but agreed that her twin was indeed crazy as hell.

"So, now you're in the drug business?!" continued Tracy angrily. "And he's going to be giving you drug money in return of what you gave him?"

"No silly," smiled Monique. "I don't want any money back. He can keep whatever he makes. It's not money I want. It's power! With Joe in charge of NYPD, and Drama being the richest drug dealer in the streets only means one thing; Monique runs this city!!!"

"Girl you done bumped your head," said Tracy shaking her head still not believing her sister could be so crazy and dangerous.

Monica laughed so hard she damn near fell out of her chair.

"You don't give a damn about Joe or Drama, do you?" asked Tracy clearly upset at her sister's action.

Monique thought seriously and hard for a moment about the question and then with a sincere look on her pretty face replied, "Not really. I mean, I love them to a certain degree Tray, but they're expendable."

"Oh snap," laughed Monica. "The girl's mind done got trapped in the art of war books daddy always had us reading."

Tracy did not find any of it funny. She couldn't believe her sister's words and actions. She knew her sister loved the limelight but never did she think to this magnitude.

"Forreal," said Monique seriously. "It's only one man I love with all my heart and that's daddy. No man can ever replace him," she said as the room had suddenly gotten a sad feel to it.

"Of course no one can ever replace daddy," said Tracy after the silence on Monique's statement. "But it's not about replacing daddy. That can never happen. You doing what you're doing have nothing to do with daddy."

"Tray," sighed Monique not digging the fact that her sister was making a big fuss over things, "all I'm saying is the only ones I love in this world with all my heart equal to myself is daddy, you, Monnie and that baby she have in her stomach. I'm saying, if the two of you love Barkim and Bryan with all your heart then I applaud you," she said lightly clapping her hands together before continuing. "But I haven't met a man besides daddy that moves my heart in such a way. And on another note, I love to fuck; really I do but any nigga will learn that there's no locking me down through the dick."

"She's gangster!" laughed Monica damn near falling out of her chair again.

"Maybe it's daddy's fault," continued Monique not paying her twin any mind. "I mean, the way he use to treat us and the things he said and did makes it hard for any man to measure up to what being a real man is suppose to be."

Tracy reached across the table and comforted her sister by holding her hands. She knew Monique was still hurting while mourning the
death of their father. She just could not deal with it.

"Let me just do me," said Monique pulling her hands back. "I
have everything under control."

"Do you, Moe?" asked Tracy.

"Yes Tray I got this," she answered hoping this was the end of
the conversation about how she was dealing with her father's death.

There were times when she would sit in her room for hours thinking about her father and coming up with different tactics on her next
move. It was one of the many things she had learned from him. He
told her to always plan five steps ahead and if she put herself in the
ememy's shoes, she would come up with the best method of attack.
He also taught her how to wage war indirectly instead of always doing
it openly. He said, the many art of war revolutionary books only
showed how to think but it was she who would still have to do the ac-
tual planning in situations. He stressed that war was based on decep-
tion and surprise and ordinary and innocent people should totally be
off limits when possible. But it was not just the training of doing hits
that stood out in her mind when thinking about her father. She remembered the love, the caring, the advice, the support in whatever
the girls wanted to do in life, the time he spent with them, the fun, the
punishments, the conversations and the many other things that made
them who they were. He taught them how to cook, drive and most of
all to think for themselves. He did not raise followers and one of his
favorite sayings was, 'if you wanted to be mind controlled then you
should join the military or any local street gang but that kind of thinking wasn't what he could give them'.

"So, what are we going to do about the last two hits daddy was
suppose to do?" asked Monique out of the blue.

"Daddy is gone," answered Tracy. "So, we don't have to do it.
He's no longer here and it's not like the people who paid him expects
us to do it."

"But what about daddy's name?" argued Monique not wanting to hear the change of heart speeches Tracy had come to recite over the past few months. "We have to represent that."

"No," said Tracy. "Daddy represented his name well enough when he was here. It's over, Moe."

"You don't understand," sighed Monique loudly. "Everybody he did business with should get what they paid for. And it's only two more hits daddy was suppose to do. We can take care of that, Tray."

"You know what?" replied Tracy squinting her already chinky eyes into two mean slits. "You're only thinking about yourself, Moe. This isn't even about daddy. You just want to use his connects and get caught up in this hit woman/Moe runs the city fantasy. Moe, I have never abandoned you and I never will. But after we take care of this last hit, it's over for us. No more hit women bullshit for us! You hear me?!" she said loudly with a look on her face letting her sister know that she had better taken her seriously.

"Alright, alright, alright," laughed Monique. "But it's two hits not one."

"Only one," she replied back. "Daddy said he definitely didn't want us to even think about the Henry Mack hit. He wasn't even sure if he wanted to take it. He said it was too dangerous and even thought about sending Mr. King's money back to him."

"But he didn't send it back," argued Monique.

"You're hardheaded," sighed Tracy. "And one day we're going to pay for it."

"Don't worry," smiled Monique, "when or if that day comes I'll pick up the tab. Now let's go pay Mr. Rodriguez a visit," she said standing up from the table.

Tracy sighed and said, "Monnie, stay here. We'll take care of this. If Barkim calls, tell him to call back tonight."

G Banks   Miz

"I'm going!" said Monica standing up.

"Monnie, sit your pregnant ass down!" laughed Monique. "We got this. We'll call you on our way back."

"You better," pouted Monica sitting back down and eating ice-cream from the bowl in front of her. She figured she'd watch a little television before calling Bryan.

Monique and Tracy went up to their rooms to get ready and come up with a plan and go over it, looking at all of the possibilities. They had become so good that it didn't take them no longer than twenty minutes to put something solid together that was most likely to work.

When they were satisfied, they got inside of Tracy's Jaguar and headed towards their destination and target.

"Let me see the picture one more time," requested Tracy as she drove.

Monique pulled a photo from her purse of a fragile Puerto Rican man with short hair and handed it to her sister.

Tracy stopped at a red light and looked at the picture long and hard before driving again. They could not afford to make any kind of mistakes.

They parked the car a block away from the hotel.

"Are you ready?" asked Tracy opeing her door.

"As ready as I'll ever be," smiled Monique as she opened her door and stepped out of the car as well.

Tracy opened the trunk and took a small metal canister from in-side of it. She placed it inside of the big empty handbag she carried and then slammed the trunk back down before walking away quickly to catch up to Monique.

Once they got in front of the big hotel in lower Manhattan, Tracy entered alone and quickly walked over to the elevators. She was happy to see an empty elevator when it came down to the busy lobby area. People carried their luggage in a rush as most tried to register a room. She got on the elevator without looking suspicious and took it to the top floor.

After twenty minutes, she returned back down to the lobby area frantically screaming as she ran to the registration's desk alarming the small white woman behind the desk.

"The building is on fire!" she screamed in a panic. "Oh my God! My one year old baby is upthere! Someone please help me!" she screamed as she theatrically paced in circles with tears coming down her pretty face. Crying was easy; all she had to do was think about the death of her father.

The white woman behind the registration desk quickly went into action. She pulled the fire alarm and picked up the phone on her desk calling the fire department.

People in the lobby had already begun to run in panic when they heard Tracy screaming about the building being on fire and her baby being trapped upstairs on one of the floors.

When another woman ran out of the elevator screaming that the building was indeed on fire all hell broke loose. People ran towards the door screaming and stepping all over each other to escape the blaze that Tracy had set to every carpeted hallway floor in the building.

As she looked around at the panicking crowd, she hoped no innocent people would get hurt because she did not want that on her conscious. Her eyes had then focused on the two federal agents hurrying into the hotel's lobby holding onto a frightened and fragile Mr. Rodriguez. They were being knocked around by the panicking crowd trying to get out of the burning building.

Tracy quickly joined the crowd and was successful in pushing the small man away from the two agents with the help of the crowd.

The two federal agents looked around in a panic for their witness and began pushing people out of their way trying to locate their unprotected witness they needed for an up and coming trial.

Tracy looked around trying to locate Monique. She knew she should have carried a weapon as well just in case things didn't go as planned. Just as she were about to get worried, she looked down into the lifeless eyes of the small Puerto Rican witness being stampeded on by the crowd with a knife protruding from his heart. Monique was maybe in the car already waiting for her, thought Tracy as she pushed her way out of the building's front door.

Chapter Thirty One

"Now this is some bullshit if I ever heard it!" cursed Detective Cornwell. "We have two bodies on our hands that I'm sure we would have eventually solved and what does the lieutenant do? He takes us off of the fucking case and closes our whole investigation when we were getting close. That fucking prick! We didn't even get a chance to track down the three girls our witness told us about. And we didn't get a chance to look into the Mr. Bader case thoroughly as well. I mean come on, Mr. Bader was a white businessman for crying out loud! You would think the department would like to track down his fucking killer!" he said angrily.

"But you know what, Jim?" asked his partner Detective Russo as he drove through a red light. "I have a very strong feeling that there's a lot of corruption involved in these two particular cases. I don't know," he sighed.

"Maybe the mob had a hand in both killings," he continued, "and is now flexing their muscle with the higher-ups in the department to just you know, brush these two cases under the rug. I mean, it doesn't make any sense."

"No, I'll tell you what it is!" stormed Detective Cornwell looking over at his partner. "It's that fucking nigger police commissioner. First a black president and now this nigger. How the fuck did he get that position anyway? One day he's a regular homicide detective, and the next day he's police commissioner? Why the hell did Commisioner Donohue retire for anyway?"

"I have no idea," answered his partner. "But I'll tell you this much. I believe someone very powerful is pulling some strings!"

$$\$\$\$\$\$\$$$

"You know my girl don't want me around you in these streets, right?" laughed Barkim.

"Yeah I heard," smiled Drama standing in front of the new house in Laurelton, Queens that Tracy purchased for she and Barkim.

Parked at the curb was Drama's brand new black Range Rover, and across the street in the cut where you can barely see them were Slave and Lunch; the two young boys that did anything he ordered them to do. That consisted of mainly catching bodies in the streets. They already killed major drug dealers and gangsters. He gave them just enough money for them to be alright but still depend on him. He didn't want either to start feeling themselves or get lazy. This was a tactic he had learned from Monique and he carried it out to perfection with his soldiers. He had definitely come up in the game. Almost everyone in the five boroughs and prisons were talking about him. He was now considered to be one of the heavyweights in the game and whenever someone mentioned whether he had a gangster killed, he would simply smile leaving the accusation in the air for speculation. He drove through the New York City streets in Range Rovers, Mercedes Benzes, BMW's, Lamborghini's and many other expensive vehicles people were in awe of. There were no more shorties selling hand to hand for him on the corners or in the projects anymore. He dealt strictly weight and sold no less than ten kilos of cocaine every week. Everything was going great for him and thanks to Monique, he also got a heads up whenever the police were investigating him either to make a drug bust or if his name came up in another murder. So, he was definitely a step ahead of the game.

"I don't know why your girl don't want you around me," said Drama as he jacked his pants up with two thumbs exposing a new swag to his style.

"Because your ass is caught up in all kinds of shit out here in these streets," answered Barkim. "I hear you got crazy beef. Anyway, that's what Gee told me."

"Nah," smiled Drama. "Niggas don't want no problems with the kid. They might talk shit on the low but they know not to let that shit get back to me. I take all threats seriously. Anyway, you should get with me. I'm pulling in a lot of motherfucking paper and I can use you on my team. No soldier shit, straight partners."

"No I'm good," he declined the offer. "I'm working construction, I'm in the union and me and Tracy is about to open a business. So, I'm good for now, and in a minute I'll really be straight."

"Aiight," said Drama looking at his diamond infested watch. "I have to get out of here but I'll slide back through whenever you give me a call."

"That's cool," said Barkim with his hands in his pockets. "Be careful. I heard Joe is really out to get you. And he knows you're still creeping with Monique. So remember, you may have a team but his is stronger, bigger and more dangerous."

"That's a matter of opinion," smiled Drama.

Barkim looked at him as if he had completely lost his mind. Just thinking about not taking Joe seriously was insane.

"You have to be the dumbest nigga I know," he said. "What you're up against is bigger than Joe. Now let me ask you something. When you take Monique out to the clubs, dinner and everywhere else, how is she treated?"

"Like she's suppose to be treated," laughed Drama. "I mean, anyone that's with me is treated good. Especially her. If it wasn't for her, I would still be selling nickels and dimes. So, when it comes to her, I go all out. Plus, that's my baby. Niggas is scared to even look at her, because they know I'll have their asses washed up. I'll do anything for her. I'm saying, I'm sure you'll do the same for Tracy."

"I would," agreed Barkim. "But Tracy doesn't have any hidden agandas."

"And Monique do?" asked Drama perplexed.

"I'm not saying that either," explained Barkim. "I'm just saying, she's fucking with two powerful men and she's not really committing to either of y'all. So, she might be playing some kind of game or something."

"Tracy put that shit in your ear?"

"No," he answered truthfully. "It's just an observation I made, that's all."

"I feel 'dat," said Drama. "But truthfully, that shit don't even matter. Like I said, I'll still be fucked up if it wasn't for her. So, fuck it though like fuck it though."

"I hear you homie," laughed Barkim. "Just be careful. Now get the hell out of here before Tracy gets home. I have to finish getting this little party together before she arrives."

"That's cool. Tell her I said happy birthday. I know my baby Monique will be here," he smiled. "Yo, I don't know why you didn't invite a nigga."

"Man, you know why. It will be just my luck if she brings Joe with her. Plus, it's not like it's going to be a big party or anything. Just a handful of people."

"Where were you earlier?" asked Drama changing the subject. "I called your crib but wasn't getting an answer."

"Oh," answered Barkim, "I had to go with Monica's fiancé Bryan to the airport to pick up Tracy's grandmother and her moms."

"Her moms? I thought you said her moms was in jail and they didn't get along."

"I did, but she got out of jail a few weeks ago and I had to convince Tracy to invite her to the party. I told her to give her a chance and try to forgive her. People can change. So, they've been talking on the phone and everything so far seems to be cool. Right now we're just waiting on Tracy, Monique and Monica to get their asses here."

"Aiight then playboy," smiled Drama giving him a pound and hug. "Hit me on my cell nigga."

"You got it," he said as he watched Drama walk back to his Range Rover.

When he saw Slave and Lunch step out of the shadows, he was surprised to have not noticed them earlier. Maybe Drama was smarter than what he gave him credit for, he thought as he turned around and walked into the house.

Barkim smiled to himself because it felt so good to finally be out of his grandmother's house. Plus he no longer had to put up with the asshole p.o. he had in Brooklyn. The parole officer he now had was a very attractive lightskin woman who was not all over him; so as long as he stayed out of trouble and did what he was suppose to do. That consisted of working and not leaving New York State without permission. She came from the Manhattan parole building but was now one of Queens best parole officers. Monique knew her supervisor and people in Albany and had offered to make some moves to get him off of parole or have his parole inactive and he was more than willing to take her up on the offer. But Tracy would have none of it. She said one favor from her sister entitled a favor back and she was not having her man caught up in any of her sister's mess.

Barkim peered inside of the empty room he and Tracy painted yesterday. It was the only room in the house that was not furnished as of yet. He smiled reminiscing of yesterday's event with her. She was painting the wall with a roller when he entered the room kissing her on the side of her neck.

"Ummm," smiled Tracy as she turned around to face him. She still looked beautiful with paint covered jeans and specks of paint decorating her smooth chocolate skin. She also wore a white pair of tennis shoes, a red teeshirt and a white painter's cap on her head.

"Come here beautiful," said Barkim pulling her to him and kissing her deeply. Right there on the white sheet covered floor, they made love with paint all over them.

He smiled at yesterday's love making and then walked into the kitchen where Tracy's grandmother, her mother Darita and Bryan sat talking and listening to the small radio on the counter. The delicious food prepared for Tracy's birthday could be smelled. One look and you would think it was Thanksgiving as opposed to a birthday party. On the table sat a big turkey, rice, beans, potatoe salad, chicken, mac and cheese, collard greens, sweet potatoe pies, yams, etc. On the counter sat the most beautiful cake with twenty nine unlit candles.

"Is that her," asked her mother Darita as soon as Barkim entered the kitchen.

"Nah that wasn't Tracy and 'em," he answered taking a seat at the table. "That was one of my friends."

"Is he coming to the party?"

"No he's not coming," answered Barkim.

He looked into her eyes and could see that not only had she been through a lot, but also possessed a great deal of life's hard lessons. It was he who talked Tracy into inviting her mother and grandmother to the party. At first she was unsure and nervous about it but then decided to just trust her man's judgement.

It was no problem for Darita to get a pass from her parole officer to visit her daughter in New York. Now she just hoped everything would go well between she and Tracy who she had given up and abused as a child.

The grandmother and Bryan sat there quietly listening to the small portable radio enjoying the oldies they played on one of New York's best radio stations; Kiss FM.

"My friend wanted to come," smiled Barkim, "but these days he's not one of Tracy's favorite people."

"I may not be either," said Darita sadly.

"Everything is going to be okay," he said reassuringly. "I hear y'all building a pretty good relationship since you've been home."

"Yes," she replied nervously looking down at her hands, "but that's over the telephone. This is in person. I just hope and pray that everything—"

"Surprise!!!" yelled Tracy, Monique and Monica laughing as they entered the kitchen after noticing that they damn near scared the grandmother, Darita, Barkim and Bryan out of their chairs.

"Girl," said Darita clutching her heart, "Y'all try'na give me a heart attack? Good thing I brought plenty of underwear because the ones I have on may be ruined."

Everyone laughed as the girls hugged and kissed the grand-mother and Darita welcoming the both of them to New York City as well as into Tracy and Barkim's home.

Tears of joy fell from Darita's eyes as she held on tightly to the girls; Tracy in particular.

"Happy Birthday baby. You are sooo beautiful," she smiled as they disengaged. Darita knew a lot of years had passed, a lot has changed and she could not make it up by trying to be a mother now. Her daughter had already been raised by G-Banks and he did an ex-cellent job, she thought as she looked at the beautiful young woman in front of her who was not a baby anymore. She knew she would always be Tracy's biological mother, but was content with being her friend. Total forgiveness and trust took time and she was more than willing to earn both from her daughter.

Monique and Monica had also forgiven their mother Clurisa and had even made plans to visit Chicago again in the next coming months. Especially after learning that Derrick had died due to his ail-ments. Monica felt nothing of the news, while Monique laughed bitter-ly and popped open a bottle of Rose Moet to celebrate as if justice had finally been served.

"Let's eat," said Monica taking a seat at the table after kissing her quiet fiancé, Bryan. "I'm starving! Remember I'm feeding two people now," she smiled patting her stomach.

"First let's pray," said Tracy.

They all formed a circle around the table, held hands and closed their eyes as Tracy led them in prayer.

"God, thank you for bringing all of us together today and for allowing me to see another birthday. For we all know that tomorrow is not promised to anyone. And please God, take our daddy Gregory Banks's soul into heaven if you haven't done so already. He was a good man, and my sisters and I love him more than life itself. We all wish he was here in the physical form on this blessed day you've given us, though we do feel his spirit among us always. And God, please continue to look over everyone at this table, Amen."

"Amen," chorused everyone before sitting down to eat. Everyone noticed the three girls wiping the tears from their eyes. They truly wished their father, G-Banks were here on this special day.

Chapter Thirty Two

"Baby, is everything okay?" asked Tracy concerned.

"Drama just got shot," said Barkim while quickly slipping on his pants and grabbing his sneakers.

"Oh my God!" exclaimed Tracy with her hand to her mouth.

"That was him on the phone," he continued. "The fool don't want to go to a hospital. He said something about cops may snatch him up there. I don't know. "

"Where did he get shot?"

"In the shoulder," answered Barkim while putting on his shirt. "Now I have to go and get this fool and get him to a hospital before he bleeds to death."

"Wait a minute baby," said Tracy quickly jumping out of the bed. "I'm going with you."

"Nah, stay here. I don't need you seeing all that blood and freaking out and shit. You know how you girls can be."

"Trust me, I can handle it," said Tracy hurrily putting on a white and grey Kappa sweatsuit and white Nikes.

She then grabbed her keys and cell phone and quickly followed Barkim out of the house.

"Where to?" she asked pulling away from the house in the new white Mercedes Benz she recently bought Barkim on Valentines Day.

"Brooklyn," he answered. "St. Johns and Utica."

It was 9 PM and dark out so Barkim hoped they would be able to spot Drama on the block where he said he would be.

"What did he say happen?" asked Tracy as she made her way down Atlantic Avenue leaving Queens coming into Brooklyn.

"He didn't say," he answered. "He just said he was shot and couldn't risk going to a hospital. He'll tell me all about it when I see him. The boy needs to leave that life alone."

Twenty minutes went by and after making a few turns here and there, Tracy pulled up on the block where she was given the directions to.

As soon as she and Barkim rolled their windows down looking for Drama, a girl and a guy came out of the shadows. When they got closer, Barkim recognize the guy to be Drama holding his injured shoulder. He said something to the girl and she disappeared. Barkim then got out of the car and opened the door and he slid inside.

As soon as they both were in the car, Tracy drove away.

"What happened?" asked Barkim peering in the backseat at his friend.

Before answering, Drama shot a quick glance in Tracy's direction deciding to talk in front of her or not. She did come with his friend to get him.

"Niggas put a hit out on me," answered Drama clutching the hole in his shoulder. "But we got the nigga that put it out and the niggas that was suppose to do it. My 'lil nigga Lunch got killed, Slave got away and so did I, but with a bullet to the shoulder. It was bodies left everywhere so don't take me to no hospital. The police probably already have the gun that shot me."

"You're gonna bleed to death," said Barkim. "We have to get you to a hospital before you fuck around and die."

"Nah man," he said looking out of the car's window. "I can't go out like that. If you're going to do that you can just let me out of the car right here."

Tracy thinking fast pulled her cell phone from her pocket and dialed a number as she continued driving. She then got her party on the line.

"Hello?...This is Tracy...No...I called to speak to you...Well, I have an emergency situation and I need your time and assistance now...I can't talk about it over the phone. Okay, I'll see you then."

She closed her cell phone and headed back out to Queens.

"Where are we going?" asked Barkim.

"To get him some help," she answered. She did not supply anymore information as she concentrated on the road.

Drama leaned back in his seat, dropped his head back and relaxed. His shoulder was burning and he was losing a lot of blood as he began to feel dizzy.

They finally reached their destination and Tracy pulled up and parked in front of a big red and white house.

They got out of the car, walked up to the house and Tracy rung the doorbell. Within seconds the door flew open and there stood Bryan.

"Come on in," he said stepping back and allowing them to enter.

"My friend Drama got shot," explained Tracy as they walked into the house, "and he can't go to a hospital so I need you to help him out."

"A hospital would be better," said Bryan not really wanting to get involved with this Drama character. He remembered everything Joe said about the thug, and he wanted no parts of it.

"I just told you he can't go to a hospital," said Tracy angrily. "Now are you going to help him or not?"

Not wanting to fall out with her, Bryan put his hand to his mouth and thought for a moment before speaking.

"Okay," he said, "let's look at it."

Tracy helped Drama remove his shirt. Bryan pulled a white handkerchief from his pocket and wiping away some of the blood as he looked closely at the wound.

"Okay," he finally said after looking and wiping. "The bullet entered this side and exited cleanly out of the other side. He can follow me and I'll bandage him up and give him something for the pain."

He then walked away with Drama following closely behind.

"I don't know why this nigga won't leave this street shit alone," said Barkim angrily shaking his head from side to side.

He and Tracy entered the livingroom and sat on the couch. Tracy said nothing regarding his statement. She sat there in her own thoughts. She didn't like the fact that her sister had totally manipulated Drama without he even realizing it. Had it been someone else, she would not have cared. However, this was her man's best friend and anything Drama went through, Barkim would feel the stress of it as well which meant that she too would feel the brunt of it.

"Excuse me a minute baby," she said standing up. "I have to make a phone call."

She then walked into Bryan's kitchen to use the house phone. It hadn't dawn on Barkim that she had her cell phone in her pocket. Had he remembered he would have known that she wanted to talk in private. His mind was totally occupied with thoughts of his best friend, Drama.

"Moe?" said Tracy into the phone. "Guess where I'm at."

"Girl, I'm about to go to bed," laughed Monique. "So just tell me where you are so I can get my beauty sleep."

The two began talking in code in case someone was listening.

"Well sleeping beauty," said Tracy, "you better wake up. Your baby just burned his shoulder playing around the stove."

"Which one?!" asked Monique hurrily getting out of bed wanting to know more.

"Your youngest child," she answered. "You know child abuse cases makes the news nowadays so you should start being a little more responsible."

"Is the burn serious?"

"Of course it is! But it's not life threatening. The burn center was too far away so Bee put cocoa butter and a band aid on it."

"Tray," laughed Monique, "he is not a little boy anymore. I'm a good mommy and I raised him right. That incident was just something that boys go through at that age. It makes them tougher. And no matter what your mind is telling you, for the tenth time let me say that I am not responsible for every little boo boo the boy makes."

"That's true but let me tell you something," said a clearly upset Tracy into the phone. "Due to you not being a better mother, anything your son does affects my son being they are first cousins. And what affects my son truly affects me! I'm sorry, but you are not fit to be a mother."

There was a long pause at the other end of the phone.

"So you think I should put him in foster care?" asked Monique meaning jail.

"Hell no!" yelled Tracy into the phone. She knew her sister could have Joe set him up in no time.

"Just put him up for adoption," she said meaning let him go.

"But he's still going to be a bad little boy. Maybe I can still abort his ass," laughed Monique.

Killing him was definitely out of the question, thought Tracy looking crazily at the phone in her hand before speaking into it.

"No! There will be no abortions!" she said angrily.

"I'm just playing," laughed Monique. "I got mad love for my baby. I'm about to come and pick him up. Are you still at Bee's house?"

"Yes, we are."

"Okay, stay 'til I get there."

Tracy hung up the phone and walked back in the livingroom where Barkim sat waiting.

"I see Bryan's not finished yet," she said walking in and sitting on Barkim's lap.

"Nah," he said. "Man, they've been in there for awhile. I hope he can stop the bleeding. What if the bullet hit a main artery or something?"

"He's going to be okay baby," comforted Tracy playing in her man's curly hair.

"I just talked to Monique," she said changing the subject. "She's on her way here."

"Where's Monica?"

"She was also at the house but probably sleep or is on Facebook. That's all she does these days. Eat, sleep and mess with CafeWorld."

"Hey, hey," smiled Bryan walking back into the livingroom with a bandaged up Drama following behind, "that's enough of insulting my fiancé."

"I gave him something for the pain," he explained tossing Barkim two small plastic see through containers of pills. "One is for the pain and the other is so it doesn't become infected."

"Thanks," said Barkim standing and helping Drama put his shirt back on. The blood on his shirt had dried up and the bullet hole in the shirt was visible.

"Monique is on her way here," said Tracy sitting back down. "She wants us to wait until she gets here. Is that okay with you, Bryan?"

"Of course," he answered gesturing for them all to sit back down.

Drama sat down leaning his head against the soft pillow on the back of the sofa.he didn't know what Bryan gave him but whatever it was had him relaxed and feeling no pain. He briefly thought about finding out what it was and putting it out on the streets.

Bryan, Tracy and Barkim talked for twenty minutes until they heard the sound of the door bell.

"Excuse me," said Bryan getting up to answer the door.

When he returned, he was followed by Monique looking as fabulous as ever. She wore a brown Anne Kline shirt and tight blue jeans tucked at the bottom inside of a pair of brown Coach's suede Noreen boots.

She greeted everyone before turning her attention to Drama.

"What's up gangster?" smiled Monique. "Is my baby okay?"

When Drama's eyes fell on her, he smiled as he slowly stood up to give her a hug. He was really happy to see her. She passionately kissed him as everyone in the room looked away. It was something about him that turned her on like no other. They kissed and fondled one another as if no one else were in the room.

"Lunch got killed," said Drama.

"What about Slave?" asked Monique with eyebrows shooting up.

"He's good," answered Drama. "He got away."

Monique was sorry to hear about the death of Lunch, but for some strange reason felt relieved when hearing that Slave was okay. She really took a liking to the young boy. He had no family and survived in the streets on his own.

"Come on," said Monique tugging on his shirt. "I'm taking you home."

"Here's his medication," said Barkim handing the two small containers to her.

"What I'm going to put on him is better than any medication," she laughed as she took it.

"Later y'all," said Drama being led out of the house.

Monique was very sexy and just thinking about her last statement made Barkim a believer that she was more than capable of doing every word she had just spoken.

He then gave Bryan a handshake and thanked him for his time and medical assistance.

"Come on babe," he said to Tracy. "Let's go home."

"After all the stuff I had to put up with I'm definitely getting some tonight," she smiled as Bryan laughed opening the door for their departure.

Chapter Thirty Three

"I think we should not do this one," said Monica sitting at the kitchen table across from her two sisters.

They were inside of the Long Island home they were raised in.

"The dream I had was too real," she said shaking her head from side to side.

"Then let's not do it," responded Tracy. "Like I said before, daddy is gone and we're not obligated to do any hits."

"Well," Monique sucked her teeth, "I'll do it myself then. The two of you act like you're scared or something."

"It's not about being scared," argued Tracy. "It's about being smart and knowing when to leave things alone. After thinking about it, daddy didn't even want to do the Mr. Mack hit. And remember what he told us, 'Don't even entertain the thought of doing this hit.' Those were his exact words. Also, you see Monnie had that dream this morning that we took the hit and got killed in the process. No, let's leave this bullshit alone. And don't start with that 'you'll do it by yourself' mess because you know we won't let you."

"I'm saying," said Monique getting fed up with her sisters for not wanting to do it. "It won't be as difficult as you two think it would be. We have been to the place already and mapped everything out. This is the last hit and we are done for good. I promise!"

"According to my dream," laughed Monica, "if we try to do it, we are definitely done for good."

"Tell us about the dream again," requested Tracy.

"Oh boy!" sighed Monique. "Not again!"

Monica laughed and started from the beginning.

"We were in a big park when we saw Mr. Mack. He had on a long white coat and bright yellow shoes. We were making fun of what he had on and then Moe stopped laughing and said 'come on let's make our move.' But for some reason I began begging her to leave the man alone but she wasn't trying to hear me. Mr. Mack was walking by himself in the park with his head down and Moe started running behind him with her gun in her hand. But when she got close, he spun around with a gun in his own hand and began firing. Every bullet that came out of that man's gun hit Moe. She was dead before she hit the ground. Me and Tray was stunned and couldn't move. And that's when I caught eye contact with Mr. Mack. I've never been so scared in my life. He had cold grey lifeless eyes and when he raised his gun again, me and Tray didn't have a chance. He really shot us up real bad."

Monique sighed and said, "That's because the two of you didn't pull for your guns. And maybe that's why I got shot. Both of you hesitated and you never hesitate in war. Listen, Mr. Mack is a dead man. That's why his eyes were lifeless. All you two had to do was pull your guns and bury him."

"That simple, huh?" replied Tracy sarcastically. "Well, what about the dream I had two days ago of daddy telling me not to get into anymore trouble?"

"Now everybody is having dreams," sighed Monique throwing her hands in the air. "Well, let me tell you mines. My dream is to represent daddy's name to the fullest as well as ours. And the ultimate way of doing that is to pull off what daddy himself had doubts about doing! So, if you ladies will excuse me I have a very important date with Mr. Mack," she said getting up and heading out of the kitchen to go get ready.

Tracy and Monica sat quietly for a moment before speaking.

"We can't let her go by herself," sighed Tracy. "Daddy would turn over in his grave if we did."

"I know," agreed Monica. "Come on, let's go."

Both women got out of their chairs and raced upstairs. They had to get ready and go over the plans with Monique again.

Monique decided to wear a red Kate Mack's dress that showed off her perfect figure. Tracy and Monica settled for jeans and light jackets. All three women concealed a .380 Caliber handgun with silencer attached. After being satisfied with their appearance, they left the house.

They rode in Monique's Mercedes Benz going over every little detail of their plan. Everything had to be right. One mistake can cause a life time of grief. Or even worse; death!

Monique pulled up in front of a big brown building in lower Manhattan. She parked the car and cut the engine.

"Are you two ready?" she asked her two sisters after taking a deep breath. "Remember, no hesitating in war."

The girls were silent for a moment and then Tracy said, "Let's just get this over with."

Monique stepped out of the car first with a smile and throwing on the sexiest walk as she entered the building through the front entrance.

Tracy and Monica had then exited the car and entered the building through the side door entrance where it appeared to be deserted. They looked around for cameras and were happy to see that none had been installed since their last visit. Tracy looked at her watch and everything seemed to be on time as she and Monica climbed the stairs to the seventh floor.

As soon as Monique entered the building's lobby, she was glad there was no one stationed at a desk or security guard post. The big lobby was empty. She did not want to kill any innocent people just to get to her target but if she had to she wouldn't think twice about doing it. To her it was strictly business and nothing personal. She was different from her sisters. She was a bit more ruthless.

Things looked the same from the day she and her sisters planned out the hit, and now she thought this hit to be easier than what she previously thought. She had the element of surprise on her side.

Monique smiled to herself as she pressed for the elevator and looked around the big empty lobby. She glanced at her watch and right on schedule entered Mr. Mack and two of his body guards. They entered the lobby talking boisterous and laughing loudly. G-Banks had always told his girls that when men talked boisterous it was because they were afraid or unsure of themselves. But Monique saw neither in the face of the man that approached the elevator and stood behind her. He looked very powerful and very sure of himself. She looked back at the man and saw the same look of knowledge and wisdom in this man's eyes that she had saw in the eyes of her father, G-Banks.

"Hello pretty young lady," smiled Mr. Mack as he looked Monique up and down. His body guards immediately stopped laughing. They no longer looked like their boss's buddies. They looked serious and professional as their perfectly trained eyes scanned the lobby as if to check was anything out of place.

Mr. Mack was a looming figure. He was tall, darkskin, heavyset and spoke with a deep booming voice. He wore the most expensive suits money can buy, and the diamond ring on his pinky finger shined so bright, it looked as if it was made for the sheer purpose of hypnotism.

"May I help you pretty lady?" he smiled as they waited for the elevator to come down to the lobby.

"No I'm okay," smiled back Monique. "I have a little business meeting on the ninth floor."

"You must have a meeting with the real-estate broker Mr. Flemming," said Mr. Mack looking into her eyes. "He works for me. Actually, I own this whole building. It cost me a pretty penny too. But nothing for what I would have paid had I purchased it now. Today I can sell it for three times as much as I bought it for. A very wise investment if I should say so myself," he bragged.

"You must have had it for a very long time," said Monique encouraging conversation to make the men relax.

"Yes," he smiled, "for a very long time."

Monique wished she had the opportunity to pull her gun out and kill him and his body guards right now, but she knew that would have been suicide. His body guards were much too professional. They simultaneously watched the lobby as well as her every move with their hands under their suit jackets; no doubt holding their weapons.

The elevator had finally arrived to the lobby and the door opened up with no one inside of it.

"Shall we?" asked Mr. Mack holding his hand forward so Monique can enter first. After she stepped inside, one of the body guards stepped in behind her and then Mr. Mack and the other body guard followed suit.

When the elevator door closed one of the body guards looked up cautiously at the ceiling of the elevator as the other one pressed the seventh floor as well as the ninth.

"Thank you," smiled Monique.

"You're welcome," replied Mr. Mack speaking for the body guard.

"If you like," he said to Monique, "I can escort you up to the ninth floor and of course I wouldn't mind putting in a good word to make sure you get a good deal on the business transaction you are planning to make."

"Now why would you do that?" she asked. "I mean after all, you did say Mr. Flemming works for you. So, I am quite sure the business deal would turn out in your best interest anyway. If it didn't that would make you a terrible businessman."

"Smart as well as beautiful," he laughed very loudly while staring into her eyes.

The elevator had then stopped on the seventh floor and Monique was ready to spring into action. However, what she saw when the elevator door opened paralyzed her with fear. Tracy and Monica were held at gun point by three of the biggest black men Monique had ever laid eyes on.

"Get out of the elevator," ordered Mr. Mack calmly to her as one of his body guards grabbed her purse to see what it contained inside of it.

Monique stepped off of the elevator and when her eyes met those of her sisters, her eyes said sorry; because she knew they were going to die on account of her. As G-Banks told his girls numerous times, "'All things don't always go according to plan.'"

Chapter Thirty Four

Mr. Mack's office was huge! It was bigger than most apartments. It took up damn near the entire seventh floor. However, the only furnishings in the big spacious room was a desk and six comfortable looking chairs. The tile covered floor had plastic all over it as if murders took place here on a regular basis. The walls were sound proofed so no one can hear the screams of Mr. Mack's many victims. The girls sat in three of the chairs that occupied the room, and the five body guards were surrounding them waiting on their boss's next order.

"Now we can make this easy or we can make this very hard," said Mr. Mack calmly as he paced the room with his hands clasp together behind his back.

"I want to know," he continued, "who sent you, how much were you paid, and how many other people are involved. If you tell me the truth I will spare your lives. But if you don't then you will all die. Very painfully I may add," he said menacingly.

The girls knew Mr. Mack was lying. A man of his caliber did not spare lives. Any man in his position wouldn't. No matter what or how much information they gave, he would not let them leave alive. To do so would only give the girls a second opportunity at a later date to accomplish what they failed to do today.

Tracy, Monique and Monica sat in the chairs with their legs crossed not saying anything. Of course they were scared but did not show it. That was another thing G-Banks taught his three girls. To never show fear in the sign of danger. He said that it only encouraged the tormentor to act out more relentlessly.

It was no need for the girls to be tied up. The body guards stationed themselves in positions where the girls could not do any harm even if they were given the opportunity. They were already disarmed and knew they were going to die. It was only a matter of how. One thing was for certain; they would never reveal anything to the dangerous man pacing back and forth in front of them demanding answers. They would never betray their father; not even in death. They remembered his many lessons about being in situations like this. He stressed that if ever they should die, they should do so with honor and self respect. He said to never think of loved ones, your freedom or anything that may be a weakness to break you down. So in Monica's mind she didn't think about a baby inside of her nor did she think of Bryan. Nothing mattered anymore as she awaited her fate. Barkim was the furthest thing from Tracy's mind. And Monique did not think of the love she had for her two sisters as she looked at the man before her with a cold stare. She didn't mind dying, she only silently prayed for one opportunity to kill her tormentor. Mentally, all three girls were in their own worlds and did not even look at one another. For they knew that would surely break them.

"I see we are not getting anywhere," said Mr. Mack as he stopped pacing.

"So what should I do with you three?" he asked but more to himself.

Three of the huge body guards who captured Tracy and Monica stood close together as if they were waiting anxiously to kill. Their trained eyes stayed on Mr. Mack as he began pacing and talking again. Out of the three huge body guards, it was one who stood in the middle that looked the most dangerous of the trio. All three of them stood over six foot six with bodies as big as NFL football players. Then there were the other two body guards that weren't as big as the other three but looked just as capable at killing. These two stood closer to Mr. Mack and their eyes watched the girl's every move as they waited for their next order.

"Ahhh!" said Mr. Mack pointing his index finger towards the ceiling as if he had just come up with a solution.

"Methods of delivering pain can become so thought provoking at times," he said walking towards his desk.

He then sat down, pulled a drawer open and began placing an assortment of weapons on top of the huge desk. He had a gun, a syringe needle with a few grams of uncut heroin, a hunting knife and a very small wooden bat. He stared thoughtfully at his selection for nearly two minutes before picking up the small wooden bat.

"Yes," he smiled as he stood up holding the bat in one hand walking towards the girls. "You should see the ugly damage this little thing can do to pretty women. Perhaps, a few hard hits in the face and head with this will make you three remember how to speak. This is the last chance to save yourselves. After I take a swing, I may not want to hear anything."

The girls said nothing as they stared ahead waiting for whatever was to come to them.

"Okay," said Mr. Mack. "Have it your way."

He lift his hand holding the bat high in the air, and was about to come down with massive force to the side of Tracy's head when the three huge body guards quickly went into action pulling out their guns and firing. The two small bodyguards also went into action pulling their guns and firing as well. The huge room became very small, and it became a battle field of loud thunderous gunfire.

Tracy, Monique and Monica fell to the floor as the bullets flew. The sounds of all kinds of guns exploded and the smell of gun powder and death decorated the air.

After what seemed like an eternity; silence filled the big office. No one moved.

The girls finally and cautiously looked up but only to see the two small bodyguards and Mr. Mack sprawled out on top of one another against the desk with blood coming from the bullet holes in their heads.

They then looked in the opposite direction and to their dismay; into the eyes of the three huge mean looking bodyguards pulling away their guns as they stared down at the girls on the floor.

"Get up!" ordered the meanest looking of the three. "And sit back in the chairs."

Slowly the girls did as they were told.

"Leave us," he said to his two companions.

The two men exited the office and closed the door behind them.

"My name is James Smallwood," said the huge lightskin man as he grabbed a chair in the office, placed it in front of the girls and sat down.

He was glad to see that the girls were still a bit shaken up and knew he had their undivided attention. They had no idea who he was and wanted to know all there was to know about him.

"You three almost got yourselves killed," continued Mr. Small-wood. "Monica, that includes the little baby you're carrying."

Her eyes as well as her sisters' shot up in surprise for she wasn't even showing yet. They searched this man's face and searched their minds for some kind of recognition of him but came up blank.

"I know just about everything there is to know about you three," continued Mr. Smallwood. "Because I work for the Black Don. Actually, we were all amazed that your adoptive father, Gregory Banks had taught you three so well."

He then shook the room with his deep booming laughter.

"Old G-Banks," he smiled. "I loved him like a brother. The Black Don loved him like a brother. Now let me give you the Black Don's message that he ordered me to deliver to you three. He said to tell—"

"Who are you, and who the hell is the Black Don?" asked Monique cutting him off. This was the first time any of them spoke since being captured.

"It isn't you," said Mr. Smallwood, "and that's what brings us all here today. Now isn't it? Don't interrupt me anymore. Let me fill you three in on what's going on. First and foremost, I had a verbal contract to bodyguard Mr. Mack as soon as the Black Don received the word that G-Banks had taken the hit to dispose of him. The Black Don felt that it was of importance to get involved, because of his love for your father. Due to his very unfortunate health, it was a strong possibility that G-Banks or daddy as you call him, would have died from gunfire instead of illnesses. Your father had doubts about doing the hit because he knew his health wasn't right and Mr. Mack was too strong to take lightly. But when your father takes a job he will take the risk of being killed to satisfy the contract. He committed himself. Now us getting involved made it that much easier for Mr. Mack to be killed if we so desired it. Before the Black Don convinced him to take three of us to be well protected, the man travelled with ten bodyguards of his own. Of course after seeing what three of our men can do in comparison of his ten, he quickly agreed. And after you three's first hit," he smiled, "we knew the torch would be picked up after your father demise. The Black Don considers himself the uncle of you three because of his close relationship to your father, so he had his eyes on you for a very long time. And that is why Mr. Mack's verbal contract had expired the moment the Black Don learned of your plan."

"How did he know?" asked Monique in awe.

"He knows everything," smiled Mr. Smallwood. "Some of us in the family refer to him as God!"

"Now if you don't mind," he continued while looking away from Monique. "I would like to give you three the Black Don's message. First Tracy, the Black Don said to inform you that you are not to do anymore hits, especially on petty street drug dealers who are not in your league."

Tracy was surprised because no one; not even Monique and Monica knew that she had killed Mike and Tone.

"And Monica," he continued, "no more hits for you either. Be a better mother than the mother you had as a child. And he said to tell you that Bryan is a good man and he's good for the revolution; stay with him. And last but certainly not least, Monique. You are definitely your daddy's child. The Black Don says and I repeat, definitely no more hits for you. You do not run the city. The Black Don does. In fact, he runs most of the cities where the drugs are distributed, and black owned businesses have flourished for our people. Legal and illegal. It was not your doings that made Joe the first black police commissioner of New York City. The mayor took your suggestion after being pursuaded by the Black Don. Oh and of course the drug connect that the young boy Drama received through your workings; only came about after the Black Don gave the go ahead. A call was made that you had called," he explained to a very shocked and surprised Monique.

"So from now on," he said standing up and walking towards the door, "no more bullshit. No more hits. It's over!"

"Wait a minute," said Monica.

"Who is the Black Don?" she asked anxious to find out.

Mr. Smallwood smiled as he turned around to face the girls.

"Some call him Frank," he answered. "But his friends calls him Pee Wee. And to the police that he evaded to this day calls him Mr. Frank Matthews," he said spinning on his heels and walking out of the office leaving Tracy, Monique and Monica to stare at the closed door with their mouths open.

EPILOGUE

Monica had a baby boy that she and Bryan had named Gregory, in honor of her father G-Banks. The two had gotten married and everything was going well.

Tracy and Barkim were now engaged. She knew she finally found the man that can give back the same love as he received. She loved him like she loved her father, and it wasn't nothing he wouldn't do for her. They opened a few businesses and Barkim knew prison was no longer in his plans or future. Due to doing the right thing and listening to his parole officer, he was no longer on parole.

Monique was still Monique. She continued to practice all she had learned from her father, and she also took in the young boy Slave. She really liked him and grew to love him. She became a mother figure in his life; something he never had, and exposed him to the greater things in life that made it worth living. She was now single. Drama was on the run for shooting a state trooper on the New Jersey Turnpike. And Joe got tired of accusing Monique of cheating and had gotten involved with a congresswoman. Two months later he was forced to resign for getting caught up in a very nasty political scandal that prompted a politician to commit suicide. Tracy and Monica both believed Monique was up to her old tricks again, but she swore she had nothing to do with it as she laughed her laugh.

Tracy's grandmother had died of natural causes. She was eighty six years old. May she rest in peace.

Her mother Darita had gotten back on her feet and did not relapse with drugs. She was determined to get her life together and spend as much time as she could with her friend and daughter, Tracy.

Monique and Monica's mother Clurisa was still mourning the death of Derrick but was now doing much better. Especially since her daughters moved her to New York so they could all be closer.

Barkim's little brother Gee was now trying to walk in Drama's shoes. His name on the streets was associated with three guys that have been killed. Guys feared him and girls loved him. All respected him. Barkim tried unsuccessfully to show him that the only things received from the streets were death and jail. Gee would have to learn the hard way.

A short note to the reader

I hope you enjoyed this book. The violence was not written to be glorified, but to entertain just as a movie would.

However, child abuse, rape, sexual abuse, molestation or any other name it is called, is a very serious issue in this society that we live in. Most of the time, it is not reported or talked about. Not even among those we say we love and trust. But in order to heal you must remove the band-aid. Let the air or I should say ear, do its' job. If you are going through this, had went through this, or feel you are about to go through this, seek help by speaking to someone you trust or calling the below organizations who cares. If you are not in the New York City area, they can still help you by directing you to the same caring organizations in your area. Thank you for supporting Miz and Pencushion Publishers.

For Battered Women

RapeCrisis Intervention/Crime

(212)577-7777 or 800-621-4673

Victim Program

24 hrs a day, 7 days a week.

Columbia Presbyterian Hospital

212-305-9060

622 W. 168th st. NY NY 10032

Rape Crisis Program

St. Vincent's Hospital and Medical Center

Crime Victim Treatment Center

212-604-8068
St. Lukes/Roosevelt Hosp.

41-51 E. 11th st. NY NY 10011
212-523-4728

411 W. 114th St. #6D NY NY   10025

Sex Crime Report Line   212-267-rape
Please call if you need help! They are there 24/7.

FAT MAN

You and your sister are now my strength

But your death is now my weakness

I wish I never left you's for prison

So many nights are sleepless

And I can see as clear as day the first time I held you in my arms

I promised to protect you, won't let the world bring you harm

But now God has called you, he's taking you up above

And this absence is killing me, squeezing my heart like a glove

When that day came, I got the news over the phone

I felt the guilt of leaving you's, my world as still as stone

But if I was there on July 28th, there wouldn't've been tragedy,

Only smiles on my 5 year old's face

I still would've known, I'd be coming home to you

But Khazyier Fat Man Memphis Pugh, mommy still loves you

I cry everyday, even if it's silently in my heart

How could a bond so strong just be torn all apart?

You are so special, you just couldn't be here

The lord seen that light in you, that's why he needed you there

Down here on earth, I'm struggling day to day

I live with all our memories & your handsome little face

Your sweet little voice constantly ehoes in my head

I'm still stuck on stupid, I can't believe my son is dead

I need you in the flesh, need you back in my sight

I miss holding you, squeezing you, kissing you goodnight

I know everything I say, your little ears hear

I don't know how I'm gonna get through this every year.

Precious Adam

Order Form:

Pen Cushion Publishers
PO Box 85
New York, NY 10116
(718)844-0686
pencushion@gmail.com

CHECK ONE: MONEY ORDERS ONLY

Bishop $14.95

The Bulldog Crew $14.95

Hater's Animosity $14.95

G Banks $14.95

Purchaser Information

Name_____

Adress_____

City_____

Quantity Ordered?

Orders shipped directly to Correctional Facilities, Pen Cushion will de-
duct off of the sales price. $11.99 plus Shipping $3.20 per book.

Total......$15.19